Moth Busters

Freaky Florida Mystery Adventures, Volume 1

Margaret Lashley

Published by Zazzy Ideas, Inc., 2019.

Copyright

Dedication

TO MY BROTHER EARL, who exemplified all that is good and kind and true about the redneck spirit.

And to "Florida Man," who is all that is the exact opposite.

What Readers are Saying about Moth Busters ...

"I READ A LOT, AND KINDLE suggested your book. This book is laugh out loud funny. Is everyone in Florida crazy? I have read Tim Dorsey, Carl Hiaasen, and Randy Wayne White. Those writers are funny but they need to watch out for you."

"A funny cozy, science fiction, thriller, mystery all rolled into one great story!"

"I read the whole book in two days, something I've never done before! I just couldn't wait to find out what was going to happen next!"

"Margaret Lashley has a knack for creating funny, small town strange, off the wall, but so endearing type of characters."

"If you enjoy laugh-out-loud comedy, this book is for you!"

"Plenty of mysteries and slap stick humor with a backwoods redneck cousin thrown in the mix. I almost felt like I was reading a cross between Terry Pratchett and Piers Anthony."

"The twists and turns of the story line kept me eagerly turning the pages to see what would happen next and kept me thinking as well. Loved the small town feel of the book and the very real to life characters. Great start to a new series!"

Prologue

THE MAJORITY OF SCIENTISTS believe there's an elegant order to the universe. But then again, most of them have never spent any time in Florida.

Sometime around 1987, the oddly shaped chunk of land dangling off the southeastern corner of the United States began to be overrun by a strange creature—a hominid who, prior to the invention of Google, had remained completely unknown to the human genome.

He's identified collectively as "Florida Man."

Exactly how, when, or why this subspecies first appeared in Florida is still highly debated. However, mainstream theorists agree on one point—the creature's complex migratory behavior is typically prompted by "the forcible removal of his person" from his former place of employment and/or familial abode.

Once freed from normal societal obligations, Florida Man's primal urges, compounded by alcohol, old Jimmy Buffet songs, and/or warrants for his arrest, compel him to climb into an orange AMC Pacer with $23.46 in his wallet and keep driving south until he runs out of money, beer, gas, brain cells, land mass, or some tragically interchangeable combination thereof.

Like any invasive species, Florida Man's influence on the native population has been widespread and devastating. In fact, Florida Man has single-handedly changed both the state's reputation and its constitution.

Florida's longtime moniker, "The Sunshine State" is soon to be replaced with "The W-T-F State."

In addition, due to the exponential increase in Florida Man's bizarre behavioral tendencies, the state legislature is now considering a revision to the state motto, "Florida: In God We Trust." Current proposed alternatives include:

"Florida: Never Wear Pants Again!"

"Florida: Stupors. They're not Just for Breakfast Anymore!"

"Florida: Sure, You Can Pay for that with a Live Alligator!"

And my personal favorite, "Florida: Really, God? *Really?*"

Florida Man has been caught on video surveillance tape burglarizing cars wearing nothing but a ball cap and a bra, dancing atop a patrol car to ward off vampires, breaking into homes to suck people's toes, and shoplifting puppies with a python in his pants.

And that was just last week.

"Florida Man" is to the Sunshine State what the "People of Walmart" are to retailers—an embarrassing, unavoidable, yet morbidly fascinating source of revenue and perverse entertainment.

As a native Floridian—and somewhat decent, law-abiding citizen—I thought I would remain immune to the plague of unchecked lunacy corrupting our once-fine state.

But I was wrong.

I didn't go searching for Florida Man. But somehow, nevertheless, he found me.

Or, at least, I *think* it was him ....

Chapter One

I WISH I COULD SAY I'd been doing something glamorous or heroic when the world as I knew it skittered off its axis. You know—saving a baby, cracking a drug cartel—that kind of thing. But the truth was, I'd been working security detail at a mall.

I was *Paul Blart Mall Cop*—without even the lousy Segway.

I'd been sitting on a bench outside the mall taking a coffee break when it happened. I spotted a guy in green crocs and tiger-striped hot-pants helping himself to a bicycle with the aid of a pair of bolt cutters. After spilling my coffee down the front of my shirt, I ran after him.

Next thing I knew, I heard a bang.

Then the lights went out.

When they came back on, well, I couldn't see it at the time, but my whole life had shifted trajectory. I was about to collide head-on with fate.

Who knew it traveled around in a 1967 Winnebago?

I got shot between the eyes on a Thursday afternoon by a freak packing a Saturday-Night Special.

It wasn't the first bad joke the world had played on me.

I also had a bachelor's degree in Art Appreciation.

I WOKE UP IN AN UNFAMILIAR bed in an unfamiliar room. Everything was so ... *white*. And peaceful. And quiet.

Either I'd died, or I'd been committed to a psych ward.

I sucked in what felt like my first breath in ages. The place smelled like plastic. And disinfectant. And ....

Fritos?

Slowly, I turned my thumping head to the left. My cousin Earl was passed out on a vinyl recliner beside me. Atop his potbelly, a family-size bag of corn chips rose and fell in rhythm with his breathing.

"Earl?"

My voice sounded like it was underwater. A twinge of concern upped the volume in my throbbing head.

"Earl?"

Earl snorted himself awake, then glanced over at me.

His eyes nearly doubled. He shot up out of his chair as if it were an ejector seat. Fritos flew everywhere.

"Bobbie!" he shouted, then caught himself.

Earl wasn't one for outward displays of emotion. Not the caring kind, anyway. We'd been rivals for nearly thirty years. There was no point in him getting all sappy now.

"You're awake," he said with a bit more reserve.

"You've got a real knack for the obvious," I cracked. My words echoed weirdly inside my skull. "What happened? Where am I?"

"In the hospital. You got ... uh ... shot between the eyes."

Earl's voice caught. He winced and slapped on a snide grin. But the tears brimming in his eyes contradicted his charade of callousness.

Tears? Crap. That can't be good.

"I remember now," I said. "There was that guy at the mall—the one in hot-pants .... He *shot* me?"

"Yep."

I tried to sit up, but the IV tube in my arm protested against it. "How bad off am I?"

"The good news is, your thick skull stopped the bullet. Lord knows you don't need any more brain damage."

Either Earl's humoring my dying ass or it's not that bad.

"Right." The left side of my mouth attempted a sarcastic smirk. "So what's the *bad* news, Frito Bandito?"

My cousin wagged his eyebrows. "Well, you've done got yourself one hell of a Kentucky waterfall."

"What?" I scowled and reached toward my head, pulling the IV tube along for the ride. My fingers landed on a tender lump in the middle of my forehead, then moved higher to the swath of smooth skin atop my partially shaved head.

"Argh! Gimme a mirror!"

Earl's cheeks dimpled, but he kept his mouth shut and handed me the mirror lying on the table beside my hospital bed.

I peered at my reflection. My face went slack. The top of my head all the way to my ears had been shaved bald. The rest of my long, auburn hair clung limply to the back of my skull like a greasy clown wig. I dropped the mirror onto my chest in disgust. "Ugh!"

"Sir!" a woman's voice sounded from behind Earl. "I told you to notify a nurse as soon as he regained consciousness! Are you in pain, Mr. Drex?"

"That's *Miss* Drex," Earl said.

"Oh. Pardon me." The nurse looked down at the chart hanging at the end of my bed, apparently unconvinced.

"No worries," Earl said. "Common mistake."

As much as I hated to admit it, Earl was right. I'd never been the "girliest" of girls. My newly receding hairline wasn't helping on that score.

"How are you feeling?" the nurse asked.

"Okay, I guess." Considering the circumstances, I felt surprisingly good. Sure, my head throbbed. But it was no worse than the hangover I'd self-inflicted last weekend.

"I'll get Dr. Brown." She shot Earl a raised eyebrow. "Sir, it would be good if you gave Miss Drex some privacy when he arrives."

Earl bobbed his shaggy head at her. "Yes, ma'am."

I studied my bear of a cousin. Despite his display of bravado, his brow had more furrows in it than a freshly plowed corn field.

"It's okay," I said to the nurse. "Like it or not, he's the only family I've got."

"As you wish."

As the nurse left, Earl's cellphone chirped. He glanced at the screen and shoved it back into the pocket of his blue mechanic's coveralls.

"Who was it?" I asked. "A customer?"

"We should be so lucky."

"How long have I been here?"

"Three or four hours."

"Geez! Who's running the garage?"

"Uh ... nobody. In case you haven't noticed, we're *both* here."

Panic shot through me. "Help me up, Earl. I can't afford to be in the hospital! My health insurance from the mall job doesn't kick in until next month."

"Yeah, about that—"

I sat up and peeled the tape from the IV in my arm.

Earl objected. "Now hold up there a second."

I scowled. "No! I might *look* like hell, but I feel fine."

"Well, to tell the truth, you don't look much worse than you did on prom night. Remember? You had that monster zit on your forehead and—"

"Shut up and help me get out of here! Do you have another set of coveralls with you?"

"Down in the truck."

"Go get them. And hurry!"

EARL AND I WERE HALFWAY down the hospital corridor—two shady mechanics in shabby blue coveralls—when a doctor walked by us. I think he would have mistaken us for janitors if he hadn't recognized my fancy haircut. Or maybe it was the bandage between my eyes ....

"Roberta Drex?" he asked, turning to stare at us as our paths crossed. "I'm your attending physician, Dr. Brown."

Earl and I kept walking, pretending not to hear. The doctor called after us. "What are you doing out of bed Ms. Drex?"

I turned to face him. "Uh ... leaving. I'm sorry, but I can't afford to stay here."

The doctor appeared more annoyed than surprised. "You can't afford *not* to. You were unconscious for several hours. Don't you want to know what's wrong with you before you leave?"

I scanned the doctor's face. If I was dying, he didn't give it away. "Okay. Give it to me straight. What's wrong?"

Dr. Brown glared at me, then wilted. "Well, to be honest, we did an initial brain scan, but couldn't find anything."

I glanced over at Earl's smirking face. He opened his mouth to say something stupid, but I shut him down with a look that could wither gonads at fifty paces.

"So, in other words, there's nothing really wrong with me. Thanks, Doc. I'll be leaving now."

Dr. Brown grabbed my arm. "Hold on a moment! Yes, the initial scan indicates your brain appears undamaged. But you were struck by a ricocheting bullet, Ms. Drex. While it slowed considerably before it impacted your skull, there could be undetected residual effects."

I frowned. "Like what?"

"Any number of things. But right now, the damage appears to be contained to skin abrasions and hematomas confined to the non-subdural dermis."

Earl crinkled his nose. "That sounds bad."

I sighed. "It's just doctor talk for a scratch and a bruise. Am I right, Doc?"

"Yes," Dr. Brown admitted. "You're one lucky lady."

"Yeah. Getting shot in the head. That's my kind of luck, all right."

"A sense of humor. That's a good sign, too. Patients have been known to lose theirs as a result of head trauma."

"Too bad," Earl quipped. "So much for the power of prayer."

I shot Earl another dirty look and turned to the doctor. "Then I'm good to go? Like I said, I really can't afford to be here."

The doctor pursed his lips. "Well, I'm still concerned. You lost consciousness longer than typical. You may have suffered a concussion. Still, there appears to be no brain swelling. The MRI we took should tell us more. To be on the safe side, I'd like to keep you overnight for observation."

I winced. "Listen, I appreciate your concern and all. But a night here would cost me more than I make in a month." I poked my chin in my cousin's direction. "Can't Earl here keep an eye on me?"

The doctor glanced at our threadbare coveralls and sighed. "I can't hold you here against your will. But you'll have to sign a form saying you refused treatment. I'll have the nurse give you a list of concussion warning signs. Promise me if you have any symptoms you'll come back to the hospital immediately."

"Sure. I promise." I sighed as relief emanated from my wallet.

Earl saluted the guy. "You can count on me, Doc."

Dr. Brown's face sagged with symptoms of early-onset regret. He blew out a breath and led us to the nurses' station. I signed the waiver form while a nurse gave Earl a pamphlet on concussions and a bag of bandages. After thanking them, we headed toward the exit.

We were halfway down the hall when my head began to hum. I flinched, then did a double take.

Standing in front of the visitor's lounge was the guy in the hoodie. The man I'd caught stealing a bike outside the mall. The guy I'd chased. The same punk who'd shot me with his Saturday-Night Special.

I gasped and elbowed Earl in the ribs. "What's *he* doing here?"

"Who?"

"That guy."

"Where?"

Anger boiled up inside me. "Over *there*, Earl. By the vending machine. That's the guy who *shot* me!"

Earl shook his head like I was crazy. "That ain't him."

My eyes narrowed. "Yes it is. How many other people would be wearing tiger pants and lime-green Crocs?"

Earl patted my shoulder. "Around here? Could be anybody."

I scowled. "Dang it, Earl! I guess I'm gonna have to run him down all by myself. Geez! I always have to do *everything*. Get out of my way!"

I took a step toward the guy and blanched. He was gone.

"Where'd he go?" I took another step.

Earl caught me by the arm and spun me around. "Stop it, Bobbie."

"Let go of me!" I tugged against my cousin's bear-claw grip. "We've got to go after him!"

Earl looked me in the eye. "Hold your horses, Cuz. I'm telling you, I'm a hundred percent sure whoever you saw wasn't the kid who shot you."

I glared at my cousin. Only a *man* could be a hundred percent sure of anything.

"How can you *say* that?" I hissed.

"'Cause the punk who shot you got runned over by a monster truck heading for the mud-bugging flats. He's *dead*."

"Dead?"

"Squashed flatter'n road kill. Well, everything but his Hello Kitty backpack."

Chapter Two

ON THE HOUR-LONG DRIVE from the hospital in Gainesville to our hometown of Point Paradise, Earl wouldn't stop ribbing about me "seeing ghosties," "losing it," and my "screws coming loose."

By the time we made it back to the auto garage, I'd convinced myself that the world was full of jerks in tiger-skin hot-pants. The guy I'd seen at the hospital couldn't have been the same one who'd shot me. There'd probably been a sale on green crocs and Hello Kitty backpacks at Walmart, and now the town was crawling with looka-like doofuses.

The whole thing had been a figment of my imagination.

As I climbed out of the truck, I caught my reflection in the side mirror and remembered that my half-shaved head was, unfortunate-ly, no figment.

I blew out a breath. Then I stomped across the parking lot and up the stairs leading to my apartment above the garage. I fumbled the door open, marched into the kitchen, and fished a pair of scissors from a drawer. Then I stood in front of the hall mirror and began whacking away at my remaining locks.

"Practicin' medicine without a license is illegal in Florida," Earl said, coming in behind me.

"I'm pretty sure it's illegal *everywhere*," I said sullenly. "And this *isn't* a medical procedure."

"Sure it is." He snorted. "It's a mullet-ectomy."

My eyes narrowed. I stared at my reflection in the mirror, blew out a sigh, and snipped off the last strands of hair hanging behind my left ear. The long clump fell to the floor, along with what was left of my vanity.

I turned my head to get a side view of my homemade hairdo. It was all I could do not to groan out loud.

A choppy band of inch-long auburn hair encircled the back and sides of my otherwise bald head. If that weren't bad enough, an angry red crater pulsed like a mini volcano in the center of my forehead.

If Bozo and the Cyclops had a baby, it still wouldn't be this ugly.

Earl laughed. "You know you're famous now, right?"

"Famous?" My pulse lurched. "Good grief! Please tell me you didn't talk to any reporters!"

Tiger Pants Shoots Cyclopoid Mall Cop. Good lord! I could end up on the home page of the Florida Man website!

Earl smirked and raised an eyebrow. "Just one. Turns out Third-Eye Blind's looking for a new mascot."

I bit down hard against a sudden, stinging pressure behind my nose. Crying wasn't my style. Especially not in front of Earl Shankles. But geez! How much more was I supposed to take?

"I need a wig," I hissed.

"Nah. I think you look great." Earl chuckled and rubbed his hands together. "I guess some money's gonna change hands tonight."

"What are you talking about?"

"Come on, Bobbie. Half of Point Paradise thinks you're really a guy. Now that you're going bald, people round here will be calling in their bets. You can count on it."

A vein pulsed in my left temple. "Could you cut me a break, just this *once*? I got shot in the head, for crying out loud." My reflection in the mirror made me wince afresh. "What am I gonna do? I can't go around looking like *this*."

"Just do what we guys do when we go bald."

I braced myself for another insult. "*What?*"

"Wear a hat."

"Oh."

Earl held out his Redman chewing tobacco ball cap. I nearly choked. In the saga of our redneck family, the grubby cap was legendary.

"Lucky Red" had been handed down to Earl by his father. He'd been wearing it the day he'd caught a twelve-pound bass in a fishing tournament on Wimbly Lake. The scale-busting lunker had won my uncle a shiny trophy and a brand-new bass boat. It was the most luck our family had had in generations.

Lucky Red was one of Earl's few prized possessions. Lending me the cap was the closest thing to "I love you" my cousin had ever expressed to me.

"Thanks." I reached for the cap.

Earl yanked it away. "It's a loaner, mind you."

"Fine." I snatched the cap from Earl, stared at the dirty brim and scowled. "Great. Looks like I'll have to wash it first."

Earl burst out laughing.

Part of me longed to join in, but the rest of me snuffed out the urge.

Perfect. Here I am, borrowing "luck" from the very man who stole all of mine in the first place.

Good one, universe.

Har har har.

Chapter Three

"DOCTOR SAYS YOU SHOULD take it easy," Earl said, towering over me with his luxurious headful of shiny, black hair.

After just sheering myself like a sheep, I found myself envious of him for *that*, too.

Great. Like I need another reason.

"Yeah. I know," I said sullenly, and carried Lucky Red into the kitchen. Earl trailed along behind me, annoying me to no end with his persistent existence.

"I could've carried you up the stairs," he said.

"I'm not an *invalid*, Earl!"

"I know that! Sheesh. I'm only trying to help."

"Sorry." I gave my cousin the best smile I could muster under the circumstances, then reached into the cabinet under the sink and pulled out a spray bottle of Windex. "It's just that, well, I'm used to taking care of myself."

I spritzed the ball cap while Earl hovered over me like an incompetent, micromanaging supervisor.

"I know you are, Bobbie. But you don't *have* to. You want me to stay the night on the sofa?"

"No."

He folded his huge arms over his barrel chest. "Well, I'm staying anyway. Somebody's got to keep an eye on you."

"*Fine.*"

I scrubbed the cap with a sponge while Earl wandered around the shabby, two-bedroom apartment that had been my parent's place for thirty years. When Dad passed away six months ago, I'd come back to try and salvage the family business.

It wasn't going well.

"This place looks like a museum to your folks," Earl called out from the living room.

"Yeah. It should. It was *their* place, after all." I hadn't had the heart to change a single thing since I'd moved in. "It feels like sacrilege for me to even be here."

Earl poked his head back into the kitchen. "Why would you say *that?*"

"You know why." I kept my voice flat. "They never wanted me in the first place. I'm the prodigal son who turned out to be the pitiful daughter."

Earl opened his mouth, but shut it without saying anything.

I put Lucky Red in the sink and filled the basin with warm, soapy water. "Listen, I'm gonna let your hat soak for an hour while I go take a nap."

Earl held up a piece of paper and shook it at me. "Keep the bedroom door open. This here list from the hospital says I should check on you every fifteen minutes."

My throat tightened. "Okay. Whatever."

I stomped to my parents' old room, kicked the oversized work boots from my feet, and flopped onto the bed. I wasn't tired. I just wanted a moment's peace.

Alone.

By myself.

Without Earl.

I stared at the picture on the nightstand. Inside the cheap frame was an image of my father, Robert Drex, sitting behind the wheel of a red, 1964-1/2 Ford Mustang. He was parked in the lot in front of the shop. A shiny, new sign above the garage's service bay doors proudly proclaimed *Robert's Mechanics*. My mom, Edith, stood below the sign, her back against the wall. Her mother, my Grandma Selma, stood beside her, holding me in her arms.

Nobody was smiling.

Why the hell did I come back to Point Paradise? To help Mom out? To save Dad's mechanic shop? To show Earl who's boss once and for all?

I chewed my lip. Who was I kidding? I was no business woman. It wasn't *all* my fault, but the shop was now so far in arrears I'd had to take that job at the mall just to keep the lights on. And Earl? He wasn't even grateful! I mean, where else could a redneck jerk like him find work? Who would hire the moronic lug except my father?

The door to my bedroom creaked open. Earl stuck his head inside. "You doing okay?"

As if working as a mall cop hadn't been embarrassing enough, I'd somehow managed to make myself even *more* dependent on my idiot cousin. It was absolutely the last damned thing in the world I wanted.

"Yeah, I'm fine."

Earl eyed me skeptically. "Okay. But I'm leaving the door open wider. So it don't squeak and wake you up."

"*Fine.*"

"You need anything?"

"Only to be left alone."

Earl's dumb, pleasant face soured a notch. "Can do."

Earl disappeared behind the door. I bit down hard against my anger. I knew I should be nicer to him. He was trying, after all. But it was so much easier for him.

He had won.

I tossed and turned, my mind seething over Earl Shankles. He was my first cousin. My life-long tormentor. The usurper of my father's affections. The whole reason my life had turned out like this ....

BACK WHEN EARL AND I were kids, I'd spent every afternoon helping out around my dad's garage after school. By the time I was eight, I could do oil changes, switch out spark plugs, replace dead batteries, and fix flat tires.

But everything had changed when I turned eleven. I'd hit puberty and had the audacity to turn out to be a girl after all. My mechanic-in-training days came to a screeching halt. My father dropped me like a hot soldering gun, banishing me from his service bay forever.

With his fantasy son reduced to wearing a training bra, my father had picked Earl to be my replacement. My cousin not only took my place as flunkey at my dad's shop—he stole my father's heart and never gave it back.

As soon as high school was over, I ran off to college and found someone else to break my heart all over again.

I guess I showed them.

I blew out a sigh and stared at the ceiling.

What did Earl have that I didn't? Why did Dad give him what rightfully belonged to me?

When I'd come home for my father's funeral, I'd discovered that Earl had taken over running my father's business. I figured it had been easy pickings for him. My mother had never wanted anything to do with the garage. I'm sure she'd gladly handed over the reins to Earl.

Well, I'd set that business straight on day one. I'd taken back charge of the books and Earl Shankles' paycheck. Mom had been relieved. So relieved, in fact, that she'd taken the liberty of running away with our postman, David Applewhite, two days after Dad's funeral. A week later she'd called to let me know they'd gotten married at a drive-thru chapel in Vegas.

Mom gets married again at sixty, and I can't even get a second date
....

I glanced at the clock. Earl would be making his rounds any minute. I rolled over and sighed for the hundredth time.

For crying out loud, just go to sleep, Bobbie!

But I couldn't. Something inside me was making me madder than a wet hornet. I felt trapped. Dragged down by circumstances beyond my control.

The door creaked open. I shut my eyes and pretended to be asleep. Logically, I knew it wasn't Earl's fault that my father had chosen him over me. But I couldn't dislodge my resentment.

In the game of life, I was a dodgeball target.

And tonight, thanks to a random act of stupidity, I needed my crummy cousin to make sure I didn't lapse into a coma.

I turned over on my other side and made myself a solemn vow.

There was *no way* I was going to let myself die in this lousy, run-down, piss-hole of a place in the middle of freaking nowhere.

That fate I planned to leave to Earl Shankles.

Chapter Four

WHEN I WOKE UP, IT was daylight. The old clock radio next to my frowning family's photo read 9:38 a.m.

I stumbled to the kitchen, lured by the smell of brewing coffee. As I poured myself a cup, I noticed Earl's Lucky Red cap was in the windowsill, nearly dry.

I heard the toilet flush. Earl emerged from the bathroom looking proud of himself. I didn't want to know what for.

"Mornin'," I begrudged as a peace offering.

"Mornin', Sleeping Beauty. You feeling okay?"

"Yeah."

"You know you snore louder than Candy Vincent?"

I scowled. "How do you know how loud Candy Vincent snores?"

"Uh ... rumors."

"Yeah, right."

Earl made himself a cup of coffee as I took a seat at the kitchen table. After he'd stirred in enough sugar to induce a diabetic coma, he joined me.

"While you were out like a light last night, you got a couple of calls on your cellphone."

"My mom?"

Earl glanced away. "Uh ... no. Reporters mostly. When I told them you were gonna live, they kind of lost interest."

"Story of my life."

Earl stared into his coffee mug. "Your boss at the mall called, too. He said times are tough. Had to make some layoffs. Blah, blah, blah. Bottom line, no need for you to worry about coming back in."

"Great. Any other good news?"

"Some cop called. Said he met you at the mall last week. What's his name? Paul Newman?"

"Terry Paulson."

Earl smiled softly. "Yeah. You always *were* good with names."

Especially when the person looked better *than Paul Newman.*

"What did he want?" I asked.

"He said he wanted to marry you."

I blanched. "What?"

Earl laughed. "Well, to use his exact words, he said he 'had a proposal for you.'"

My nose crinkled. "I wonder what he meant by that?"

Earl wagged his eyebrows at me. "Maybe it's an *indecent* proposal. No, wait. Maybe this guy's opening up a new ghost-buster division. See any more *haints* last night?"

I shot him a sour face. "Only the ghost of my dearly departed hair." I ran my hand along the red stubble. "Crap. What am I gonna do? I can't go see Detective Paulson wearing an ad for chewing tobacco on my head."

Earl grinned. "Don't worry, Bobbie. While you were snoring your lungs out, I thought of something. Here. I found this in granny's place next door."

Earl held out a shoebox.

"What were you doing snooping around in Grandma Selma's apartment?" I demanded.

"Cool your jets. She was *my* granny, too."

"Gimme that!"

I yanked the shoebox from Earl's hands and lifted the lid. Inside was a short, curly wig made of blue and silver polyester fibers.

Poor Grandma. She'd worn her best Sunday wig to the grave with her.

I took the cheap wig out of the shoebox and held it up to the light.

Earl snorted. "Don't tell me you're actually thinking about wearing that thing."

"No. But seeing as how I don't have a lot of options, maybe Beth-Ann can fix it. See you later."

I got up from the table.

"Where you going?" Earl demanded.

"I'm gonna get a shower, then I'm going to see Beth-Ann. If she can work a miracle on this thing, I'll be heading over to see Detective Paulson afterward."

"Do you really think you should be driving?"

"It's either drive myself to Beth-Ann's or stay here and let you drive me crazy. I think I'll take my chances on the road."

Earl threw up his hands. "Have it your way."

"I will. You've had it your way long enough."

"What's that supposed to mean?"

"Nothing." I sucked in a deep breath and blew it out. "Earl?"

"What?"

"Thanks for lending me Lucky Red."

He shot me a suspicious look. "Yeah."

I grabbed the cap from the windowsill and headed down the hallway.

"I hope Windex kills germs," I hollered back at Earl. "I wouldn't want to catch a staph infection from this thing."

Chapter Five

"BE CAREFUL OUT THERE," Earl said as I climbed into my father's red Mustang. "Don't go getting yourself lost."

"Not much chance of that."

How could I end up any further off track than Point Paradise?

I cranked the engine. As I let the vintage muscle car idle for a minute, I stared at the flashing yellow light that marked the intersection of Norville Street and Obsidian Road. Or, as we locals called it, "The corner of nowhere and oblivion."

My father's business, Robert's Mechanics, was the only semi-viable business on the otherwise desolate crossroads. Cattycorner from it was an appliance store turned junk shop, which changed renters every six months or so. Next to that dump was another junk shop that had given up the ghost for good when it caught fire this past summer.

That fire had been the last nail in the coffin of my father's ambition to put Robert's Mechanics and Point Paradise on the map. He'd bought both junk places across the street for next to nothing, which was still more than they'd been worth. I tried to sell the properties to keep the garage afloat, but so far there'd been no takers. Not even a nibble.

In a way, I was glad Dad hadn't lived to see the junk shop across the street burn down. When I'd first come back, I'd been gung-ho on Dad's dream to reinvigorate the tiny town. But after six months of dealing with deadbeat renters and garage customers' rubber checks, my sentiments had taken a nosedive.

More and more, my ambition concerning Point Paradise was to drive away and never look back. I'd even begun to fantasize about torching the place as I fled. To me, Point Paradise had become the dreary deathtrap of my dead dad's dreams.

I sighed, shifted the Mustang into first, and pulled out of the parking lot. I headed east on Obsidian Road toward Waldo, the nearest clump of buildings big enough to be incorporated into an actual town. That's where my friend Beth-Ann's beauty shop was, and Dana's Café, where I was to meet with Detective Terry Paulson later in the afternoon—provided the wig-gig went well.

About half a mile down Obsidian Road, I passed the only other business in Point Paradise. It was an abandoned gas station converted into a drive-thru convenience store.

Owned by some guy from Waldo, the dive was run by Artie Jacobs, who'd lived up to his high school prediction of being least likely to succeed. Considering where we'd all come from, he had every right to be proud. Around here, there'd been a hell of a lot of competition for the title.

I spotted Artie sitting in his chair by the cash register. Per tradition, I honked and waved. Before he could wave back, I gunned the engine and blew past him, grinning like Jack Nicholson in *The Shining*.

Pathetic, I know. But in a town this small and this broke, you took your cheap thrills where you could find them.

At the end of the road, I hooked a right and headed south on US 301 toward Waldo. Feeling antsy, I lifted the ball cap and scratched my itchy scalp. Tiny stubbles of hair were already growing in. I wondered how long it would take for my auburn locks to reach ponytail length again.

Beth-Ann would know. She was a good friend and a miracle worker when it came to hair. I hoped she still had one doozy left in her bag of tricks for me.

I was sure as hell gonna need it.

Chapter Six

A FEW MILES OUTSIDE of Waldo, I passed a roadside billboard and hit the brakes out of habit. Besides being the butt of innumerable "Where's Waldo?" jokes, the tiny town had earned itself two national distinctions—neither of which was ever brought up in polite conversation.

Three years ago, Waldo had been designated the nation's worst speed trap by AAA. After discovering Waldo's seven police officers had written nearly twelve thousand speeding tickets that year, AAA had paid to erect the billboard I'd just blown past. It used to read, "Speed Trap Waldo 6 Miles" in black and yellow, the most readable color combination to the human eye.

The billboard was abandoned now, as was the entire Waldo police force. The incident had raised such a stink that the entire department had been disbanded and their duties turned over to the Alachua County Sheriff's Department.

Two years later, the Florida Legislature gave Waldo its other national distinction by passing a law banning traffic-ticket quotas for law officers. They named it the "Waldo Bill." As for the notoriety the town received, the rest of us were secretly jealous.

Everything exciting always seemed to happen in Waldo.

A rural-route school bus buzzed past me on US 301. It was most likely heading toward Hawthorne, the nearest town with a public school.

Poor saps.

I thought about how Beth-Ann and I had met on a bus just like it when we were sixteen. She'd climbed aboard wearing black jeans, a black T-shirt, black boots, black hair, black fingernails, black eye makeup, and black lipstick. I'd never seen anyone like her. Beth-Ann had been the first "Goth" kid at Hawthorne High—maybe the only one in all of Alachua County.

I turned the Mustang off US 301 onto Country Lane and smiled, remembering the first words Beth-Ann had ever said to me.

"Normal is for losers."

She'd given my boy's jeans, chain wallet, and close-cropped red hair the once-over, then sat in the seat next to me and delivered that line. Then she'd offered me a bottle of black nail polish. I'd been so stunned I didn't even try to stop her as she took my hand and painted my nails. It was my first-ever manicure.

I bit my lip and glanced down at my fingernails. I could use a manicure now, actually. But it would be a waste of money I didn't have. Besides, there was no point. Carburetors didn't care if you had soft cuticles.

I pulled the Mustang up to a little wooden cottage and cut the ignition. Beth-Ann worked out of her house. She'd converted the detached garage into a beautician studio. A hand-painted sign hanging over the garage door read, "Beth-Ann's Beauty Parlor. Yes, I Know It's A Garage."

I walked around the corner of the garage and down the footpath lined with pavers. The side entry door was ajar. I pushed it open the rest of the way.

A chalk-pale face looked up from sweeping the floor. Still sporting black hair, black lipstick, and thick eyeliner, Beth-Ann wasn't about to give up her Goth dream anytime soon.

"Holy crap!" Beth-Ann said as I took off the Redman cap and gave her a gander at my red monk's ring. "Did you get attacked by a psychotic clown or something?"

"No. Just shot between the eyes." I flounced onto her salon chair.

"I heard about the shooting, Bobbie. Good thing you've got a thick skull."

I whirled around in the chair. "Really? You, too? I'm fine, by the way."

She rested her hands on my shoulders and winked at me. "I know that, Bobbie. Otherwise, I wouldn't be teasing you."

I shot her a tight smile. "Speaking of teasing ...." I pulled the wig out of the shoebox. "Can you do something with this?"

Beth-Ann's face puckered like she'd smelled a fart. "Geez, Bobbie. I'm a beautician, not a magician."

I let out a sigh. "Okay. It was worth a shot." I got up out of the chair and took a step toward the door.

"Wait!" Beth-Ann said. "Let me check my wig box. I think I've got something in there you could use."

"You've got a *wig box?*"

Beth-Ann opened a cabinet and pulled out a cardboard box.

"Yeah. You know. Donations. Leave-behinds. Hey, it's a woman's prerogative to change her mind—and her hairstyle." She glanced at my head and winced. "You of all people should know that."

She rifled through an old Amazon box that appeared to be harboring the dehydrated husks of an entire generation of tribbles.

"Aha! Here it is!" Beth-Ann held up a bright-red wig. "Sit back down, sister."

With no better option springing to mind, I flopped back into the barber chair. Beth-Ann stretched the wig out like a shower cap and placed it over my semi-bald dome. She tugged it left and right, and spun me around for a gander in the mirror.

"Ta da!"

I gulped. I'd gone from Kentucky Waterfall Woman to Sharon Osborne on a bender in under thirty seconds. Combined with my garage coveralls, the look was perfect—if I wanted to masquerade as *Woody Woodpecker* working the night shift at a Texaco.

"You're kidding," I said.

"Hey, beggars can't be choosers."

I blew out a breath. "How much is it?"

"For you? Nothing. Compliments of the house."

"That's *some* compliment."

Beth-Ann shrugged. "If you'd rather go on looking like a redneck Franciscan monk, be my guest."

I sighed. "You're right. What the hell."

"I've also got a clothes box, in case you ever decide to change out of those mechanic's coveralls. I haven't seen you in anything else since you came back, Bobbie. Why are you always wearing them, anyway? Some kind of sick penance?"

"I run a mechanic's garage, in case you forgot."

"I know. But not 24-7. Your life isn't *over*, you know."

I scowled. "You sure about that?"

"Yes." Beth-Ann shot me a look. "What happened to you? You used to actually *like* other humans."

"Sorry. It's just that ... I dunno. Carl did a number on me. And that whole thing with Earl. What is it with guys? They think they run the universe."

Beth-Ann shot me a sympathetic smile. "Guys only have the power we give them. Just like everything else in life. So, when are you going to get your life out of that greasy garage and back in the sassy saddle with me?"

I smirked. "Soon." I turned to go, then hesitated. "Hey. Any chance you can do something with my face?"

Beth-Ann stared at the scabby crater between my eyes.

"Like I said, Bobbie. I'm a beautician, not a magician."

She eyed my deflated face and winked. "Aww, come on. Have a seat. Lemme see what I can do."

Chapter Seven

I GAVE MY SPIKEY RED wig a quick tug, ponied up a bit of feminine chutzpa, and sauntered into Dana's Café.

I'd come to meet Detective Terry Paulson about a proposal. Part of me hoped my cousin Earl had been right, and the proposal would be an indecent one. Pathetic as it was, this meeting was the closest thing I'd had to a date since Artie had asked me for a lift when his car broke down.

Not wanting to appear desperate or overeager, I'd turned down Beth-Ann's offer of more alluring attire and stuck with my usual outfit—my dad's fraying coveralls and oversized work boots. The problem was, the heavy boots made it impossible to pull off an actual saunter. Instead, I tripped over the threshold and stumbled into the coffee shop like a drunken hobo.

Paulson watched it all from a table for two.

Despite my cheeks burning with humiliation, my heart leaped at the sight of him in uniform, just as it had when I'd met him for the first time at the mall last week.

I shot Paulson a smile, swiped habitually at my auburn bangs, and froze for a second when I realized they were no longer there. In their place was a bandage the size of a monkey diaper.

"Well, look at you," Detective Paulson said in a voice that lilted with flirtation. "I have to say, I liked your hair longer. What'd you do? Get shot in the head or something?"

I couldn't decide whether to kiss him or kick him in the groin, so I smiled. "Very funny."

Paulson's smirk faded. His brow furrowed. "I heard the news. I'm sorry I wasn't there to help when it happened."

I pursed my lips and shrugged. "No worries. Gainesville's way out of your jurisdiction anyway."

Paulson winced. "True. But what I meant to say is that I'm glad you're okay. You're not going back to that job at the mall, are you?"

I shook my head. "No. You take one lousy bullet between the eyes, and they throw you out like last month's fryer grease. My manager called this morning. I've been laid off."

"Ouch. I *thought* you looked upset. Is that what's bugging you?"

Ugh! Every time I heard someone ask, "What's bugging you?" I thought of some flea-infested rodent ... or Carl Blanders, my ex, which, in my book, was pretty much the same thing. But at the moment, it was Detective Paulson who was getting under my skin. I wanted to slap his smug, irritatingly attractive face—then roll around in the hay with him. But not actually *roll around in the hay.* Being naked in a pile of dirty, pokey, dried-up stems of grass sounded itchy—and downright uncomfortable.

I looked up from my wandering thoughts. Paulson was studying me with a pair of laser-beam eyes the color of glacier shards.

"Uh ... no," I said. "Nothing's bugging me. I just hate that expression."

"Well, in this case, the term 'buggy' fits."

"What do you mean?"

"Have a seat." Paulson half-stood and gestured for me to sit.

"I prefer to stand." I curled my hands into fists to hide the motor oil under my fingernails. I didn't want to get too near Paulson. There was no need for him to discover my signature cologne was Quaker State.

"Have it your way." Paulson leaned back in his chair. "After Jack Barker, uh ... *left,* I found a report involving Mildred Vanderhoff. Apparently, the old gal's gone off her rocker."

"You must be new in town," I quipped, then remembered that Paulson was. In fact, it was rather miraculous there was a police officer there in Waldo at all.

Three years had passed since Waldo's infamous speed-trap debacle. Four months ago, the town had finally been reissued its first dedicated police officer, Jack Barker.

At fifty-three years of age and three-hundred pounds, it wasn't exactly surprising when Barker had suffered a heart attack. Two weeks ago, they'd hauled him out of this very café and up to Gainesville for treatment. I'd heard a rumor that Artie had been at the scene, and had finished Barker's half-eaten donut.

The official story was that Officer Barker was on sick leave, recovering. But we all knew he was at a gastric bypass clinic getting his colon resected. Detective Paulson had been assigned to fill in during the interim, while Barker whittled down his waistline.

I took a step closer and curled my fingers around the back of the chair opposite Paulson. "Of course, being new in town, you wouldn't know this, Detective Paulson. But old lady Vanderhoff's been Point Paradise's resident crazy cat lady since as long as I can remember. She's a rite of passage for kids around here." I smiled coyly. "In fact, you're nothing but a dork until you've mustered up the courage to ring her doorbell and run."

"You don't say." Paulson grinned. "So, did *you?*"

"Sure. When I was six. On Halloween. She came to the door wearing a green monster mask. Made me drop a load in my pedal pushers—along with my pillowcase full of candy."

Yes. That's the way to talk sexy to a man, Bobbie. No wonder you haven't had a date since Blanders ....

"But that's ancient history," I added hastily.

Paulson's left eyebrow arched. "Let's hope so."

I glanced down at my frayed coveralls. My cheeks burned. I wanted to crawl under a rock and drag brush up to its edge to cover up any trace of my ever having existed. But that wasn't an option. So, instead, I slapped on an expression of casual interest, toed my father's scruffy right boot, and asked, "What does the report say?"

"According to Vanderhoff, someone keeps calling her home phone. They say weird things and hang up."

I shifted onto my other foot. "Well, like I said, it's probably the neighborhood kids earning their stripes. In case you haven't noticed, they do *everything* on the phone nowadays."

Paulson shot me a salacious smile, then leaned over and removed a file from his briefcase. He opened it and read aloud from the pages within. "Vanderhoff says, and I quote, 'When I pick up the phone, I hear *beep-beep-beep*, and a robot tells me to do naughty things.'"

I bit my bottom lip. "Huh. Okay. That's weird. Even for Vander-hoff."

Paulson shot me a boyish grin. "I know, right? I mean, who uses a *landline* anymore?"

That one earned him half a genuine smile. "When did she start getting the calls?"

Paulson's blue eyes shifted back to the report. "Ever since she came back from Beth-Ann's Beauty Parlor a week ago last Wednesday, apparently."

"You're joking."

"That's what Jack's report says." Paulson tossed the file onto the table in front of him. It spun half a circle and came to rest with a corner hanging off the edge. "Read it yourself."

"Why? What's it got to do with me?"

Paulson's grin faded. "Well, I thought about what you told me last week. Are you still interested in becoming a private investigator?" He glanced up at the bandage on my forehead. "I mean, after this mall cop incident?"

My gut flopped. I'd never been less sure of something in my entire life. But if I didn't become a P.I., how else was I ever going to escape Point Paradise and motor oil under my nails—not to mention Earl's farty Frito breath?

"Yeah. I'm sure," I said, and rolled my eyes up toward my forehead. "This little thing? Nothing but a flesh wound."

Paulson shook his head. "Mall cop." He tapped a finger on the report. "I can't believe they made you risk your life for ten bucks an hour."

"That's why I took that P.I. training course on line. To get licensed as a Class CC Intern." I hung my head. "Problem is, I need two years of on-the-job training to get my real investigator's license." I looked up and smiled wryly. "Then I'll be eligible to die with the dignity of knowing I was making *twenty-four* bucks an hour."

Paulson grinned. "I take it you finished the course?"

"They tell me the diploma's in the mail."

He whistled. "Wow. You can get a certificate for anything over the internet nowadays."

"Thanks," I said sourly. "So, did you just call me in here to bust my chops or what?"

Paulson winked. "If I did, is that a crime?"

Considering how broke I am? Yes. I wasted at least a buck fifty in gas to get here. You could've asked me about the diploma over the phone.

"I guess not," I said, and turned to go.

Paulson's voice sounded behind me.

"Wait, Bobbie. You need work."

I froze in place. What I *really* needed was cash. But the word "work" was close enough. I turned back around. Paulson's face wasn't exactly serious, but it wasn't mocking, either.

"I'm listening," I said.

Paulson stood. I couldn't help but do a mental inventory.

Tall? Check. Dark? Check. Handsome? Double check.

"You still with me?" he asked.

My eyes traveled from Paulson's manly frame to his piercing blue eyes. "Yes, sir."

"Good. Because when I came across this file, I immediately thought of you. I mean, what better practice for a newly licensed CC intern?"

"What do you mean?"

"You can take on the case of the Crazy Cat lady. A CC for a CC. Get it?"

"Ugh," I groaned. "I get it. What's it pay?"

Paulson winced and made a sucking sound out of the side of his sexy mouth. "Officially? Nothing. It'll be practice. Like an apprenticeship, of sorts."

My interest disappeared along with my smile. "No thanks."

"Listen, I can't pay you on the books. But how about a wager?"

I frowned. "What do you mean?"

"You solve Vanderhoff's problem, and I'll give you twenty bucks out of my own pocket."

Given the current state of my financial affairs, his offer was disconcertingly appealing. "Why would you do that?"

"Because, with Jack on vacation, I'm busy with bigger fish to fry than an old lady who sat too long under a hairdryer." He flashed his charming smile. "Come on. Help me out with Vanderhoff."

I stared into his mesmerizing blue eyes until one of them winked.

"It'll be fun, Bobbie," Paulson coaxed. "You can be my new 'low man on the totem pole,' so to speak."

Great. Now even Paulson doesn't see me as female. My work here in Point Paradise is complete.

"How could I refuse an offer like that?" I said sourly, and reached for the file.

Paulson yanked it away.

"I'm not done," he said and grinned seductively. "I said it was a *wager*. If you don't solve the case, *you* owe *me* something."

"What?"

"Dinner."

Huh. Maybe this wasn't just a pity call after all.

I should've been happy about that. But my gut fired off a warning knot.

Don't get involved with Paulson.

The guy's charming, sky-blue eyes were like a window into my soul. If history repeated itself, the view from that window would be the last thing I'd see before I jumped through it and splattered my guts all over the sidewalk, right next to my broken heart.

Geez. When did I get to be such a romantic?

"Fine." I grabbed the file. Paulson hadn't specified what *kind* of dinner I'd owe him if I didn't solve the case. As far as I knew, a McHappy Meal still cost way less than twenty bucks.

So it was a wager I couldn't lose. At least, not financially.

"I'll solve it. You'll see," I said, and turned to go. I attempted a dramatic exit, but tripped on my oversized work boots and fell to one knee, right next to a trashcan.

Awesome.

I put a hand on the rim, hauled myself up, and willed myself not to look back.

Then I stomped out the door of Dana's Café, cursing the dead man who'd left me to fill his stupid shoes.

Chapter Eight

IT WAS A FEW MINUTES after four o'clock when I left Detective Paulson in Dana's Café and headed back toward Point Paradise. From Waldo, Robert's Mechanics was ten miles away, down rural backroads habituated mostly by hunters, lost tourists, and the flattened carcasses of animals with poor depth perception.

Being stuck in Point Paradise amongst the forgotten Florida backwoods of sawgrass and pines, to me Paulson's arrival had been the most interesting thing to happen since Earl found a two-headed turtle out in Wimbly Swamp last year.

The image of Paulson's handsome face coaxed a smile from my sullen lips as I drove south on Obsidian Road. In a better mood than I'd been in ages, I slowed down as I approached the Stop & Shoppe drive-thru. I thought about buzzing through just to give Artie something to bitch about, but decided against it.

I was working a case now. I needed to act like a professional.

Vanderhoff's house was a few blocks behind the Stop & Shoppe. It was one of a tiny cluster of modest ranch houses built in the 1950s, back when people were still gullible enough to buy swampland, and Point Paradise was still gullible enough to think it had a future. The developer had dubbed the place Cherry Manor.

Cherry Manor. Yeah, right.

No cherry trees grew in Florida, and there were certainly no manors within thirty miles of Point Paradise. In fact, I was pretty sure that, except for the size of the oak trees growing in the front yards, nothing had changed in Cherry Manor since the post WWII boon that had sparked its construction in the first place.

The Mustang's engine coughed when I switched off the ignition in front of Vanderhoff's house. From the sound of it, I needed a new air filter. I made a mental note of it. But right now, the granny who'd gone goofy was top on my priority list.

I climbed out of the car and walked up the plain concrete sidewalk leading to the plain concrete porch of her plain concrete-block house.

I rang the bell.

A lumpy green face appeared in the small window in the front door. It was the same grotesque mask that had caught me off guard that fateful Halloween three decades ago. This time, however, I didn't crap my coveralls.

Given the overall state of my life at the moment, I decided to count that as a win.

I waved to Vanderhoff.

She opened the door.

Dressed in a red turban and a faded muumuu, she looked like the love child of a ménage á trois between Zoltar, the Grinch, and any random backwoods redneck me-maw.

"Is that you, Mrs. Vanderhoff?" I knew it was, but I was working an official case now, and wanted to follow P.I. protocol: Always establish the identity of individuals before questioning them.

Vanderhoff's features shifted indistinguishably underneath the yellowish-green glop on her face. "What are you doing here, Bobbie? My car ain't broke down."

"No, Mrs. Vanderhoff. I'm here helping out Detective Paulson."

She eyed the yard behind me. "Where's Jack Barker?"

"Vacation."

"Oh yeah. How's he doing?"

"Fine. Can I come in?"

"Why?"

"Just want to ask you a few questions. About those phone calls you've been getting."

"Oh. Sure. Come on in. Let me wash my face."

She ushered me into her living room and motioned me toward a faded, flower-print couch. I sat down and glanced around. Despite being her neighbor for decades, I'd never actually been inside her house before.

I hadn't had the nerve.

After all, her house was Point Paradise's equivalent of *The Munsters'* place. I laughed to myself.

What had I been afraid of back when I was a kid? The old lady's harmless.

Then I stopped laughing.

Across the room, an ancient porcelain doll in a tattered lace dress stared at me. From her perch atop a wingback chair, she looked like a miniature corpse pissed off about being jerked out of her coffin.

I swallowed hard and glanced to my left. In a dark corner sat a curio cabinet stuffed with more dolls. Each of them glared at me from their overcrowded, glass prison.

A jolt of cold electricity shot down my back.

Geez! Are these like ... voodoo *dolls? Is this how Vanderhoff gets her revenge on the kids who bother her? Oh my lord ... has she got one of ... me?*

"So what do you want to know?" Vanderhoff asked, startling me so badly I shot up off the couch.

"Uh ... questions ...." I fumbled for words as I waited for the crawling sensation beneath my red wig to subside. "I hear you ... uh ... you told Jack you've been getting weird phone calls."

I studied Vanderhoff's face and decided she'd looked better with the avocado mask.

She sucked her teeth. "Yeah, they're weird, all right."

Suddenly, she jabbed a hand in the pocket of her faded muumuu. In P.I. mode, I braced myself in the event evasive action would be required. The old lady was crazy. For all I knew, she could've been packing a Colt 45—and I didn't mean malt liquor.

Her hand emerged holding a TV remote. An odd mixture of relief and disappointment echoed through my gut.

"Bobbie, you remember that show, *The Jetsons?*"

"Yeah." I straightened my slouching shoulders and shook off the willies. "I mean, yes, ma'am." I pulled a notepad and pencil from my purse to record the account.

"Well, the guy who keeps calling me sounds like that robot, Rosie. Only if she was a man, you know what I mean?"

Not really.

"Sure, Mrs. Vanderhoff. What did the robot say, exactly?"

The old lady leaned in closer to divulge her confidential information.

"*Beep-beep-beep,*" she whispered into my face.

My fingers relaxed around my pencil. I waved away the cloud of stale smoker's breath that came along with her confession and said, "I see. Did you say anything back?"

Vanderhoff shook her turbaned head. "Well, no. I hung up on him. I mean, who knows what 'beep' means in robot language? He could've been making an obscene phone call for all I know."

Right. Robocop's taken up a new career making perverted robo-calls. Case solved.

I bit my lip and tried to appear professional. I figured maybe flattery would loosen up the witness. "Yes. Well, that's certainly one interpretation, Mrs. Vanderhoff. And, might I say, you took a very smart approach, hanging up on him."

The old woman smiled, causing her dentures to slip. "Thanks, Bobbie."

"So, how many times did Robo ... I mean, *the robot* call?"

"Three or four times. I wasn't gonna bother the police, Bobbie. But when he told me to commit a crime, that's when I called Jack."

"A crime?"

"Yep. After he quit all that dad-blamed beeping business, that deviant demanded I get over to the A&P and steal six bananas."

Something inside me went slack. It might've been my will to live. "Well, that's quite specific. And ... did you?"

"Did I what?"

"Steal the bananas."

Vanderhoff's eyes doubled in size. "No way! I'm not a dad-burned thief!"

"Of course not." I dialed my tone to conciliatory. "I'm sorry. Tell me, why do you think the robot called *you*, Mrs. Vanderhoff?"

She scratched her head with a yellowed fingernail. "I don't know. Maybe he thought I was easy. There ain't a lot of eligible bachelorettes here in Point Paradise, as you well know."

Okaaaay ....

I doodled a cross-eyed lunatic in my notebook. "Is there anything else you can remember that I should know?"

Vanderhoff studied me for a moment. "Yes. For the record, I think it was pretty low what that scoundrel, Carl Blanders done to you, honey."

"Thanks, Mrs. Vanderhoff."

"I mean, dumping you for Candy Vincent after all them years. It ain't right. After all, you still got some of your looks left."

I eyed her sourly. "Thanks."

"Candy Vincent's a tramp, if you ask me," Vanderhoff rambled on. "Who names a kid Candy and expects her to be anything but a tramp? Am I right?"

"Yes. You're right. Thanks. And I'm sorry about what's happened to your niece Mandy."

The old woman winced. "You know, that new haircut of yours kind of reminds me of her."

Really? Poor Mandy.

Vanderhoff sighed and reached into the other pocket of her muumuu. My back stiffened. What would she pull out this time? A butcher knife? A doll head? A tub of guacamole?

Before I could grab her arm to stop her, Vanderhoff pulled out a fist and thrust it at my face. I flinched. When I opened my eyes, she unfurled her gnarled fingers to reveal a handful of green pills.

"You want a Paxil, honey?" she asked. "It helps. And you sure look like you could use one. I heard you got shot, but your skull was too thick for it to do any real damage."

My jaw clamped tight enough to straighten bent metal.

I have got *to get the hell out of this stupid town!*

"No thanks, Mrs. Vanderhoff. I have to go. But here, let me give you my number in case this robot guy calls again, or if you think of anything else that might be relevant."

I handed her one of my cards. Besides the online course and the fee for the state exam, a set of cheap business cards was the only investment I'd made in my budding P.I. career. I didn't even have a gun. Nobody I knew offered a lay-a-way program for a Glock, and slingshots were *so* third century.

Vanderhoff took the card. "Okay, Bobbie. I'll stick it on the fridge with one of the magnets Mandy sent me."

"Good plan." As I turned to leave, my footstep caused an oak floorboard in her living room to squeak.

Vanderhoff grabbed my arm. "Did you hear that?"

"Hear what?"

"The floor. It just said my name. *Mil-dred. Mil-dred.* Didn't you hear it?"

I shot Vanderhoff the kind of hope-against-hope smile people in movies offer serial killers on the off chance it'll persuade them not to chop them into cat food. I modeled it after the doomed smile I'd seen on the faces of all of those dead-eyed dolls camping out in her living room.

"Yes, I heard it," I said. "*Mil-dred*. Plain as day. You have a good night, now, Mrs. Vanderhoff."

I hurried out the front door, slamming it behind me. When I stepped off the porch and glanced back, Vanderhoff's turban-topped face was staring at me through that small windowpane in the door like Norman Bates in *Arabian Nights*.

A chill squirmed through my spine. I sprinted to my car, my nerves half shot. I'd just interviewed my first P.I. subject, and I'd just committed my first P.I. mistake.

I'd lied to the client.

As I tumbled into the driver's seat of the Mustang, I rationalized that I hadn't *really* lied to Vanderhoff. Not completely.

It was true that I hadn't heard the floorboard squeak "Mil," but I'd definitely heard it say "dread." In fact, like a spider with icicles for legs, dread had crawled all the way up my spine and was spinning a frosty web in my brain.

Is this what it's like to be a P.I.? Geez!

The only reason I even signed up for that stupid course was so I could keep tabs on my dates—if I ever got another one. Never again was I going to be the last one to know someone was cheating on me—and with Candy Vincent, no less!

I reached into my stash of Tootsie Pops and pulled out the last sucker in the bag. It was green. I hated green. What kind of flavor was *green?*

I unwrapped the sucker and popped it into my mouth anyway—for the same reasons I'd taken this bizarre, hand-me-down assignment from Paulson in the first place.

I was broke. I was angry. And I was out of options.

I snorted out a jaded laugh.

Those three traits seemed to come with the territory for anyone unlucky enough to be trapped in Point Paradise.

A sudden flash of light to my right caught my attention. I looked over to see the lights had gone out in Vanderhoff's living room. There was nothing more I could do there tonight, so I cranked the engine and tossed the nasty green Tootsie Pop in the Mustang's ashtray.

Then a weird feeling came over me.

I'd just had my most interesting night in months. The strange encounter with Vanderhoff had left me invigorated, oddly spooked, and feeling a bit in over my head.

Oh my word. Is this what it feels like to be ... alive?

I'd almost forgotten.

I rolled up the car window and pictured the rugged, charming face of Detective Terry Paulson. He'd been the first person in a long time to cut me a break.

With only an intern's CC license, I wasn't supposed to work a case without a full-fledged P.I. alongside me. Florida required I obtain two years of on-the-job training before I could I call myself a *real* private investigator.

I smiled. Paulson's arrival had been like manna from heaven. I mean, where the hell else was I going to find someone willing to give me a shot?

Paulson had bent the rules by letting me interview Vanderhoff on my own. But in a tiny, nowhere kind of place like Point Paradise, the rules tended to slide when you knew everyone on a first-name basis.

Besides, what could be the harm in me poking around? The worst that could happen was I'd end up having to buy Paulson a cheeseburger—and maybe get myself laid.

But neither of those things were going to happen tonight.

So, with nothing else to go on and nothing else to do, I shifted into drive and pointed the Mustang in the direction of Waldo and the A&P. Somebody was going bananas. Whether it was me or old lady Vanderhoff was still up for debate. As I headed down the road, I had no illusions about my prospects. I was still a pawn in the game of life. But for the first time in ages, I actually felt like playing.

Chapter Nine

THE A&P TURNED OUT to be a bust. No weirdos lurking around, at least not by Florida standards. Everyone had on the right amount of clothing and no one was holding a sign reading "Will Work for Beer."

I made the most of the trip by picking up a loaf of Wonder bread for toast in the morning, then headed for home.

As I got near the Stop & Shoppe, I thought it might be fun to buzz through, just to make Artie haul his humongous butt off his chair and wait on me. But after scrounging the bottom of my purse to pay for the bread, I didn't have enough money for a lousy Tootsie Pop. So instead, I settled for flipping him the bird as I cruised past.

In the fading light, I leaned out the window to see if Artie had seen my single-digit salutation. I'd expected to see his familiar scowl hovering above his scraggly soul patch and double chin. Instead, my eyes landed on something even more disturbing.

I blinked.

No. That can't be.

I slammed on the brakes. And, after executing the fastest three-point turn on record, I zoomed back to the Stop & Shoppe. It was still there.

I hit the brakes, rubbed my eyes, and took another look.

Still there.

Against all logic, a pair of red, glowing orbs hovered in the darkness about six feet above the roof of the run-down convenience store. I grabbed my cellphone to take a picture. When I looked up again, they were gone.

What the—?

I figured they must've been some kind of reflection, so I pulled up under the sagging awning that served as the Stop & Shoppe's low-rent drive-thru. Artie was busy sawing logs in his executive armchair, his feet up on the counter by the cash register.

The fat bastard had slept through the entire thing.

That figures.

I revved the engine, startling a loud fart out of Artie.

"What?" he grumbled, rubbing his beady eyes. It was uncanny. Artie possessed the same basic body shape and face of a middle-aged manatee.

"You see anything funny this evening?" I asked.

"Funny?" Artie leaned sideways, causing his chair to creak in a way that sounded both painful and precarious.

"Yeah. You know, *unusual.*"

He scowled. "No."

I shifted the Mustang into park. The engine sputtered out.

Damn air filter.

I wrapped my fingers around the key and was about to re-restart the ignition when I heard scratching coming from the awning overhead.

"What's that?" I asked.

"Probably rats." Artie gave a disinterested shrug. "Or tree limbs, maybe. The skinflint owner don't spend a dime to keep this place up. Just last week I had to—"

"Hush!" I cocked my head toward the ceiling.

"What?" Artie shot me a scowl. "You doing pest control now, Bobbie?"

"Shut up, Artie! *Listen!*"

The scratching sound continued, traversing the length of the roof awning from the roadside toward the back, where the Stop & Shoppe butted up against the woods.

I got out of the Mustang and sprinted past the end of the awning, then strained to see the rooftop. I couldn't make out squat in the darkness.

"You got a flashlight?" I yelled at Artie.

His chair squealed. "Sure," he hollered back. "For six-fifty. You want batteries it's another four bucks."

"Ugh." I shook my head and walked back to the Mustang. As I peeled out of the Stop & Shoppe, I glanced back. No red orbs.

Hospital shooters? Robot phone calls? Now these stupid glowing orbs? What next? Sasquatch in a tutu?

As the Stop & Shoppe disappeared in my rearview mirror, I made a mental note to add a flashlight to my P.I. kit—once I *had* a P.I. kit.

From the looks of it, I was going to need one.

Either that, or I needed to seriously consider making an appointment with a psychiatrist.

Chapter Ten

MY CELLPHONE RANG. I cracked open an eye and searched around in the tangled bedsheets for it.

"Hello?"

"I've got one for you."

My brain cramped. "What do you want, Earl? I'm still half asleep."

"It's nine-thirty."

"It's my day off, okay?"

"True mechanics never take a day off."

"Ugh. I got shot in the head, remember?"

He snorted. "How long you gonna ride *that* gravy train?"

"Earl, I'm only gonna ask one more time. What do you want?"

"Like I said, Bobbie. I've got one for you."

"Listen. I'm in *no* mood for one of your dumb jokes."

"It's a *customer*, you dingdong. Unless you don't want one."

My brain perked to life at the prospect of a paycheck. I bolted upright in bed. "Oh. What are we looking at?"

"Right now? A guy with a moustache that could win a Groucho Marx contest. And for the record, it's only *me* who's looking at him, Sleeping Beauty."

"I *meant* what are we looking at for *work*, smartass. Flat tire? Oil change? Please say it's major mechanical failure."

"I dunno. He walked here."

I squeezed my cellphone so hard it chirped. "Are you saying he doesn't have a vehicle? If this is another one of your stupid pranks, Earl, I'm gonna fire you."

"No prank. The guy needs a tow. I'm thinking it could be worth a few bucks. Should I tell him to get lost? You've got better things to do?"

I heard the *ka-ching* of a cash register—as it tumbled off a cliff. "Don't let him go anywhere! I'll be down in three minutes."

Earl laughed. "I'll do my best to keep him entertained."

"No jokes, Earl. Especially that stupid one about the gear shaft. You hear me?"

My phone went dead. I jumped out of bed and peeked through the blinds. From the dusty window of my apartment above the mechanic shop, I could see Earl talking to some guy dressed in black. He hadn't been kidding after all.

I let go of the blinds and made a mad dash for the bathroom. I figured I had no more than three minutes before Earl told that gearshaft joke and we lost the only customer we'd had in a week. I pulled a T-shirt on over my head, wriggled into my father's coveralls and humongous work boots, and clomped down the stairs.

I bet the guy's onboard computer's on the fritz. They mess up everything.

I considered computers—especially *onboard* computers—to be the ruination of life as I knew it.

About the same time cars became equipped with them, I'd become equipped with boobs. Dad had given me the boot, and my cousin Earl had gotten the benefit of sopping up all my father's knowledge—*and* his time.

With all Dad's attention on Earl, my mother had finally gotten her chance to make me into a girl. It hadn't gone well. I guess by then I was too far off the grid.

Mom and Grandma Selma didn't know what to do with a girl who refused to wear a dress and who tied dolls to fence posts and shot out their eyes for BB-gun practice. After a while, they'd given up on the whole idea of domesticating me. "Don't bother me and I won't bother you," became a routine which lasted until I took off for college.

Even so, when Dad died and Mom up and ran off with Mr. Applewhite, it really threw me for a loop. Given her submissive nature, I didn't think she had it in her to go rogue.

Mom had left me all alone to run the garage with Earl. I'd have fired the jerk on day one, but I didn't know anything about those blasted onboard computers.

So my cousin and I had formed our own sort of weird alliance. He'd remained head mechanic at my dad's shop, and I'd become "the boss"—in other words, the person responsible for dealing with the bills, the customers, and the paperwork. But it was no "don't bother me and I won't bother you" relationship.

Just the opposite.

Earl and I bothered the hell out of each other—for sport.

I stumbled to the bottom of the stairs and caught sight of my reflection in the mirror by the door. Nothing like forgetting you're a bald cyclops to give you a friendly jolt in the morning. Better than a double espresso.

I gasped, fumbled back upstairs, and grabbed my wig. There was no time to fix my face. But, thankfully, nobody expected much in the way of appearance from a mechanic.

Secretly, I considered it one of the best perks of this whole lousy job.

Chapter Eleven

THE DOOR LEADING TO the parking lot squeaked as I pushed it open. An orange streak of late-morning sun hit me across the face, making me wince like a three-eyed vampire.

"This here's the boss man, Bobbie Drex," Earl said as I tumbled out the door and shuffled over to them. "Or, as we like to call her, 'the boy with boobs.'"

So much for establishing myself as the authority figure.

I sneered at Earl. "Did I mention that you're fired?"

Earl grinned, confident in his irreplaceability. He nodded and deadpanned, "Yeah. Just let me go collect my severance package."

"It's hard to find good help nowadays," I said to the guy with the moustache, extending my hand for a shake.

Anywhere but Florida, the guy would've been considered an odd duck. He wore a vintage fedora, which he tipped at me in an old-fashioned gesture of courtesy. As he did, I noticed he also had a knot on his forehead. Unlike mine, however, his was big enough to smuggle a boiled egg inside. His lip was busted as well. I figured he must've been in one hell of a bar fight recently.

"Name's William Knickerbocker," he said. He winced slightly when he raised his hand to shake mine. "Or as some folks like to call me, 'the boy *without* boobs.'"

Everybody's a smartass.

"How about I call you Bill?" I said dryly.

"That works, too. My vehicle's about two and a half miles down the road that way." Bill winced again as he raised his arm to point south down Obsidian Road. "I need a tow and repairs."

"What are you driving?"

"An RV."

Ka-ching!

"I think we can help you out with that, Bill. But I'm not sure about *you*." I took a furtive glance at his bulging forehead. "What are you? Some kind of professional barroom brawler?"

He grinned. "No. But it's amazing how often I end up looking like one." He touched his forehead. "This is just your typical head-against-the-windshield goose egg."

My eyebrows ticked up a notch. "You were in an accident?"

"Yeah. I think I hit a deer or something."

"A deer, you say." I exchanged a knowing glance with Earl. Venison beat an empty stomach any day of the week, even if it *was* road kill. It was fine, as long as you got there quick enough.

"What about *you*?" Knickerbocker asked, his eyes on the red knot between my eyes. "Where'd you get *that* beaut?"

"Oh. I, uh ...."

"She just had her demons exorcized," Earl quipped.

Knickerbocker's left eyebrow shot up. I looked past him at Earl. He was behind Knickerbocker, his face twisted into an idiotic expression aimed at making me lose my composure. I clenched my jaw to squelch the burning desire to kick Earl where the sun don't shine.

"Earl, darling?" I said between my teeth, "When you're done having a seizure, could you please give Bill here a lift back to his vehicle? Hook it up to Bessie and tow it back."

Earl's face switched to his normal, easy-going grin. I hated how easily he could shift gears.

"Yes, boss man." He moseyed toward the garage's only working service bay.

Bill blanched. "*Bessie?* You're going to pull my RV with a *cow?*"

I smirked. "Not exactly."

The sound of an angry diesel engine thundered from inside the service bay.

I nodded toward the garage. "*That's* Bessie."

Knickerbocker turned around just as a huge, black, four-wheel-drive monster truck emerged from the bay. Equipped with a 540-horsepower Hemi engine and tractor tires taller than me, Bessie could yank Godzilla out of Tokyo.

Earl steered the massive truck out of the garage and idled it next to Bill and me. "Hop in," he said to Knickerbocker.

"You wouldn't happen to have a stepladder, would you?" Bill asked.

"Fresh out." I patted my pockets. "Earl, Bill here said he hit a deer. Be sure and check that out."

Earl winked. "Yes, boss man."

Knickerbocker reached over his head to open Bessie's passenger door. He grunted as he hauled his tall, lanky body inside the cab. The effort made him wince and lick the seam on his busted lip.

He closed the door and Earl hit the gas, tearing another pothole in the crumbling asphalt parking lot. The pair disappeared past the flashing yellow light and down Obsidian Road.

Once they were out of sight, I slipped into the garage, unfastened the padlock on the electrical box, and flipped over a few breakers. A couple of overhead lights blinked on, and an air compressor began to hum.

I smiled to myself. I didn't care if Knickerbocker was a tourist, a weirdo, or even an escapee from nearby Stark Prison.

We were flat broke.

With any luck, the repairs on his busted vehicle would generate enough money to pay last month's light bill before they cut off the juice.

Chapter Twelve

FROM MY APARTMENT ABOVE the garage, I spotted Bessie passing underneath the flashing yellow light at the intersection. Hitched to the monster truck's rear was the most dilapidated hunk of junk I'd seen since my last trip to the Waldo antiques center.

Crap. So much for hitting the motherlode. I guess I'm gonna need Detective Paulson's twenty bucks after all.

As I watched Earl ease the rusty, algae-covered hulk of an RV into the service bay, I punched a number into my cell phone.

"Paulson? It's Bobbie Drex here with a case update."

"Well, don't *you* sound all official-like?" he crooned. "Let me guess. Vanderhoff's got early-onset Alzheimer's?"

"Good one. No. I think there may be more to it than that. I drove by the A&P last night. There was some weird guy hanging out in the parking lot in a yellow Volkswagen Beetle."

It was a lie. There hadn't been so much as an alley cat roaming the parking lot. But if my mother had taught me anything, it was that if you gave someone enough detail, you could make *anything* sound plausible. Besides, it was for a good cause. I was so broke twenty bucks would've doubled my net worth.

"Really? A yellow Volkswagen?" Paulson asked. The news seemed to catch him off guard. "Did you get a license plate number?"

My throat tightened. "No."

"So what's the possible connection between the Volkswagen and the calls Vanderhoff's getting?"

I cringed. "Well, I don't know. I didn't say I'd cracked the case. I just have a gut feeling there's more to Vanderhoff's story than your theory that a beauty parlor hairdryer cooked her brains."

"Right. Speaking of which, have you gone by Beth-Ann's to check out the dryer?"

Crap. I should have thought of that when I was at her place yesterday.

"It's on my follow-up list for today."

"Good. Just do me a favor."

"What?"

"Don't go chasing strange vehicles around in the dark. At least, not without me."

I grinned. "No worries there, I promise." That *wasn't* a lie. I didn't have money to waste on gas. The Mustang only got fifteen miles to a gallon. On a good day. Downhill.

"Okay. Call me when you've got something," Paulson said.

"Roger that."

I clicked off the phone and tromped down the stairs and over to the service bay. When I got there, Earl was deep under the hood of the RV, giving Knickerbocker the diagnosis on his raggedy-ass old Minnie Winnie.

"Threw a rod," Earl was saying. "Right through the gear shaft."

I wasn't sure if Earl was being serious or had just delivered the punchline to the joke I'd expressly banned him from telling. I checked Knickerbocker's face. He seemed unconcerned either way.

"Can you fix it?" Knickerbocker asked.

Earl shrugged. "Sure. But do you really think it's worth spending the money on this old hunk—"

I kicked Earl in the shin. Hard.

His surprised eyes met mine, and I shot him a look that could curdle an enamel paint job. He winced and rubbed his leg.

"What a classic," I said, beaming at Knickerbocker.

"Uh ...," Earl fumbled. "I mean, I have to say, sir, she's a real beauty."

Knickerbocker's battered face sagged a little more. He let out a sigh. "Listen. I know she's no looker, but she's got sentimental value. Do what you can for her, would you?"

"Don't you want to know the cost first?" Earl asked. He glanced over at me and withered again under my angry glare.

Bill shook his head. "No. Whatever it costs, it's okay." He turned to me. "As long as you take cash, that is."

"We definitely take cash," I blurted before Earl had a chance to say anything else idiotic. He might've been a mechanical genius, but he was the crappiest salesperson in the known Milky Way Galaxy.

"We'll get to work on it right away," I said. "Earl will figure out the parts you need. You put down a deposit that pays for the parts, and we'll get them ordered right away."

Knickerbocker smiled absently. "That sounds good. How long will it take to fix?"

"I'd say not more than three to six days," Earl said, "depending on availability of parts."

"You have someplace to stay?" I asked Knickerbocker.

"I can't stay in the RV?"

I shook my head. "No. It'll be up on the lift."

"And maybe in a few pieces, I suspect," Earl said.

Knickerbocker shrugged and smiled in a vague, pained kind of way. "Then I guess I'm going to need a place to stay."

"I've got a small in-law apartment upstairs," I blurted. "I could rent it to you for say, eighty-nine dollars a night?"

Knickerbocker looked at me strangely, then let out a groan. His eyes rolled up into his head, and he collapsed backward, right into Earl's waiting arms. My cousin caught him by the torso, then laid him out on the floor of the service bay like a side of beef.

"I'd a passed out, too," Earl said. "You shouldn't a gone over fifty-nine bucks, tops."

"This isn't funny, Earl. The guy may have a concussion or something. Help me get him up the stairs."

"Shouldn't we call a doctor?"

"Who? Dr. Greenblatt? He moved away two months ago."

"Oh, yeah." He looked me in the eyes. "Good thing you and me can't afford to get sick."

I didn't try to argue with Earl's logic. It made more sense than anything else going on at the moment. I grabbed Knickerbocker's legs, Earl hooked his arms under his shoulders, and we toted him toward the stairwell.

As I wrangled the door open with an elbow, Earl's stomach growled.

"Oh," he said. "I almost forgot. I searched around, but couldn't find no signs of a deer. This feller here must'a hit something else."

I sighed.

So much for free venison stew tonight.

Chapter Thirteen

I STARED AT THE STRANGER sprawled out in Grandma Selma's old bed.

Earl and I had carried Knickerbocker upstairs to her tiny in-law apartment. It was attached to my parent's place by a short breezeway. I hadn't been inside it for months. The air inside smelled faintly of dust and her perfume.

We'd laid Knickerbocker on the bed and pulled his shirt off to assess him for injuries. Between his neck and left shoulder, we'd discovered a large bruise ringed with broken skin. It was sort of oval-shaped, and as big as the bottom of a plastic jug of Castrol Motor Oil.

I'd figured the injury must've come from the shoulder strap on his seatbelt. Knickerbocker's RV was too old to have airbags to soften the impact.

Earl, on the other hand, had insisted the injury was a Sasquatch bite. I'd shot him another choice selection from my repertoire of scathing looks, handed him my life savings, and sent him off to the A&P to fetch some aspirin, rubbing alcohol, and two cans of chicken soup, whatever was cheapest.

While Earl was away, I'd stayed behind to keep an eye on our unanticipated patient. Equipped with the hospital's handy-dandy concussion watch list, I sat on an old wicker settee and intermittently glanced over at Knickerbocker, biding my time by scanning articles from a selection of outdated magazines I'd filched from the recycle bin at Beth-Ann's.

I was engrossed in a fascinating article on new and exciting ways to reinvent green bean casserole when Knickerbocker groaned. I jumped up and sprinted to his side.

"Are you okay, Mr. Knickerbocker?"

He opened his eyes. Either his irises were black, or his pupils had swallowed them whole.

"Mr. Knickerbocker?" I repeated.

His eyes pointed in my direction, but whether he could see me or not, I couldn't tell. He muttered something that sounded like a foreign language, then shifted his dazed eyes to his left, as if he was searching for something.

"It's okay," I said soothingly. "You're okay." I touched his arm. He jerked away.

"Mr. Knickerbocker!" I said louder. "You're okay. Can you hear me?"

"Huh?" He grunted, and turned back toward me. His dilated pupils were now rimmed with green.

"You're safe with me," I said.

"Where am I?" he asked.

"My grandmother's apartment. You passed out."

"Oh."

"I sent Earl for supplies," I said, then heard a rumble. I went to the window. Earl was pulling Bessie into the parking lot, having spent, literally, my last dime.

I walked back over to the bedside. "I don't mean to be crass, but I'll need money before we can go any further."

Knickerbocker's head lolled on the pillow. He glanced down at his naked chest. "Go any further? Are we ... uh ... did we just—?"

My back bristled with Southern indignation. "Before we can order parts. For your RV."

"My RV?"

"Yes. You said you hit a deer."

"Oh. Deer. Right. Did it survive?"

My eyebrows inched closer together. "I don't know. We didn't see any signs of it around the accident site."

"Why am I here ... in this bed?"

"You fainted. You hit your head in an accident. You walked here. We towed your RV? You don't remember?"

"Uh ... sure. But why am I half naked?" Knickerbocker lifted the sheet and took a peek under it. "You didn't see my ... uh ... *lizard*, did you?"

A snort of laughter erupted from behind me. I turned to see Earl standing there holding a paper grocery sack, grinning like a lottery winner.

Earl smirked at me, then eyed Knickerbocker. "Been a long time since *that one there's* seen a lizard."

Knickerbocker reached up and touched the goose egg on his forehead. His brow furrowed. "So you *didn't* see it?"

"*I* didn't," Earl said. "But having just freshly arrived, I can only speak for myself."

I punched Earl's arm. "Stop it. He's delirious."

I turned to Knickerbocker. "Now you lay back and let me disinfect your wounds."

"You remember what bit you?" Earl asked as I took the bag, opened the bottle of alcohol, and poured some onto a wad of toilet paper.

"Bit me?" Knickerbocker asked.

"He's talking about the wound on your shoulder," I said.

I shot Earl some side-eye, then sat on the edge of the bed beside Knickerbocker. I dabbed at the half-circle of bruised, slightly broken flesh.

Knickerbocker winced. "Feels like a cracked clavicle," he said. "Must've been the seatbelt."

I turned and sneered at Earl. He crinkled his nose at me.

"I hate to bring this up," Earl said, "but it'd be good to get some money down on them parts before the supply stores close for the day."

"Parts?" Knickerbocker asked.

"Your RV broke down, remember?" I asked.

"Sure." Knickerbocker tried to sit up, but fell back onto the pillows. "Sorry. I feel ... uh ...."

"Should I call a doctor?" I asked. "You don't look so good."

"No doctors!" Knickerbocker said with more energy than I thought he had left in him. He tried to sit up again, but gave up and leaned back on the pillows. "I hate doctors."

Earl's eyebrows raised to his shaggy hairline. "I hear *that*."

"Look. In the glove compartment," Knickerbocker said. "I keep money in there. Take whatever you need."

My right eyebrow arched. "Aren't you worried we might ... you know ... cheat you?"

"Yeah. Or rob you blind or something?" Earl added.

Knickerbocker studied us both through a pair of half-dilated, bloodshot eyes.

"Don't take this personally," he said. "But from the looks of you two, I don't think you've got enough ambition for anything like that."

Chapter Fourteen

I CLOSED THE DOOR TO the bedroom, leaving Knickerbocker propped up on pillows with a glass of tap water and a selection of *Southern Living* magazines circa 1997.

"What do you think we should do?" I whispered to Earl as we walked down the hall toward the kitchen. "He seems confused. Do you know anything about treating a cracked clavicle?"

"Not a thing," Earl said. "But if I'm right and that fella got hisself bit up by Bigfoot, he's probably got some kind of poison fever, you know, causing him to be all delusional and whatnot."

I closed my eyes and blew out a breath. Talking to Earl was like trying to have a conversation with Jethro on the *Beverly Hillbillies*. He had the same country twang, the same dumb luck, and the same irritating happy-go-lucky attitude. He also had an uncanny knack for calling things accurately, despite having no intellectual pursuits beyond *Auto Trader* and *Pimp My Ride*. It was downright infuriating.

"It's not a Bigfoot bite!" I hissed at Earl. "It's from his seatbelt. He said so himself."

"What about all that lizard mumbo-jumbo? That don't make him a very reliable witness, if you ask me."

"He's probably confused. From the accident."

Earl shrugged. "Or he's some nut-job fresh outta the looney bin."

I glared at Earl. I wanted to dismiss his comment out of hand. But doubt threaded its way across my mind like one of my Grandma Selma's cross-stitches. And that spider with icicle legs crawled out from under my wig again and made a beeline for where my bra hooked in the back.

"I don't want to be alone with him," I blurted. "Earl, you make the soup. I'll go check out the glove compartment."

"Yeah. Let's see if his cash is just a delusion too." Earl crinkled his nose. "Uh ... how do I make it?"

I looked up at the six-foot-four lump of uselessness. "Soup? You're kidding. You open the can, Earl. You pour it in a pan. Then you cook it till it boils."

"What kind of pan?"

I groaned, shook my head, and stomped down the stairs.

Halfway down, I turned around and stomped back up the stairwell. "Where are the keys?"

Earl grinned, pulled them out of the breast pocket of his coveralls, and dangled them in front of me like a cat toy. I swiped them from his hand and blew him a raspberry.

What a jerk!

I UNLOCKED THE DRIVER'S door of Knickerbocker's crappy old RV. It had a built-in cab, and I figured it measured around twenty-four feet long. Despite the exterior looking as if it were ready for the junkyard, I was surprised to discover the interior was almost mint.

One glance at the shiny chrome controls jutting from the aqua-painted metal dashboard and I was eight years old again—a kid in a candy store.

Sweet.

From the looks of it, the Minnie Winnie had to have been manufactured in the late 1960s, back when groovy was still a thing worth striving for.

Of course, the windshield was a total loss. It was shattered into an opaque hodgepodge of tiny ice cubes. The driver's seat also had a gash on the left side, near the headrest. Nicotine-hued foam rubber spewed out from the gaping slit in the aquamarine vinyl like raw chicken fat.

I glanced around the floorboards and passenger seat. No receipts. No junk food wrappers. Not even a roadmap or a coffee ring. If this guy was living in his RV, you'd never have known it. I laughed to myself.

He must be totally OCD.

I tried the glove compartment. It was locked. I fumbled with the key ring and tried the smallest key. It didn't work. I tried the next one. The key slipped in. I turned it, and the metal glovebox fell open like a slack jaw.

My own jaw followed suit.

Inside the glove compartment sat row upon row of neatly bundled cash—the kind of money you'd expect to nab from a successful bank heist.

I closed my mouth and cautiously picked up a packet. I fanned through the bills with my thumb.

Twenties. Fifty of them. A cool grand.

I picked up two more paper-banded packs and noticed a silver glint behind them. I shoved aside a few stacks. A 9mm Glock came into view.

I gasped.

I'd wanted a Glock since I was eight years old.

As I reached for the gun, a thought made me recoil as if I'd been attacked by a rattlesnake.

Who is this guy? Black clothes. Wads of cash. Driving in the middle of nowhere—in the middle of the night. There's no way he can be good news.

I should call Officer Paulson!

I patted down my coveralls. Five heavy-duty utility pockets and not one of them contained my cellphone. I mentally kicked myself in the ass, then stuffed three bundles of bills into my right hip pocket. I stacked the others back neatly, locked the glovebox, and was about to leave when curiosity got the better of me.

I swiveled the seat around, got up, and crept into the main cabin of the RV.

Beyond the reach of the overhead service bay lights, the RV's interior grew dim and veiled in a grayish gloom. As my eyes adjusted to the faint light, a modest kitchen, a small banquette, and a fold out couch built into the wall came into view.

Typical, old retro-style RV.

Beyond the main cabin, I could see a small hallway. At the end of it was a metal door. I walked to the edge of the hallway for a closer inspection.

The door looked like something from a lock-up unit. Four deadbolts secured the door above the doorknob. Four more below. Definitely not original equipment.

The hair on the back of my neck bristled.

Why would anyone do that?

A noise in the garage sent me whirling around on my thick, rubber heels.

Crap! Knickerbocker's coming!

My upper torso twisted toward the front of the RV. The bottom half wasn't quite so quick. I tried to take a step, tripped on my boots, and did a belly flop onto the floor of the main cabin.

"Oof!" I grunted as I hit the floor, the wind knocked out of me.

I lay there a second, taking inventory of my body parts, then hiked myself up on one elbow. As I waited for my breath to catch and the stars to clear from my corneas, I caught a movement from the corner of my eye.

I turned my head and found myself face-to-face with a pair of yellow-green, reptilian eyes.

Chapter Fifteen

THE REPTILE'S BULBOUS eyes stared blankly at me from inside a ten-gallon terrarium. It had been tucked beneath the banquette in Knickerbocker's RV.

I grunted and hauled myself to sitting on the linoleum floor.

Well, what do you know? Knickerbocker really does have a lizard.

"LOOK WHAT I FOUND," I said to Earl as I walked into the kitchen of Grandma Selma's apartment toting the terrarium.

"Well, I'll be. That looks like a lizard, all right." Earl shook his head. "Too bad, Cuz." He winked at me. "For a minute there, I thought you'd done got lucky."

"Hardy har har." I set the terrarium on the counter and pursed my lips to stifle a grin.

"Earl, that's not all I found." I pulled the stacks of twenties out of my pocket and fanned them in front of Earl's face. "I guess you can go ahead and order those parts now."

Earl's eyes grew as big as boiled eggs. "Lord a'mighty! How much you got there?"

"Three grand. But there's more if you need it."

Joy and avarice mud-wrestled on Earl's face, providing me with some much-relished sadistic pleasure.

"You got that soup ready?" I asked.

"Yeah." Earl took an iron skillet off the burner and poured its contents into a bowl. The whole while, he kept one eye trained on the money, until I shoved the bills back in my pocket.

"I'll carry the soup," I said. "You carry the lizard."

"What about the saltines?" Earl held up a waxy paper sleeve of crackers. "You can't have soup without saltines."

"You spent my last bit of my money on ... ugh!" Then I remembered the money in my pocket and lightened my mood. "Fine." I set the bowl on a plate and tossed a handful of crackers around the edges. "Happy now?"

Earl eyed my bulging money pocket. "I guess."

"Grab the lizard and follow me."

We crept down the hall, both of us quiet for a change. I balanced the plate and bowl precariously on one set of fingertips, like a French waiter, and tapped on the bedroom door with my free hand.

No reply.

I pushed the door open. The bed was empty.

"Mr. Knickerbocker?" I called out.

The floor-length curtains moved. Knickerbocker peeked out from behind them.

"Uh ... I brought you some soup. And Earl here has your ... uh ... lizard."

Knickerbocker's bloodshot eyes lit up at the sight of the terrarium. "Gizzard!"

Earl shot me the look he usually reserved for customers who pull into our garage and ask if we have clean restrooms.

"I'll set her down right here on the bureau," Earl said, and gingerly placed the glass terrarium on top of granny's ancient oak chest of drawers.

Knickerbocker took a step toward us, then loomed sideways, as if he'd just gotten off a Tilt-a-Whirl. His hand landed on the bed, catching his fall.

"Get back in bed right now," I said. "Eat your soup. You need to build your strength."

Knickerbocker smiled weakly and complied. He crawled into bed and took the bowl of soup I offered with two shaky hands.

"Saltines. Nice touch," he said, and slurped the soup as if he hadn't eaten in weeks.

Earl ogled the small, lime-green lizard through the glass of the terrarium. "If you don't mind me asking, Mr. K, why're you traveling around with a lizard of the reptilian persuasion?"

Knickerbocker looked up from his soup and shrugged. "No barking. No walking. No litter box. Gizzard only needs one thing. Crickets and fresh water."

"That's two things," I said.

"Oh. Right," Knickerbocker said absently. "Do you think you could get her some?"

"Crickets or water?" I asked.

"Both."

I looked over at my cousin. "Sounds like a job for you, Earl."

He pouted. "Why me?"

"Because I'm heading back over to Beth-Ann's."

Earl grinned. "Aw, come on, Bobbie. That wig looks fine. Besides, you don't have to get yourself all dolled up on my account. Or is it on account of *someone else?*" He shot Knickerbocker a wink.

I sneered. "It's not about either of you."

I hadn't told Earl about the case I was working with Officer Paulson, or about getting my private investigator intern certificate. I wasn't in the mood to live either one of those personal gems down just yet.

"Can I bring you back anything?" I asked as I walked toward the bedroom door.

"How about a comb?" Knickerbocker said. He ran his hand over the top of his head and seemed genuinely surprised to discover he was as bald as a cue ball.

I turned away so neither man could see my eyes roll around in their sockets.

Great. Another weirdo man to take care of.

Thanks, universe. That's all I need.

Chapter Sixteen

ON MY WAY TO BETH-ANN'S beauty shop, I noticed four or five buzzards circling above the woods a few miles south of Point Paradise. In this rural area, lots of people dumped their trash instead of paying for pickup, so I didn't think much of it. I drove on, intent on nailing my second interview as a P.I. intern.

No mistakes this time, I chided myself. *Beth-Ann's a friend, but I can't let that influence my professionalism.*

"HEY, YOU," BETH-ANN said as she swept up a heap of black, wavy hair. "Just gave myself a trim. You need one?"

"Ha ha. You're a riot." I glanced at my wig in the mirror, frowned, and gave it a quick adjustment.

"What's up, then?" she asked.

"Not much." Taking a note from my training course, I tried to act casual, in order to put the interviewee at ease. "Just searching for intelligent life. You seen any lately?"

Beth-Ann grinned. "In Waldo? Not even a molecule. You?"

"Nope. But I *did* meet a man."

Beth-Ann's face shifted from studied indifference to juicy-gossip intrigue. "Really?" She leaned on her broom handle. "Spill it, girl!"

I shrugged. "Not much to tell yet. He came into town today with a busted RV. He's boarding in Grandma's apartment for a few days."

"What's his name?"

"William Knickerbocker."

Beth-Ann rolled her huge, violet eyes. "Ugh! I hope he's cuter than he sounds."

"Meh. Not really. Kind of skinny. Bald. Not my type."

Beth-Ann's shoulders slumped. "Figures. Not even potential as a new client." She bent over and scooped the hair up into a dustpan. "So what else is up?"

I puffed out my chest a little. It went unnoticed due to my over-sized coveralls. "Paulson gave me a case to work on."

Beth-Ann's eyes twinkled with interest. "The sexy detexy? He gave you a *real* case? Tell me every juicy detail!"

"Well, that's kind of why I'm here. The case involves old lady Vanderhoff. She says she's been getting weird phone calls. "

"Vanderhoff?" Beth-Ann crinkled her nose. "Oh, geez, Bobbie. Paulson's playing you! Can't you see that? He probably wants to get you somewhere dark and secluded so he can get in your pants."

I grinned. "Jealous?"

Beth-Ann sneered. "Damned straight." She sighed, then laughed. "Vanderhoff's crazy. Remember that time she saw Jesus' face in a potato chip?"

I pursed my lips to a bloodless line. "Ruffles, no less. Don't re-mind me. Earl grabbed it out of her hand and ate it."

We locked eyes and both said, "Ruffles have religion."

We laughed a moment, then Beth-Ann shook her head. "Ruined that poor woman's chance at a *National Enquirer* spotlight. You know she still talks about it?"

"No!"

"Yep. Every time she comes in, near about."

I grinned, then cleared my throat, straightened my shoulders, and shifted into professional P.I. mode. "Seriously, Beth-Ann. What would Paulson have to gain by sending me on a wild goose chase with Vanderhoff?"

"What does any guy get out of torturing a woman?" Beth-Ann scowled for a second, then smirked at me. "I can't believe you're gonna be a detective! Tell me. How much is he paying you for the case?"

I bit my lip. "If I figure out who's behind the calls, I get twenty bucks."

"Twenty bucks? Geez. What a tightwad. And if you *don't?*"

"I have to take Paulson to dinner."

Beth-Ann shook her head. "And you don't think *that's* you getting played? Sorry girl, but license or not, you're no *Magnum P.I.*"

I sighed and drummed my grease-stained nails on a washbasin. "I went to her house last night."

"Whose house?"

"Old lady Vanderhoff's."

Beth-Ann's face went paler, if that was possible. "Wait a minute. You went *inside?*"

"Yeah."

She grabbed my forearm. "What was it like? Were there balls of tinfoil as big as beanbag chairs? Empty Cool Whip containers stacked to the ceiling? Real children's skeletons in her closet?"

"No. Actually, it looked relatively normal. Except for the dolls."

"Dolls?" Beth-Ann recoiled and dropped my arm. "Yuck!"

"I know. There were tons of them. Totally creepy."

"Did you find out anything?"

"Only that she's even crazier than I thought. She told me a robot told her to steal bananas."

Beth-Ann's eyes narrowed. "That's got your cousin Earl's name written all over it, Bobbie. I bet he put her up to it. To get back at you for leaving that rotten can of sardines under Bessie's driver's seat on his birthday."

My lips twisted over to one side of my face. "I hadn't thought of that."

Beth-Ann laughed. "Maybe you should have, detective."

"Okay. Maybe you're right. Still, just in case, do you mind if I ask you a few questions?"

"Sure."

I pulled a notepad and pen from my coveralls. Beth-Ann smirked, but only for a flash, then slapped on a semi-serious expression.

"When did Vanderhoff come in here last?" I asked.

"On Wednesday a week ago. Her bi-weekly wash and set."

I scribbled it down. "Did you use any new dyes or shampoos on her that might have caused a reaction?"

"Nope. Normal stuff. And no color that week. Just the wash and set."

"So she was here for how long?"

"From two in the afternoon to quarter past three."

I looked up at Beth-Ann. "That's pretty precise."

"I've been doing her hair for fifteen years, Bobbie. I've got that baby down to a science."

"Okay. Did she happen to sit under a hairdryer?"

"Of course. With a headful of curlers. You know the routine."

"I mean ... for maybe *longer* than usual?"

"Nope. I had another appointment right after. Nosy Nellie Parker at three-thirty. I had to keep on schedule or Nellie'd blab all over Alachua County about how my standards were slipping."

"That's the hairdryer, right?" I pointed to a chrome and purple chair that appeared to have been transported straight from the set of a low-budget, sci-fi movie.

Beth-Ann eyed me like I'd lost it. "Yes. It's the only one I've got. You and Carl sold it to me, remember?"

"Of course." I walked over to check it out. Of all the things in Beth-Ann's kitschy 1950s-vibe shop, her hair-drying chair was my favorite.

Sleek, low-slung, and boxy, the chair was upholstered in a light-lavender vinyl with a starburst pattern. Tubular chrome pipes served as its spindly-looking arms and legs.

But the part I liked best was the dryer head itself. The conical-shaped dome of stainless steel was the size and shape of the business end of a ballistic missile. It always made me think of a helmet left behind by an egg-headed alien.

I looked around for a manufacturer's tag. "What's the chair called again?"

"The Atomic Purple Salon Chair," Beth-Ann said. "Circa 1950-something. But I call her 'Girlie.'"

I grunted and scribbled it down on a notepad. I was about to leave when I noticed an earwig crawl out of one of the holes in the chrome dryer head.

"Anything else?" Beth-Ann asked. "Hate to give you the bum's rush, Bobbie, but I've got a perm coming in any second."

"No, that's it for now." I walked toward the door. "Thanks. You might want to spray for bugs. See you next week?"

"Bugs?" Beth-Ann scowled, then she zeroed in on a spot above my eyes. "Hey, you could use a brow wax."

"I think I'll hold onto all the hair I have left for right now." I opened the side door, hesitated, then turned around. Beth-Ann was bending over her dustpan.

"Hey, Beth-Ann?"

She looked up. I bit my lip, then blurted out what I wanted to ask before I lost my nerve.

"Do you believe in Sasquatch?"

Beth-Ann grinned slyly. "Did Earl put you up to this?"

When I didn't grin back, she straightened up to standing. "Wait. Are you serious?"

I shrugged and chewed my bottom lip. Then decided to laugh it off.

"Naw. I was just kidding around."

Chapter Seventeen

ON THE WAY BACK TO the garage, I wondered whether Beth-Ann was the most reliable source to confer with about the existence of hairy, ape-like creatures. Sure, she was non-judgmental. And a great hairstylist. People came from all over to get their hair done by her. But thinking about it now, maybe she was a little *too* open-minded.

A few weeks ago, after attending some kind of New-Age meetup, she'd advised me not to pray using negative words. She'd said that God couldn't hear "no" or "don't." So if someone prayed, "I don't want to be poor," all God heard was "I want to be poor," and so he granted their wish.

I was actually beginning to think there was something to it.

Ever since Carl Blanders dumped me, I'd been praying, "I don't want another no-good man in my life." Perhaps that double negative had been too confusing for the Creator of the Known Universe to figure out. Why else would another oddball loser wash up on my doorstep after I'd distinctly prayed for the exact opposite?

But then again, God had made up for it by delivering Terry Paulson to Point Paradise. The thought of his blue eyes and boyish grin made me want to call him up and flirt with him over the phone.

What the heck.

I pulled out my cellphone to call him. I figured I'd use the pretense of giving him a case update. But what did I have to report? That the brain-scrambling hairdryer in question turned out to be Atomic Purple? I frowned, nixed the idea, shoved my phone in my pocket, and turned the radio up.

I was a couple miles away from Point Paradise when I saw the buzzards again. I realized they were circling the same area where Knickerbocker had his accident. Curious, I pulled over. As soon as I opened the door, I could smell the unmistakable odor of rotting meat.

Too late for venison barbeque. But no doubt about it. Knickerbocker most certainly hit something....

With no obvious trail in the sawgrass, I followed my nose into the woods. About fifty feet into the pines, I saw a whitish-yellow lump in the leaves, up next to a pile of brush. As I got closer, I could see it was the corpse of a short-haired, mixed-breed dog. Its body was intact. Its jaws appeared to be covered in coagulated blood. Flies buzzed around it in noisy clouds.

Gross. Well, that solves that mystery.

I turned around to head back to the car.

My knees went wobbly. I nearly fell down.

Leaning up against a pine tree was another dead body. Only this one was human. Dressed in a pair of orange prison overalls, I couldn't tell if it was a man or woman. The person's throat and face had been pretty much ripped to shreds.

Paranoia swept over me like an arctic blast. *Is the killer still here? Watching me?*

My body began to shake uncontrollably.

I have to get out of here!

But my legs didn't seem to get the magnitude of the situation. They were stuck, frozen in place.

A fly buzzed around my face, then lit on my cheek. I swatted it away, horrified at the thought of where it had last landed. Nausea and dizziness flooded my senses, as if I'd suddenly become aware of the Earth spinning on its axis.

Get. The. Hell. Out. Of. Here!

With every ounce of willpower I could muster, I got my stiff, paralytic legs take a step toward the road. The second step wasn't any easier. As I attempted a third, a tree branch cracked behind me.

A hot surge of adrenaline raced through my veins, startling me out of my stupor. My legs unlocked, finally joining the rescue team.

I took off, pounding my way through the underbrush on coltish, half-numb legs. As I came to the road clearing, my father's red Mustang shone like a blazing beacon in a raging sea. I jumped in, rolled up the windows, and locked both doors—three times.

Shivering with shock, rational thought eluded me. I knew a corpse couldn't chase me. Still, I kept waiting for it to appear out of the scrub. Every molecule inside me was screaming for me to get the hell out of there and never look back.

But running wasn't an option.

I swallowed hard and took a deep breath. If I was going to do this P.I. thing, I had to suck it up and grow a pair. Besides, my shivering hands were shaking so badly I couldn't get the key in the ignition anyway.

I sat in the car trembling like a wet Chihuahua in the snow for a full ten minutes. Finally, my hands calmed down to a jitter. I reached into a pocket for my cellphone.

"Paulson? It's Drex."

"How's my favorite P.I. in training?" he joked.

"I found a dead body."

"What! Where?"

"On Obsidian Road. About two and a half miles south of the intersection."

I waited for a response. None came.

"What should I do?" I asked.

"Hold on. I'm thinking. Don't tell anyone. I'll be there as soon as I can."

Chapter Eighteen

OFFICER PAULSON ARRIVED nearly an hour later. I was kind of grateful it took him that long. I was still a bit shaky when he pulled up beside me on the side of the road. My legs felt wobbly as I climbed out of the Mustang. I leaned against it for support.

"Sorry. I was out on a case on the other side of Waldo," he said as he got out of his car. "You okay?"

"No. It was horrible. Whoever it is ... they're all mangled up. Probably by the dog."

"There's a dog?"

"Yes. It's dead, too."

"Show me."

I hesitated. "Do I have to?"

"No. But do you want to be a detective or not?"

I shook my head. "I dunno."

His expression softened. "Wait here, then. Where is it?"

"Straight ahead. You can't miss it. Follow the trail I made in the sawgrass." *As I ran like a headless chicken-shit through the woods.*

"Got it." Paulson disappeared into the pines. He returned about fifteen minutes later.

"Sorry, Drex. But I can't find anything. I'm going to need your help after all."

I nodded. "Follow me."

RELUCTANTLY, I LED Paulson through the tangled under-growth of wiregrass and palmettos to the horrific scene. I pointed a finger at the canine's corpse about twenty feet away. "There's the dog over there."

"Yes. I see it," he said. "But where's the body?"

"Behind us."

I turned slowly, eyes half shut, not wanting to see it again.

"Where?" Paulson asked.

I cracked open a flinching eye. The corpse in the orange overalls was nowhere to be seen. My mouth fell open.

"It was right over there." I pointed to a stand of pines.

"Are you sure whoever it is was dead? Maybe they got up and—"

I shook my head numbly. "No. They were dead all right."

"Uh-huh. Well, Bobbie, I hate to say it, but you *did* just experience a head trauma. And I heard a rumor you saw a phantom shooter at the hospital. Maybe you should go talk to your doctor or some-thing. You might be having hallucinations."

My gut flopped. "I could have sworn it was real."

Paulson put an arm around my shoulder. In other circumstances, I might have liked it. But at the moment, all I could see and smell around me was death. At least I knew then I wasn't into necrophilia.

"You want me to drive you back to your shop?" Paulson asked.

"No. I'll be okay."

"Then I'll follow you. To make sure you get back all right. It's my fault. I shouldn't have put you through this so soon after your acci-dent. You should get some rest."

I sighed. "You're right. Do me a favor, Paulson?"

"Sure."

"Don't tell anybody about this. The last thing I need is Earl find-ing out. He'll be on the phone turning me over to some UFO net-work or something."

"Okay. It's just a dead dog. Mum's the word. As long as you promise you'll take it easy. And go see a doctor."

I crossed my fingers behind my back. "I promise."

Right. Like I'm gonna spill my guts to a shrink and end up in the looney bin like poor Aunt Clara. No thanks.

Chapter Nineteen

THE SUN WAS DIPPING below the tree line when I pulled the Mustang onto the crumbling asphalt parking lot in front of the mechanic shop. In the runoff ditch between the road and weedy yard, Earl was squatting in the grass, hopping around on his heels like a giant frog in a black wig and overalls.

Any other time, the scene would've provided me sadistic, comic relief. Tonight, it was just relief, pure and simple.

I blew out a big breath, hoping some of the lingering horror would exit with it. I slapped on a trembling smirk and climbed out of the Mustang.

"Someone finally turn you into a toad?" I half-heartedly yelled at my cousin.

He stood up. His face bore an odd mixture of trepidation and indignation.

"Near 'bouts." He nodded toward the garage and glanced up at the second story. "That weirdo up there. He passed out in his soup blabbering something about a rubber octopus."

My trembling smirk collapsed. "What? He must be in worse shape than I thought."

Earl shot me an *I-told-you-so* look. "Sasquatch bite. I'm telling you."

"Can it, Earl."

Earl shrugged. "You're the boss."

I scowled. "I don't get it, Earl. If Knickerbocker's so bad off, how in the world did he manage to walk here this morning?"

"Shock, maybe? Or maybe he got one of them adrenaline surges. You know. Like them stories you hear about where some tiny little gal lifts up a Mack Truck to get her baby out from underneath it."

I shook my head. "Earl, I'm not in the mood to hear any more of your stupid crap tonight."

His face puckered. "It ain't stupid crap. Look it up yourself. It's on the Internet."

"I would, if I could afford to get the cable hooked up again. But all the money we earn goes to pay *your* salary." I shot him an angry scowl. "Just gimme the crickets and go on home."

Earl scowled. "Happy to oblige." His face softened. "Sure you don't need any help with that guy upstairs?"

"No. I can manage. If he's not better in the morning, I'll call 9-1-1."

"Alrighty then. Call me if you need me." Earl opened his huge, meaty palm and offered up a couple of half-squashed crickets.

"Thanks," I said as the bugs tumbled into my hand. I closed my fingers around them and felt the insects wriggle in my palm. They weren't the only things on their last legs.

The sapphire ring on my hand was the only thing of value I hadn't yet pawned to make ends meet. A gift from Grandma Selma, I hoped I wouldn't have to part with it.

"Watch yourself, you hear?" Earl said as he walked away. He turned back and shot me a look he'd stolen from my father—an odd expression between worry and pity.

My fear evaporated into anger. "Don't tell me you're actually *worried* about me," I said.

"Naw," Earl said. "It's *him* I'm a-feared for. I wouldn't want to be left alone with you for all the money in China." Earl brushed his hands off on the seat of his coveralls, turned his back to me, and headed toward Bessie.

"Yeah?" I called after him. "Well ... I hope Bigfoot gets *you* next."

Earl spun around. "Ha! So you *do* believe that fella got bit by the Sasquatch!"

"I do not!"

"Well, don't you worry about me, little Cuz. No dumb ol' skunk ape's gonna get me. Not in Bessie, he won't. I'll flatten him under my tires. Make him into a primate pancake."

I scowled. "Sounds delicious." -

Chapter Twenty

AFTER LETTING MYSELF into Grandma Selma's apartment, I crept down the hall and tapped lightly on the bedroom door. Knickerbocker didn't answer. I peeked inside to find him sleeping soundlessly in bed. I tiptoed in and dropped the two mangled crickets into the terrarium. The lizard eyed them, then stared at me blankly.

"Sorry," I whispered. "They're a bit squished."

Knickerbocker moaned. I whipped around, startled.

He was still asleep, so I snuck over for a closer look. His brow was sweaty. I touched his forehead. It felt feverish. He writhed in his sleep and mumbled something. I leaned in closer. He repeated the same two words over and over. They sounded like "rubber octopi."

Geez. Earl hadn't been kidding after all.

I was no doctor, but I was pretty sure a bump on the head shouldn't cause a fever. I checked the mark on Knickerbocker's shoulder. It was swollen and red. Had he really suffered some kind of animal bite? I thought about the padlocked room in the back of his RV. Had something—or *someone*—escaped from there and attacked him?

My mind flashed back to the dead dog in the woods.

That dog could have bit him! What if it had rabies? Oh my lord! The dog died of rabies, and now Knickerbocker's turning into a human Cujo!

AFTER CALMING MYSELF with a couple of shots of gin, I rethought my earlier man-Cujo theory. I decided to check on Knickerbocker one more time before I called animal control. Whether he was a nut or a saint, I couldn't tell. But one thing I knew for sure. Right now, that man needed my help.

I fetched a clean washcloth from the bathroom, ran some cool water over it, and wiped Knickerbocker's brow, careful to avoid putting pressure on the knot on his forehead. The bump looked smaller. And I was surprised to see tiny stubs of hair growing back all over his head.

Knickerbocker wasn't bald, after all. Just shaved. Like me.

No wonder he wore that dumb fedora.

Then I noticed something that made my spine shiver. Faint, circular marks dotted his entire scalp. About the size of quarters, they reminded me of tentacle marks.

Rubber octopi.

Good grief! Is Knickerbocker a scuba diver? Has he been attacked by a giant squid? What the hell is going on here?

He moaned again. I felt his forehead. The poor guy was burning up. I'd have to wait until morning to get any answers out of him.

I rinsed the washcloth and placed it, clean and cool, against his forehead, covering his eyes. Then I took a moment to study the odd stranger before me.

Knickerbocker was lean and muscular. Not a workout body—more of a wiry, forgets-to-eat kind of physique. He was around six feet tall. Unremarkable in looks, save for the cheesy moustache and tentacle marks. He didn't have any tattoos that I could see, so he probably hadn't done any jail time.

I doused a paper towel with alcohol and dabbed at the angry red circle of broken skin between his neck and left shoulder. He was definitely unconscious. If he'd been awake, he'd have reacted to the sting.

As I leaned closer, I could smell the muskiness of him—a kind of nervous perspiration mixed with honest sweat. I wondered how long it had been since he'd bathed. His clothes could do with a wash. So could mine, for that matter.

I left the alcohol-soaked paper towel on his wound and reached down to unbutton his pants to throw them in the laundry. As I touched the metal button on the fly of his black jeans, a surge of electricity tingled throughout my body.

Unlike the other jolts I'd experienced of late, this one wasn't entirely unpleasant. I sat up in surprise.

I know it's been a long time since I've seen a man in his skivvies, but am I really that *pathetic?*

I set my jaw to clinical nurse mode and finished undoing the button of his jeans. I began to unzip his fly, but my fingers froze. In the exact spot previously covered by his pants button was what appeared to be a second navel.

I sucked in a breath.

Two bellybuttons? Who is *this guy?*

I blinked in disbelief.

No, no, no! That doesn't make any sense.

I looked again. It was still there.

Scar tissue. From an operation. Or a gunshot wound. It had to be.

I reached out to touch it ... to put my finger in the hole ....

Knickerbocker groaned. I jumped about three inches. I quickly re-buttoned his jeans and covered him up with the sheet.

Should I call 9-1-1? Detective Paulson? The FBI? The Mutual UFO Network, for crying out loud?

I looked over at the terrarium.

I need to think this through. If he was a criminal, would he be traveling with a pet lizard? And what kind of psycho would trust me and Earl with all his cash?

There was only one thing I knew for sure. Knickerbocker was a paying customer. Didn't I owe it to him to at least give him the opportunity to explain himself?

I snorted out a jaded laugh.

That's rich, Bobbie. You owe it to him. You owe a lot of people, but this guy isn't one of them.

The cold, hard truth of it was, the guy had money. And I was in dire straits. Knickerbocker himself might not have been a godsend, but his cash sure was. Besides, there was no need to make any hasty decisions just yet.

I refilled his water glass, set out a couple of Tylenol tablets, and turned off the lamp by his bedside. Then I tiptoed over to my apartment and got the afghan my Grandma Selma had knitted for me right before she died. I made myself a nest on the living room couch and lay there, wide-eyed for ten minutes or so, thinking about phantom shooters and ripped-faced corpses and psycho killers with twin navels.

A sudden flash of lightning turned the long, flowy curtains into floating spirits of the undead. Distant thunder rumbled through the darkness like gravelly voices from the grave.

Sometimes I really hated my stupid imagination.

I got up and dragged a dining room chair up to the bedroom door where Knickerbocker was sleeping. I wedged it tight against the doorknob and went back to the couch.

As Grandma Selma always said, "Better safe than sorghum."

She always was one to mix her metaphors.

Chapter Twenty-One

BRANCHES TORE AT MY face as I fled through the woods. Something was after me. Stalking me. Something big. Something evil.

Its pounding footsteps grew louder. It was gaining on me! I didn't dare look back. I might trip and fall.

But I simply had *to see ....*

I turned my head.

In an instant, I felt myself falling.

My palms hit the dirt. I tumbled headfirst onto the moist ground. As I skittered across a thick blanket of pine needles, their pointy ends stabbed my flesh like tiny daggers. Then I slammed into a pine tree.

The rough bark gouged my skin like a cheese grater. But there was no time to assess my wounds. I pushed myself up and turned around.

Two glowing red eyes leered at me from the darkness.

A guttural growl reverberated through the thick air. The creature lunged at me, jaws snapping.

Hot spittle splatted against my forehead. I smelled the heat, the foulness of its breath, as its long, yellow claws ripped into the side of my head, tearing out my left eye. It fell to the ground and rolled into a hole a few feet away.

Oddly, I could only see through my detached *eye. From its vantage in the dirt, I made out a hairy, man-like beast wearing a black fedora.*

Its bear-like claws ripped into my throat. I tried to scream, but my larynx was already shredded. My howl fluttered out like a low, staccato moan.

Suddenly, the beast froze as if a director had yelled, "Cut!" It looked at me, confused.

"Wait a minute," it said to my detached eye. *"Smelled the heat?"*

I woke with a start, half-paralyzed with sleep. My heart thumped in my chest like a grounded boat motor. I turned my head a fraction of an inch and yelped in pain. My neck had gotten wedged against the armrest of the couch, and was now stiff as a roller-derby hairdo.

I sat up and rubbed it, making a mental note to never eat Vienna sausages after ten p.m. again. I heaved a sigh, then hauled myself off the couch to check on Knickerbocker.

I un-stuck the chair from under the bedroom doorknob and cracked the door open for a peek. He was still in bed, asleep. The clock radio on the nightstand read 6:18 am.

Good.

After checking on Knickerbocker around midnight, he'd settled down and slept peacefully through the rest of the night.

I started to go, but noticed fresh blood on his lip. A vague memory flashed across my mind. I'd thought it had been another one of my crazy, meat-byproduct-induced dreams.

Maybe not ....

I'd been changing the washcloth on Knickerbocker's forehead when it happened. He'd grabbed my arm and pulled me to him. He'd kissed me hard on the mouth. The force had reopened his split lip. I'd been caught so off guard that it'd been over with before I could protest.

Afterward, Knickerbocker had slumped back into a fitful slumber. I'd snuck out of the room and wedged the chair under the doorknob again.

Had that all been a dream? Another odd delusion?

His bloody lip said otherwise. So did the smear of blood I discovered on my chin when I looked in the bureau mirror. I was washing it away when my phone rang. I ran down the hall to catch it before it woke up Knickerbocker.

"Hello?" I whispered into my cellphone.

"You're still alive. Thank God!" It was Beth-Ann.

"Uh ... is there a reason I shouldn't be? Look, I haven't had any coffee yet and—"

"I Google-searched Knickerbocker," she said. "Obviously, you didn't."

"No. Why would I?"

"I thought you wanted to be a detective."

"Private Investigator," I said sourly. "And *unlike you*, I believe in a person's right to privacy."

I didn't see any reason to mention to Beth-Ann that my cable had been cut off months ago. Or that I had a smartphone that was way smarter than me. I mean, who could see anything on that tiny screen anyway?

"So I guess you don't want to hear what I found out, then," she teased.

I nearly choked on a wayward yawn. "I didn't say *that*."

"Get this, Bobbie. There's *no such guy* as William Knickerbocker. At least, nobody alive in the US."

She suddenly had my full attention. "You're kidding."

"Nope. Just some guy who invented some lightbulb thing back in the Dark Ages. He died, like, a million years ago."

I suddenly understood why Beth-Ann had failed both high school history *and* math. "You could've gotten the spelling wrong," I said, trying to assuage the niggling sense of unease creeping up my spine.

"I guess. But I doubt it."

"Listen. Thanks for the info, but I gotta go. I need coffee." What I *really* needed was a weapon, in case Knickerbocker was a psycho from planet Kill'emall.

"Okay. But be careful, Bobbie."

"I will." I hung up and sprinted out of my grandma's apartment and into my own. I got a pot of coffee brewing and called Earl. He answered on the sixth ring.

"What?" he growled.

"I was just wondering when you're coming in." I didn't want to tell him I was scared. In our family thesaurus, vulnerability was synonymous with weakness.

"It's Sunday, dingdong," Earl groused. "My day off. Parts won't be here till tomorrow anyway. What's your problem?"

I've got a twin-naveled space-alien, psycho-killer hiding out in my grandma's bed like the big, bald wolf.

"Nothing, Earl. Have a nice day."

I clicked off the phone, made two cups of coffee, then went down to the service bay and retrieved Knickerbocker's Glock from the RV's glove compartment.

It was time for Mr. William Knickerbocker to come clean.

Chapter Twenty-Two

KNICKERBOCKER, IF THAT *was* his real name, wasn't in bed when I pried the chair free again and opened the bedroom door. He was in the shower. I could hear the water running, and I could see his black jeans laid out on the bed.

Right next to his wallet.

I set the coffee cups on the nightstand and patted my right hip pocket to reassure myself the Glock was still there. Then I did something totally against my nature.

I rifled through his stuff.

It didn't take long. The wallet was nearly empty except for a few credit cards with the name Nick Grayson. Had he stolen another man's wallet? Inside the billfold were five hundred-dollar bills so crisp and new they looked like Monopoly money.

I unsnapped the flap to a pocket in the wallet. It fell open to reveal a tin-colored badge that could've come from a Cracker Jack box. The words Private Investigator ran along the top edge of a circle in the badge's center. Inside the circle was a strange emblem made of three triangles, kind of like a 3-D Star of David.

I re-snapped the flap, folded the wallet, and carefully placed it back in the same exact spot by the jeans on the bed.

When I turned around, a naked man was staring at me.

"Do you usually pilfer through your guests' belongings?"

Knickerbocker's voice was strangely devoid of any distinguishable tone. Or maybe I was too distracted by his other assets to notice. He was stark naked.

"Who *are* you?" I demanded.

"Who are *you?*" he volleyed.

Something indiscernible flickered across his green eyes, then they hardened to what appeared to be quiet resolve. He took the towel he was drying his head with and wrapped it high around his waist. I got the feeling he was keener to cover his twin navels than his privates. He glanced to his left, licked his bottom lip, and took a step toward me.

I stumbled backward and fumbled for the Glock in my pocket. I yanked it out and pointed the gun at him. "Tell me who you are. *Now.*"

He considered me thoughtfully. "Who do you *think* I am?"

"You said you're William Knickerbocker. But there's no such person. The name in the wallet says Nick Grayson."

"So why are you asking?"

I wasn't expecting a philosophical rebuttal. "I ... I want to know why you're using an alias. Are you on the run or something?"

"Sort of." He sighed. "No. Not really. I only give my real name out on a need-to-know basis. You didn't need to know. By the way, is that my gun?"

"Shut up! I'm the one asking the questions!"

"How am I supposed to answer them if you order me to shut up?"

I blew out an exasperated breath. This was not going to plan.

"I'm a detective," I lied. "Working undercover. What are you doing here? What's with the rubber octopus? And the tentacle marks all over your head?" I thought about asking about his twin navels too, but I was afraid it might land me in one of those, "Now I'll have to kill you," kind of scenarios.

"Hold on," he said. "Rubber octopus? That's a new one."

"You kept saying it in your sleep. Octopi rubber. Something like that."

A glint of recognition flashed across his eyes. "Oh. *Oculi rubere.* It's Latin. It means red eyes."

I relaxed my grip on the Glock a notch. "Why would you keep saying *that?*"

He hesitated for a moment as he studied me. "Uh ... because my eyes were red."

I shook my head. "Over an over? I don't think so. You were delirious. That term *means* something to you."

His expression softened slightly. "Wait a second ... you took care of me last night, didn't you."

"Yes."

He reached a hand toward me. I stiffened my stance and braced the Glock in both hands.

Knickerbocker stepped back and held up his hands. "Sorry. I just wanted to say thank you."

I shifted uncomfortably. "Uh ... you're welcome."

His eyes shifted over toward the nightstand. "You won't shoot me if I reach for that coffee, will you? It smells great."

"No. Go ahead."

As he reached for a cup, a warning signal pinged in my brain.

He could throw hot coffee in my face!

"Stop!" I shouted. "I need a few answers first."

He eyed the coffee longingly, then looked back at me. "Okay, I guess I owe you that. Shoot." His eyes widened. "I mean—don't *shoot*, shoot. Just ask your questions."

"So who are you? Knickerbocker or Grayson?"

"Grayson. Nick Grayson."

"How can I be sure?"

He smiled charmingly. "Why would I lie to you? You've already seen my lizard."

He winked a green eye at me. I blushed. Then he glanced over at the terrarium. I blushed some more. Was it possible he remembered kissing me last night? Or maybe he didn't. He *had* been delirious, after all.

"May I ask *your* name?"

"Bobbie ... I mean *Roberta* Drex."

"Nice to meet—"

"What do you do for a living, Grayson?"

He winced. "That one's a bit tricky."

I snorted. "You're a private investigator. Like me."

He nodded. "True. I am a P.I. But I'm nothing like you."

My jaw flexed. *What a jerk!*

"No, you're *not*," I said sourly.

Grayson winced. "I didn't mean it like *that*. What I meant was ... I kind of investigate more ... uh ... *esoteric* things."

"What do you mean?"

"In layman's terms? The unexplained."

"Unexplained?"

"Yes. Things that can't be explained by normal, rational, sensible logic."

"You mean like ghosts and stuff?"

Grayson smirked ever so slightly. "Well, not exactly. I'm investigate unusual events that leave physical evidence."

"Like Bigfoot?"

"If compelling evidence is found, yes."

I pursed my lips. "I don't believe in all that."

Grayson smiled. "That's okay. They still believe in *you*."

I adjusted my stance, a bit angry at being teased. "You're full of crap, aren't you?"

"Yes. And so are you, Roberta Drex. In fact, the average person walks around with over twenty-five pounds of feces clogging up their colon."

I grimaced with disgust. "Why would you know that? Why would you *want* to know that?"

Grayson eyed me curiously, as if I were a fun, new toy. "As I said, I have unusual interests."

"I think you have an unusual head injury."

Greyson glanced upward, as if to get a look at the bump on his forehead. "Yeah, that too. Look, I'm sorry if I've been a bother. Let me pay you for your troubles, and I'll be on my way."

"I don't think so." I gripped the gun tighter. "I think I should call the cops. Or the FBI."

"Go ahead. But might I suggest Homeland Security? Be sure to tell them you're holding a gun on a man for babbling about a rubber octopus. Don't forget I've got a Bigfoot bite, a shaved head, two navels, and I'm traveling in an RV with an accomplice—a lizard named Gizzard. Just don't be surprised when they haul *you* away instead of me."

He had a point. *What am I supposed to do now?*

Grayson must've read my expression like an open comic book.

"Right now, lady, the only person who'd believe your story is *me*. Listen, you can either let me go or shoot me. But if you choose option B, I would highly recommend taking the safety off my Glock first."

I looked down at the gun. Like a viper striking, Grayson snatched it from my hand. As I looked up, I heard a click. I winced, closed my eyes, and waited for the second bullet in less than a week to strike me between the eyes.

Chapter Twenty-Three

THE BULLET NEVER CAME.

I hazarded a peek out of one eye.

Grayson was standing less than two feet away from me, holding the butt-end of the Glock toward me. He'd undone the safety and was offering me back his lethal weapon.

I took it. He didn't resist.

"Why did you do that?" I asked, stunned.

"Because I want you to trust me."

"Why?"

"Because if we can't trust each other, we can never be friends."

I swallowed against the dry knot in my throat. "Friends?"

"I'd hate to part as enemies after you've been so kind."

I suddenly felt undone with confusion. Was *I* the bad guy in all of this? My face flushed with heat. Southern guilt could do that to a person. Then I remembered that if he left, he'd take his wallet with him.

"Part?" I asked, my voice a notch nicer. "Why do you have to go? I mean, what's the rush?"

"It's not safe to be around me. I try not to put my friends in harm's way."

I looked at him sideways. "That sounds noble and all, but it smells like buffalo chips to me."

Grayson looked taken aback. "What do you mean?"

"Around here, friends stick together through thick and thin."

Grayson cocked his head and smiled wistfully. "You have no idea how thin the ice can get when you skate near me."

"I was born and raised in Florida," I quipped. "I don't know how to ice skate. But I do recognize a cold shoulder when I see one."

Grayson laughed. "You're an interesting woman, Bobbie Drex. If that *is* your real name."

"It is. Believe me. I wish it wasn't."

I nodded toward the nightstand and the two steaming mugs atop it. "Now drink your coffee, Nick, before it gets cold."

I SAT DOWN AT THE ROUND, oak dining table where my parents had eaten three square meals a day for the past thirty years. Along the walls, pictures of relatives glared disapprovingly at me as I shared a meager breakfast of toast and coffee with the stranger who'd arrived yesterday in almost as bad shape as his RV.

Emboldened by a shot of caffeine, I braved a question I'd been itching to ask Grayson since he'd said the word *unexplained*. It wasn't exactly a question I could've asked Earl, for cripes' sake. Or even Beth-Ann. But given my two recent run-ins with odd visions, I was dying for a little perspective from someone who perhaps knew something more about the topic.

"Do you believe in ghosts?" I asked casually as I topped off his cup of coffee.

"Me?" Grayson's brow furrowed. "Depends on what you mean by *ghosts.*"

"The spirits of dead people." I sat down and pulled my chair closer to the table. "Do you think they're real, or simply hallucinations?"

Grayson shrugged. "What's the difference?"

My back stiffened. "Well, one is *real* and the other's ...." I trailed off, uncertain how to continue my argument.

"My point exactly," Grayson said with a light laugh. "Who could know for sure? Every person's reality is different, Drex. We believe what we *decide* to believe, against all known intelligence to the contrary."

"What do you mean?" I frowned, unhappy with his answer, and took a giant, ripping bite from my slice of buttered toast.

"Let's face it. The so-called 'facts' are irrelevant to most people. Unless, of course, they happen to support their opinions."

"What are you saying? That people are blind to the truth?"

He slathered butter on his toast. "Well, that depends on what you call the *truth*."

I jabbed a knife into a jar of fig preserves. "I think I should warn you. I'm armed and you're getting on my last nerve."

Grayson smiled. "It's human nature to seek *validation*, Drex, not *in*validation. A person's point of view, no matter how soundly laid out, is still merely an opinion. It's not an absolute."

My nose crinkled with annoyance and skepticism. "I'm still not following you. Give me an example."

"Okay. Let's see ... how about *everything* you've ever read, said, or witnessed in this lifetime?"

I nearly spewed my coffee. "What?"

"*Every* book ... even history books, science books, the great philosophers ... they're nothing more than limited interpretations of personal experiences. They're simply the musings and opinions of their authors."

"Huh?"

"Think about it. How many times has science declared something as absolute fact, then had to retract it? How many times has 'recorded history' proven to be nothing more than a self-flattering account from the winning side?"

My lip jerked upward as if yanked with a fishhook. "Lots of times, I guess."

Grayson seemed to take my concession with easy indifference. "Then again, maybe they weren't wrong after all."

"What?" My mind screeched like a needle across a record. "If you're trying to confuse me, Grayson, congratulations. You win."

Grayson sighed. "I'm not trying to be ambiguous. It's just that I believe truth is merely a temporary construct."

I blew out a breath. "Okay, if I'm going to wrap my head around this, I'm going to need more coffee. *Lots* more coffee." I got up to fetch the pot.

Grayson drained his cup and held it up for a refill. "Some philosophers believe that at any given time, we're only evolved enough as a species to embrace a certain level of social and scientific principle. So we decide what truth is, what *reality* is, based on a sort of bell curve of the *intellectual collective*."

I frowned. "What are you saying? That *nothing* is ever absolute? That nothing is ever really *true*?"

"Not exactly. What I'm saying is that truth is a *fluid* thing, Drex. Every individual has their own truth, and who's to say whether it's right or wrong?"

"That's pretty deep down the rabbit hole for a vagabond conspiracy-chaser living in a ratty RV."

Grayson's chin lifted slightly. His eyebrows knitted together, giving him a look of mock pretentiousness. "I'm *not* a vagabond. I prefer the term 'non-localized, alternative solutions investigator.'"

I smirked. "Well, I suppose you *are* entitled to *your* opinion of reality."

Grayson grinned. "Touché."

I refilled his coffee cup. "So tell me, no bull this time. What's up with the red octopus thing?"

"*Oculi rubere*. It's Latin for red eyes."

"You said that. But why were you repeating it over and over in your sleep?"

Grayson glanced around, as if to ensure no one else was listening. He leaned in toward me. "Because I came out here on a case. I'm investigating rumors of a red-eyed creature that's been roaming the pine forests and swamps around Waldo."

I nearly dropped the coffee pot. "And I thought you were full of it *before*."

"I'm not joking."

"You're really chasing a monster? Gimme a break, Grayson!"

"My alternative P.I. services happen to include the occasional tracking of cryptids," he said defensively.

"Cryptids?"

"Yes. As yet undiscovered or unexplained creatures."

"Like ghosts?"

"More substantial than that. Creatures who leave behind foot-prints."

"And dead bodies?"

Grayson's eyebrow shot up. "Perhaps. Why do you ask?"

I shrugged, uncertain of how much to reveal to him. "Have you, you know, actually *seen* this red-eyed thing you're chasing?"

"Yes. At least, I think so. On the road the night before last. Right after my RV broke down. The whole incident—or accident—whatever it was, was *odd*."

"What do you mean?"

"My RV came slamming to a halt ... as if I'd hit something." Grayson absently felt the tender knot on his forehead. "After getting up close and personal with the windshield, I looked over to my left. I would swear I saw a pair of red eyes staring at me from the woods."

Ice spider made another beer run down my spine. "Maybe it was your own reflection in the window."

"No. Couldn't've been. The driver's side window was down."

I grimaced. "Did you get a picture of it or anything?"

"No. I remember reaching over to roll up the window ... then this stabbing pain suddenly shot through my shoulder."

"It *bit* you?"

"I don't know." Grayson slowly rotated his shoulder. "It could've been the seatbelt harness. I think I cracked my clavicle. Anyway, the next thing I knew, it was daybreak. I was still sitting upright in the driver's seat. I remembered seeing the flashing yellow light up the road. I thought it was close, so I got out and walked it."

"The flatlands around here can be deceiving."

Grayson's eyebrow shot up. "You're telling me. I kept walking and walking, but the light wasn't getting any closer. I was beginning to think it was a mirage. Then, finally, two and a half miles later, I ended up at your garage."

I thought about the bite-shaped wound on Grayson's left shoulder. What if it really *was* a bite? Should I tell him about the two glowing red spheres I'd seen atop the Stop & Shoppe drive-thru? Were those the red eyes he was chasing? They certainly couldn't have belonged to deer—not unless Rudolph was doing a pre-Christmas test flight.

I decided against saying anything. Especially after all the gobbledygook he'd just spilled. If Grayson wasn't going to give me any straight answers, then he wouldn't be getting any from *me*.

But I really wanted some straight answers.

I chewed my lip. Maybe if I took Grayson to the place I'd seen the dead body, he'd stop this esoteric bull-crap philosophizing and give me some useful information. According to my P.I. training course, I shouldn't lead the witness. If I was going to do this, it would be better to take him there without telling him anything, then let him conjure up his own version of reality.

The man certainly seemed up to the task.

"I went back to the scene of your accident," I said. "I don't think what you hit was a deer."

Grayson's eyebrows rose slightly. "No? What do you think it was?"

"Not sure. You up for a ride? I'll show you."

Grayson glanced quickly at his mug. "Can I take my coffee with me?"

"Yeah."

"Okay, then. Let's go."

Chapter Twenty-Four

"IS THIS A SIXTY-FOUR?" Grayson asked as he climbed into the Mustang.

"Sixty-four and a half."

"Candy-apple red. Goes well with your auburn hair."

"Actually, it's Rangoon Red. And this is a wig."

Grayson cocked his head at me and smiled. "Really? Wh—"

"Don't ask."

"Okay." He looked down at my boots. "So what's with the clod-hoppers, Red?"

"Don't call me Red. They're my father's work boots."

"He doesn't need them?"

"Not where he is at the moment."

"Where's that?"

"You tell me, Mr. Philosopher. He's dead."

Grayson nodded. "Oh. The old Heaven-or-Hell paradox. If you're into that sort of thing."

"You're not?"

"No. But I'm quite certain there's an intelligence at work behind all that exists. Does that work for you?"

I shot him some side-eye. "Not really."

Grayson glanced to his right for a moment, as if he were consulting someone sitting beside him. He turned to face me again. "That's okay. The universal intelligence says *you* don't actually work for *it*, either."

Red flags began to wave like a NASCAR pileup. So I did what I usually did when that happened with a guy.

I ignored them.

I shifted into first and headed out of the parking lot.

"Tell me something," I said as we buzzed down Obsidian Road. "What's with the fedora?"

Grayson touched the vintage hat on his head. "This old thing? Keeps my head warm."

"It's a Dobb's Fifth Avenue from the 1950s."

Grayson shot me an appreciative smile. "That it is. Impressive."

"I worked in antiques after college."

"Smart move. I worked in entomology."

My foot nearly slipped off the accelerator. "Really? Can I ask you something?"

"Sure."

"Can earwigs really drive a person crazy?"

Grayson laughed. "I have to hand it to you. You do pose some interesting topics of conversation."

I winced. "Sorry. I've never been much for small talk."

"Me neither. To answer your question, I suppose anything could drive a person crazy if they gave it enough power."

I groaned. "Not philosophy again. Come on. I'm talking about real life. Like ... what if an earwig crawled inside somebody's ear?"

"Ah. *Anisolabis maritima*. The poor, maligned little earwig. That's an urban myth. Sure, once in a while one finds its way into someone's ear. But it's just looking for a dark, moist place to hide out. There's never been a case of one damaging anyone's brain or driving them crazy. In fact, they're one of the few insects that display maternal instincts. But then again, they also eat guano. Why do you ask?"

I shrugged. "No particular reason. We're here."

I pulled the Mustang off the road where Grayson's RV had come to a standstill two nights ago. It wasn't hard to find. A few straggling scavengers still circled in the sky above, marking the spot like Mother Nature's own GPS death drones.

"Ugh. Buzzards," I said, looking up as I climbed out of the car.

"Vultures," Grayson corrected.

"Po-*tay*-to, po-*tah*-to," I said. "Follow me."

Grayson kept close, just a step or two behind me as I searched for the trail I'd trampled into the sawgrass yesterday. The overnight rains had plumped the grass and washed the sand, making the trail barely discernable.

"Only Americans call members of the genus *Cathartes* buzzards," Grayson said behind me as I fumbled my way through the thigh-high grass. "To everyone else on the planet, a buzzard is a hawk, a bird of prey."

"Does it matter?" I asked, slightly annoyed.

"In detective work, getting the details correct is critical. Buzzards are actually turkey vultures."

"Okay, okay," I said. "They're *vultures*. But that over *there* is a dead dog."

I pointed to the carcass lying about fifteen feet ahead in a clearing just beyond a stand of pines. The animal appeared to have lost its bloat and collapsed inward. It looked like a moth-eaten fur coat.

Grayson walked up to the carcass. He squatted down close enough to disturb a swarm of flies. "It's a dog, all right. Gave somebody hell, too. The fur around its jaws is black with encrusted blood."

"What do you mean some*body*? Couldn't another animal have attacked it?"

"Sure. As long as the other animal knew how to wield a knife. See those straight, inch-long wounds in its side?"

I stepped closer and tried not to breathe. Grayson took a stick and poked at a few holes, making my stomach twist. "Knife punctures," he said, as matter-of-factly as if he were giving someone his lunch order.

I'll have a homicidal stab wound and a side of fries.

I grimaced. "You sure you didn't hit it with your RV?"

"Yes. I don't see any crushing injuries. No broken bones."

"Could the dog be the source of the red eyes you saw the other night?"

"Well, I think we can rule that out, too."

"How?"

Grayson lifted the dog's head up with a stick. The eye socket on the other side of its head had been sewn shut.

"That would be hard to pull off with only one eye," Grayson said almost merrily. "Yes. Those are knife punctures, all right. This dog put up one hell of a fight. I'm surprised the guy who tangled with it made it out of here alive."

"Uh ... maybe he didn't."

Grayson looked up at me. "Why do you say that?" He rose to his feet like a shot, then glanced all around him. "Do you see a body?"

"No. But yesterday, I *thought* I did. I must've imagined it, because when I came back an hour later with Paulson, it wasn't here."

Grayson studied me. "Are you in the habit of seeing imaginary dead bodies?"

When I didn't dignify his question with an answer, Grayson's face softened. "Look. It may be important. What did this body you thought you saw look like? Was it male? Female?"

"I don't know. The face was ... gone. Ripped off or something. Its head was a bloody pulp."

Grayson nodded. I studied him for signs of skepticism, but couldn't detect anything but earnest interest.

"What else can you tell me about it?" he asked.

"It was wearing an orange jumpsuit."

"Hmmm. Must have been an escaped convict."

"That's what I thought, too. But now I'm not so sure."

"Why not?"

"Ever since I was a kid playing in the woods, I always worried I'd come across an escapee from Starke Prison. Maybe I really *did* just imagine it."

"But you're not a kid anymore," Grayson said.

I looked away and studied the ground at his feet.

"Something tells me there's more to this, Drex. Something you're not telling me."

Ahh crap. What the hell.

"This isn't the first dead guy I've seen lately who turned out to be a mirage."

Grayson took a step toward me. "What do you mean?"

I sighed. I was in this deep. Might as well go all the way.

"The guy who shot me on Thursday? I saw him in the hospital as I was leaving. I'd *swear* it was him. But then Earl told me it couldn't have been, because he was dead. Hit by a bus."

Grayson nodded. "Time to cue the *Twilight Zone* music, huh?"

Dammit. I shouldn't have told him.

"So where was this guy you saw yesterday?" Grayson asked.

I pointed to a stand of trees. "Up against that pine over there."

I followed Grayson over to the tree. He examined the bed of rust-colored pine needles surrounding the trunk, then used a stick to clear a spot in the sand below. The normally light-gray sand was tinged pinkish-red.

"Could be your guy was no ghost."

I peered at the pink sand. "Is that blood?"

"Possibly. Hard to be sure after all the rain last night."

I glanced around the woods, suddenly horrified. "So what happened to the body? He was dead, I'm sure of it. He couldn't have gotten up or crawled away."

I wanted to ask Grayson if he believed in zombies, but then again, I didn't want to know the answer.

"See these marks and scuffs in the sand?" Grayson pointed to a set of half washed away canine-looking tracks and slash lines in the sand. "He could've been dragged off by predators. Or eaten down to nothing by your friendly neighborhood vultures."

I shook my head. "Not possible."

"Why not?"

"After I saw the body ... or mirage, or whatever the hell it was, I ran back to my car and called Paulson. It took him about an hour to arrive. When we came back here, the dog was still over there, but the body was gone. I *had* to have imagined it. Vultures couldn't have eaten it in an hour."

"Don't be so sure," Grayson countered. "A few years ago, a woman fell to her death hiking in the French Pyrenees. Before the rescue helicopter could get there, she'd been totally devoured by vultures in under forty-five minutes."

"Are you serious?"

"Yes. Nothing left but shoes and clothes and a few bones."

"Gross! How do you know that?"

"A good private investigator keeps up with those kinds of things. That, and I happen to have a subscription to the *Huffington Post*."

"Ugh! Even if you're right, and I'm not saying you are, shouldn't there be something left of the body? Or at least the orange jumpsuit? It should be easy to spot in the grass around here."

Grayson smiled like a proud professor. "*Now* you're thinking like a private investigator."

"Save your praise. I'm not really a P.I. At least, not yet. I've only got my intern license."

Grayson smiled. "I know."

My eyebrows shot up in surprise. "How?"

Grayson's smirk evaporated. He cocked his head to one side. "I'm a private investigator. I thought I'd mentioned that."

"Argh! You're exasperating!"

"Okay, okay. Ever heard of a thing called Google?"

"Of course."

"You should try it sometime."

"Ha ha. I would, but I don't have internet at home at the moment."

"At *home*? Don't you have a smartphone?"

"Yes."

"Drex, if you're serious about becoming a P.I., I suggest you learn how to use your phone. Now, let's do a little beating around the bush and see if we can find some trace of this orange jumpsuit person, shall we? He or she might turn out to be our red-eyed monster after all."

"Fine."

"And while we're at it, tell me all about this getting shot business," he said. "And the other dead guy you think you saw."

Chapter Twenty-Five

DESPITE SEARCHING FOR nearly an hour, Grayson and I couldn't find a trace of the dead person in the orange jumpsuit. Grayson thought the pinkish stain in the sand could've been blood or a layer of microbial fungus. He collected a sample for testing. If it *was* blood, it could've come from the dog. So the jury was still out on whether my concussion was causing hallucinations, or I'd simply lost my freaking mind.

"Well, that was fun," Grayson said as we climbed back into the Mustang. "I thought we were going to see a dead deer, but we ended up with a one-eyed dog who, tragically, found himself on the wrong end of Jack the Knife."

"I should call Officer Paulson," I said, sticking the key into the ignition. "Let him know about the knife wounds and all."

Grayson buckled his seatbelt, wincing at the effort. "Who is he again?"

"He's the cop assigned to Point Paradise. We're too small to have our own police department. So Paulson acts as kind of a liaison, covering our area from his office in Waldo."

"Well, you picked an interesting first case, I'll give you that. Sure beats tracking down deadbeat dads and cheating spouses."

"This isn't *my* case. I only told Paulson about it."

"Sure," Grayson said. "That's right. You can't work cases by yourself with an intern license."

"Yeah, *technically*. But I already *am* working another case for Paulson, kind of."

Grayson shot me a devious grin. "*Really?*"

I shrugged. "It's just a stupid little thing. He didn't want to be bothered with it."

Grayson wagged his eyebrows and spoke in faux Groucho Marx. "Tell me, Gracie. How stupid is it?"

I laughed. "Our village kook keeps getting weird phone calls. Beeping. Robot voices. Stuff like that. It's nothing, really. But I guess, like you said, you've gotta start somewhere."

"You're kidding," Grayson said.

"I *wish*."

Grayson touched my arm. "No. I'm serious. You ever heard of a place called Point Pleasant, West Virginia?"

"No."

"It was the site of some weird happenings back in the 1960s. People in that little town started getting weird phone calls."

I shrugged. "Yeah? Well, who doesn't every now and again?"

Grayson nodded. "Fair enough. But quite a few of them also reported being chased by a flying, red-eyed monster."

The hair on the back of my neck bristled. I turned the key in the ignition and shook my head. Could that really have been what I saw—what I tried to chase down—at the Stop & Shoppe?

"They called him the Mothman," Grayson said.

I willed myself not to say a word about my encounter. I was already halfway to crazy. I didn't need to give Grayson any more fuel to drive me the rest of the way to nutsville.

"You and Earl are gonna love each other," I said as sarcastically as I could muster. "He's a freaking conspiracy theorist, too."

"You're not?"

"Nope," I said, and mashed the accelerator. "Life itself is enough of a conspiracy for me."

Chapter Twenty-Six

"WELL, THERE GOES MY getaway plan," Grayson said as he surveyed the carnage inside the service bay of my dad's garage. The engine to his RV had been thoroughly disassembled by Earl, who'd spread its innards all over the place like he was getting ready for a jumble sale.

I winced. "Sorry. But I tried to warn you. The engine was shot, anyway. Earl's a great mechanic. He'll have it back together for you in a jiff. Three days, tops."

Grayson licked his busted lip as he digested the news. "Well, I guess I should make the best of it. Hold on a second."

He climbed inside the RV. A moment later, I heard bottles clinking around. I thought he was going to haul out a couple of beers, but he came back holding a Q-Tip. One end of it was fluorescent pink.

"What do you think?" he asked, showing it to me.

I eyed it dubiously. "Not my shade of lipstick. But I think it'd go great with your green eyes."

Grayson laughed. "I did a Kastle-Meyer on the soil sample."

"A castle what?"

"Kastle-Meyer. A drop of phenolphthalein here, a drop of hydrogen peroxide there, and voilá. Pink means positive for blood."

I crinkled my nose at the swab. "Is it human?"

"Indeterminate. I'd need to do a precipitin test to find out. And for that, I'd need more blood, a lab, and perhaps an unlucky rabbit."

"Oh."

Grayson tossed the swab into a trashcan. "Do you have lunch plans? My treat."

If I was hungry, I couldn't tell. I was still too grossed out by the whole dead dog thing.

"Tell you what," I said, "given the state of our foreheads, I think we could both use a rest. I'll make us some soup. We'll get a nap, and then head out later to an early supper. I'm not that hungry right now. Besides, I need to call Paulson and catch him up on what we found."

Grayson nodded. "Actually, that sounds good. I could use a rest. What did you have in mind for dinner?"

"There's a little Mexican restaurant in Waldo. El Molino's."

He waggled his eyebrows at me. "You had me at *Mexican*."

"Good. But, just so you know, I'm not interested."

"You're not interested in eating?"

I frowned. "No. I meant .... Look, you're not trying to ask me out, are you? I hope there's no ... you know ... *ulterior motive*."

Grayson shot me a look. "Oh. Well, make no mistake, Drex. There's an ulterior motive, all right. I didn't see a restaurant for twenty miles before my RV broke down. And I've heard the Uber service in this area sucks."

I smiled. "Give me a few minutes and I'll bring you a bowl of chicken noodle."

"Could you do me a favor?" Grayson asked.

"What?"

"Would you change your shoes for dinner? Or if you don't have any, go barefoot?"

I crinkled my nose. "Why?"

"Call me a softie, but I hate to see you dragging around in a dead man's past."

My throat grew tight. I gave him the once-over. He gave me a friendly smile.

"Okay," I said. "I'll see what I can do."

I STUDIED MY REFLECTION in the mirror and readjusted my wig. Then I fished my cellphone from the pocket of my coveralls and spent ten minutes trying to figure out how to add Paulson's number to my list of phone contacts.

Damned computers! Carl used to do all this crap for me. Why did I let myself get so dependent on him?

I gave up and punched Paulson's number into the phone. "Paulson? It's me, Bobbie Drex."

"Hello, there. Anything new with Vanderhoff?"

"No. But listen. I went back out to the site where we found the dog."

"You did? Why?"

"I dunno. Curiosity? Anyway, I found something we missed yesterday. On the dog's body. Its fur had puncture wounds all over it. Like it had been stabbed by someone."

"Stabbed? Huh. What did you do with the carcass?"

"Nothing. It's still there."

"This may be a case of animal cruelty."

"Or worse. Paulson, you know that body I thought I saw? It may have been real after all. I was thinking the dog could've been killed by an escaped con."

"Did you find the body?"

"No. But the ground by the tree? You know, where I thought I saw it? The sand had a pinkish hue. It's blood."

"That could be critical evidence, Bobbie. I'll get out there and collect samples."

"But I—"

"Listen, Bobbie. Don't worry. You did good. I'll double-check the police reports for any mention of escaped prisoners. And I'll run back over to the scene right now and bag some soil samples for evidence. Don't go back there. We don't want more contamination of the scene, in case this turns out to be something bigger than a dead dog."

"Okay. But I'd hurry if I were you. There were vultures circling."

Paulson sniggered. "Buzzards don't bother me. I've had to fight off more than a few in my day."

"Grayson says they're vultures."

"Who's Grayson?"

"A guy staying here while his RV gets fixed. He's a private investigator."

"You don't say. Was he there with you at the scene?"

"Yes. He said last night's rain washed away a lot of trace evidence."

"That's not good. Listen, be careful with this guy. He may say he's a P.I., but you never know about strangers. And with your recent concussion, you might not have the best judgment right now."

That niggling feeling of unease returned. "Okay. You're right. But I already told him we'd go to dinner at El Molino's tonight. Do you want me to ask him anything?"

"Not that I can think of at the moment. But tell him to keep his hands to himself, okay?"

I smiled. "I'll do my best."

I clicked off the phone. I was no detective, but I was pretty sure I noted a hint of jealousy in Paulson's voice. I kicked off my father's boots and adjusted my wig. Hair or no hair, it was time to give that weirdo Grayson something to boggle his already warped little mind.

Chapter Twenty-Seven

"SO THERE REALLY *is* a woman underneath those coveralls."

I stared Grayson down across a sticky, brown laminate table. We were sitting in a duct-taped-together vinyl booth inside El Molino Mexican restaurant in beautiful, downtown Waldo.

I was sporting my sexiest top that didn't have a grease stain on the front, and I'd slurped down just enough of a frozen margarita to have the guts to ask him some probing questions. I fired them off in rapid succession, before I lost my nerve.

"Okay, what gives with the octopus circles on your head? That lizard in the terrarium? The dumpy RV? All that cash in your glove compartment? Your obsession with a red-eyed monster called Mothman?"

Grayson eyed me curiously, then fired back with his own volley.

"What's with the woodpecker wig? Daddy's boots? Dressing like a man? Wanting to be a P.I.?" He sat up in the booth. "I thought you were a small-town mechanic, Drex. Turns out you're a freaking KGB interrogator!"

I shrunk back in my seat. "Sorry." I hiccupped. "But you have to admit, there's a lot of really odd things about you."

Grayson twisted one side of his mouth and blew out a breath. "Maybe you're right. But it's not good to tell someone all your secrets at once. Not when you're holding as many as I am."

His face changed from serious to playful as if he'd flipped a switch. He waggled his bushy eyebrows at me. "If we both spill our entire guts tonight, what will we have left to talk about on our second date?"

I rolled my eyes. "Date? I wouldn't bring a cockroach here on a date."

"Huh." Grayson nodded thoughtfully. "I wouldn't have taken you for someone into arthropods."

I shot Grayson a look, but got distracted when the waitress arrived with a stack of tacos big enough to feed a Free-Will Baptist hootenanny.

The smell of cumin and ground beef made me salivate. I grabbed a taco off the top of the heap. Grayson followed suit right behind mine.

"You took quite a chance, handing me back your Glock," I said and shoved half the taco into my mouth.

Grayson watched me like a lazy cat watches a mouse. "You might see it that way. But my whole life is about taking calculated risks ... on the right people, that is."

"*Calculated* risks?"

He shrugged and shot me a sly grin. "While you were wincing in terror, I took the magazine out of the Glock."

I nearly choked on my mouthful of taco. "That's not fair!"

"Why? You *still* could've beaten me over the head with it."

"Anyone ever tell you you've got serious trust issues?"

Grayson burst out laughing. "All the time. How about you?"

I suppressed a smirk and looked at the corner of the ceiling. "Maybe once. Twice ...."

"How about a toast, then?" Grayson said. "To paranoia. Mother Nature's bodyguard."

I reached for my margarita. Grayson raised his mug of beer and winced.

I flinched in empathy. "Does your shoulder still hurt?"

"A bit. But that's to be expected. I *should* be dead. What did you do to stop the poison?"

"Poison?"

Grayson's eyes lost their playful edge for a millisecond. "I meant infection."

"Oh. Nothing. Just rubbed it with alcohol."

"Huh. Who would have thought something that simple could cure a Mothman bite?"

I studied his twinkling eyes and smirking face. It was impossible to tell if Grayson was teasing me or not. I really hated that I couldn't read him. After all those years sizing people up at Blanchard's antique auctions, I thought I could read *anyone*.

There went that theory.

I raised my glass. "Like I said, you and Earl are gonna get along like gangbusters. Cheers."

Our glasses clinked together, and our eyes remained locked as we each took a sip. I looked away first, and set my margarita on the table.

"Are you ever going to answer my questions?" I asked.

Grayson's left eyebrow shot up like Spock's. "Sure. Pick one. I'll answer *one*. Fair enough?"

"Better than nothing, I guess." I thought about it for a moment. "So, all that money in your glove compartment. Did you make it as a private investigator?"

"Yes."

"How?"

Grayson shook his head. "Nope. That's another question."

"Argh!"

He smirked. "My turn. Why are you wearing that wig?"

"They shaved my head in the hospital."

Grayson took off his fedora, revealing his pale scalp. His bald dome appeared dark gray from the short stubble covering it like a five o'clock shadow.

"Finally. A point of commonality," he said.

"Commonality? You mean the hospital or the head shave?"

Grayson put his hat back on. "No more questions."

I frowned. "What are we gonna talk about then?"

Grayson smiled sinisterly. "Tell you what. How about a dare?"

"A dare?" I took another slurp of margarita to prepare myself.

"Yes. You show me your bald head, and I'll tell you about my lizard."

I nearly spewed my drink. "Your flirting skills suck, you know that?"

Grayson half grinned, half grimaced. "Sorry. I meant it as a joke."

"Whatever," I said. "Still, no deal. You're not seeing my bald head."

"Okay. Tell me why you dress like a man."

"Nope." I shot him a smug look. "*That's* another question."

Grayson studied me for a moment. "Answer it, and I'll tell you about how I earn my money."

Finally, there was a man in front of me with an offer I actually didn't want to refuse. I took another slug of margarita—this time for courage.

"I was supposed to be a boy."

Grayson blanched. "What?"

I blew out a sigh 37 years in the making. "I was supposed to be Robert Drex, Jr. But somewhere in transit, I got my wires crossed and the plumbing wrong. My sonogram 'penis' turned out to be the extended middle finger of my left hand."

Grayson sat back, his eyes dancing with intrigue. "No way."

"No. No *penis*. My parents had to add an "A" to the name they'd planned to put on my birth certificate. That sonogram was the end of dear Robert and beginning of me, Roberta—a very poor substitute, indeed."

I took another slurp of margarita and shrugged with resignation. "But hey, what kid hasn't disappointed their parents, right? I just decided to get it over with extra early."

Grayson shook his head. "Did they make you pretend to be a guy, too?"

I scowled. "No. But as a kid, I hung out in the service bay with my Dad, mostly. Until I hit puberty, that is. Then my father made me get out and stay out. Mom and Grandma Selma tried to make me into a girl, but by then, I was eleven. It was too late."

"Huh," Grayson said.

I fortified myself with another slug of margarita. "You wanna know something?"

"What?"

I glanced around, then flinched. "I've never actually worn a dress. My poor mother couldn't make me. Not even on prom night. It just felt ... *weird*, you know?"

Grayson's face took on a studious appearance, like a doctor handing out a diagnosis. "Perhaps you'd already passed some critical stage of development, beyond which you couldn't embrace pantyhose."

I laughed, relieved he hadn't judged me as some kind of freak. "Yeah. Maybe. Now, I guess I'm doomed to live out the rest of my life in jeans."

Grayson smiled. "Well, at least you didn't say mechanic's coveralls."

"Oh, hell no!" I shook my tipsy head and sloshed my drink all over the table. "This whole situation is ... is ... well. Crap. I don't know what it is."

"I don't get it," he said. "What's stopping you from just ditching this place and leaving?"

I sighed and slumped further into the booth. "Look. When my father died, I had to take over his auto repair shop. I wanted to save his legacy,"

"His legacy?"

I scowled. "Okay, I wanted to prove I was every bit as good a mechanic as Earl, okay? I sunk my life savings into that god-forsaken garage. And what did I get in return? *Broke!* That's what!" I shook my head. "That place is a freaking money pit. Earl won."

Grayson eyed me curiously. "Earl won?"

"He gets a paycheck, and I'm stuck paying the bills. You want to know why I tromp around in my dead father's shoes?"

I didn't wait for Grayson to answer.

"Because I can't afford to buy my own stupid pair of steel-toed boots! That's why!"

Grayson nodded solemnly. Then he smirked mischievously. "So, tell me Drex. What were you doing before you became the world's surliest mechanic?"

For some reason I couldn't explain, I burst out laughing and I couldn't stop.

I laughed until I snorted. Then, I laughed at my snorting. I laughed at my pain. I laughed at my stupidity. I laughed at the utter absurdity of my life. I laughed at the utter absurdity of Nick Grayson, the bald, fedora-wearing P.I. with two navels.

God, it feels good to laugh.

The waitress came over with another round of drinks.

"Ah," Grayson said. "Just what we need. Reinforcements."

He grabbed his bottle of beer, then gently placed my margarita on the table in front of me.

"Please, go on," he said, and smiled at me encouragingly. "Tell me all about your life before becoming a grease monkey."

He raised his beer bottle. I met it with my margarita.

"I was an antiques dealer," I said, then took a sip. "With my fiancé. Correction ... *ex*-fiancé. Carl Blanders." I set the drink down and shrugged. "It was a good gig, actually. Until he went and traded me in for someone with a higher Blue Book value."

"Ouch."

I sighed. "Yeah. But that's another story. Let's just say that for now, I'm stuck doing what I'm doing until I can come up with something better."

"Like becoming a private investigator?"

I studied Grayson a moment to see if he was mocking me. He wasn't. "Yeah."

"You know, I think you may have the makings of a good one, Red."

My back bristled. "Listen, Grayson. Call me a boy if you want. Call me a jackass. Call me crazy, for all I care. But like I told you before, *don't* call me Red. Do it again and I just might take a socket wrench to your carburetor ... if you catch my drift."

"I get it," Grayson said, holding up his hands. "Deal."

"Deal?" a familiar voice sounded to my right. "What kind of *deal* are you two making?"

I looked over to see Officer Paulson stomping up to the end of the booth. He glared at us, his ice-blue eyes nearly hidden behind angry, narrow slits.

"There's no deal, Paulson," I said. "We're just exchanging information."

Paulson eyed me, then Grayson. "I thought I told you not to discuss the case, Bobbie."

Grayson met his stare. "I assure you, we weren't talking about any *case*. You must be Detective Paulson. I'm Nick Grayson."

Grayson stood and held his hand out. Paulson shook it, but only after waiting a beat.

"What are you doing in Point Paradise, Mr. Grayson?" Paulson asked.

"Just a little sightseeing." Grayson looked at me and winked. "You have to admit she's quite a sight. Am I right?"

Paulson's face flushed. The tendons in his neck tightened. "Ms. Drex here is a treasure, Mr. Grayson. And folks around here ... well, we like to keep a close eye on our valuables."

Grayson nodded. "Well, I can—"

"You two have a nice evening," Paulson said, cutting Grayson off. He turned to me. "Bobbie, give me a call tomorrow. I want a full report on *you-know-who*."

Paulson turned on his heels and marched out of the restaurant.

"Is 'you-know-who' perhaps 'little-old-me'?" Grayson asked, batting his eyelashes.

I didn't answer, because I really didn't know.

Chapter Twenty-Eight

AT MIDNIGHT, THE OLD landline to my parent's business started ringing.

It'd been in continuous service since they'd opened Robert's Mechanics three decades ago. I hadn't had the heart to disconnect the number, since their old-time customers still used it from time to time. It hadn't rung in weeks. But now that I only had two hours sleep on a three-margarita hangover, it wouldn't shut the hell up.

The fourth time it started ringing, I was too boiling mad to stop myself from answering it.

"What?" I yelled into the phone.

"*Beep-beep-beep.*"

"Who is this?"

"*Beep-beep-beep.*"

"I'm hanging up, now, jackass."

"We're watching," a robotic voice said.

"Who's watching?" I demanded.

There was no reply.

The line went dead.

Great. Mrs. Vanderhoff's somehow managed to get me on robocop's telemarketing list.

I slammed the phone down and crawled back into bed. Then that tingly ice spider crawled up my spine and made a nest in my hair.

I got back up to make sure my front door was locked. It wasn't. I set the lock, then I fumbled around for something to defend myself against a killer robot.

Gun? Don't have one. Knife? No. I can't stand the sound of metal on metal.

I spotted the flyswatter on my kitchen counter. I scowled.

Better than nothing, I guess.

I picked it up and went back to bed.

I AWOKE TO THE SOUND of someone banging around in the service bay downstairs. Even when you're expecting it, Monday morning always comes too early.

Unless, of course, you're an annoying early-bird like my cousin Earl.

I got up and fumbled around aimlessly for a minute, trying to decide whether or not to tell someone about my weird phone call last night. Lord knows I couldn't tell Earl. He'd have a field day with it. I couldn't tell Paulson, either. He was already on the verge of having me psychoanalyzed.

Not that I cared that much. But if I got labeled as crazy ... well, there'd go my P.I. gig.

I padded to the kitchen and made a pot of coffee. It was still perking when a knock sounded at my front door.

I figured Earl must've been here for hours and already gone through the coffee thermos he brought with him every day.

"Come in," I called out.

"Can't. It's locked."

Oh yeah.

I shuffled down the hall in my dad's old T-shirt and sweatpants. Not ready for a dose of Earl-style humiliation, I slapped on my Woody Woodpecker wig before I cracked open the door.

"What do you want, Earl?" I hissed.

It wasn't Earl.

"Uh ... just hoping to get a cup of that coffee I smell?" Grayson averted his eyes, but only after he'd gotten a good look at me in all my morning glory.

Great.

"Gimme a minute, for cripe's sake!" I yelled, and slammed the door.

I groaned at my reflection in the hallway mirror, then readjusted my wig and rubbed the sleep from my eyes. I stared at my saggy sweatpants and lost all hope.

I opened the door. "Sorry. You kind of caught me off guard."

Dressed neatly in his typical attire of black t-shirt, black jeans, black fedora, and black shoes, Grayson looked like a member of the wardrobe SWAT team here to bust me for non-compliance.

"Not a morning person, are we?" he asked, then smiled at me cheerfully.

My eyes narrowed. "You want some coffee or not?"

"Yes. Please. Might I add, you look dapper this morning."

I scowled. "Dapper is a masculine descriptive."

"Well, those *are* men's clothes, aren't they? I swear, do you own anything actually manufactured for the female anatomy?"

I slammed the coffee cup on the table. "Jeans. You saw 'em last night. What are you doing up so early, anyway?"

"Call me *The Princess and the Pea*, but it's hard to sleep through the whine of a pneumatic drill."

I winced. "Oh. Yeah. Sorry about that. But the good news is, that means Earl's busy fixing your RV."

"Good. So what's on the agenda for today?" Grayson asked, tapping his index finger annoyingly on his coffee mug.

My nose crinkled. "What do you mean?"

"Well, seeing as I'm kind of stuck here, I thought I'd explore the local entertainment options."

"What are you talking about? There's nothing to do here."

Grayson scratched his chin. "Remind me again. Why do you live here?"

I blew out a sigh that could've extinguished the candles on a centenarian's birthday cake.

"I *told* you. I'm working on my escape."

"Oh, yes. The P.I. gig."

"Right. Which reminds me, I've got to give Paulson a report on Vanderhoff today."

Grayson's left eyebrow raised slightly. "Vanderhoff?"

"The old lady who keeps getting the weird phone calls. Hey. You didn't call the shop last night, did you?"

"No. But I heard the phone ring four times."

"My parent's old landline. Sorry. It turned out to be a prank call. Nothing but beeps and static. Then some stupid mechanical voice said, 'We're watching you.'"

Grayson's back straightened. "Interesting."

"Nuts is more like it. Should I tell Paulson? He already thinks I'm crazy for seeing imaginary dead guys."

Grayson chewed his lip for a moment. "I tell you what. You help me, and I'll help you."

"Help me? How?"

"Let me borrow your car, and I'll teach you how to bug a phone. Deal?"

I sneered. "Whose phone? Earl's? I already hear way more out of his stupid mouth than I want to."

"No. *Vanderhoff's*. We can put a listening device in her phone, and then you'll know whether she's cuckoo for Cocoa Puffs or telling the truth."

I scowled. "In my book, that's called invasion of privacy."

Grayson shrugged and locked eyes with me. "In mine it's called on-the-job training."

Chapter Twenty-Nine

I SLIPPED INTO A PAIR of jeans and my best threadbare button-down shirt. With the woodpecker wig centered on my skull and the last dregs of Mom's dried-up eyeliner applied, I almost looked feminine. I blew out a sigh, then hobbled down the stairs in a pair of Mom's inch-high red pumps to check on Earl in the service bay.

"Well, look at you," Earl teased. "I ain't seen you out of coveralls in a year. I thought you'd done sewed yourself into 'em."

I shot him some side-eye. "Yeah. Ha ha and all that. Look, you got everything you need to keep going on the repairs to Grayson's vehicle?"

"Who's Grayson?"

Oh, crap! I don't want to get into this with Earl. Not right now.

"Knickerbocker," I said. "It's his first name."

Earl eyed me mischievously. "You two on a first-name basis now?"

"He's a private investigator, Earl. He's going to help me on the Vanderhoff case."

"The Vanderhoff case? What. You a detective now, too?"

Aww crap!

"I'm working on something for Paulson, okay? Grayson's helping me out."

Earl grinned. "I *bet* he is."

"Listen, Earl. He's a customer. Nothing more. He's paid six days rent in advance, and shelled out the entire tab for the parts. He even gave me five-hundred down toward your labor costs. That's nearly thirty-five hundred bucks. Don't blow it, okay? We need the money."

"I dunno, Bobbie. Something smells fishy to me."

"Who cares? His money's good. And you know as well as I do, we damned sure need it."

Earl put on his pondering face for a moment. Not a good portent of things to come.

"You're right, boss man." He sniggered and punched me in the arm. "If you ask me, sounds like a case of 'Don't ask, don't *smell*.'"

As my eyes returned from their orbit around their sockets, I spied Grayson coming down the stairs. His polished leather shoes were the only things gleaming in the entire garage.

"Good morning, Earl," he said after shooting me a wink. "How're the repairs going?"

Earl smirked. "Don't ask, don't sme—"

I punched Earl hard on the arm.

"Ouch!" He shot me a redneck scowl. "That hurt!"

"You ready to go, Drex?" Grayson asked.

I looked him in the eye. "Never been more ready."

Grayson grinned. "Come on, then. Let's roll."

Chapter Thirty

AS I STEERED THE MUSTANG out of the crumbling parking lot of the mechanic shop, Grayson fiddled with a weird, old-fashioned looking cellphone he'd retrieved from his RV. I smiled. Maybe he didn't embrace technology either.

"How'd you become a private investigator?" I asked.

Grayson fiddled with some buttons on the device in his hand. "I read a book when I was a kid called, *So You Want to be a Detective*."

I shook my head and smirked. "It's never a straight answer with you, is it?"

Grayson shrugged and set the device in his lap. "Playing it straight all the time is no fun, Drex. Sometimes, a sense of humor is the only thing that gets you through the rough spots."

I rolled my eyes. "Yeah. Life can be a real riot, all right."

"Come on. Of all the career choices in the world, what made *you* want to be a private investigator?"

I steered the Mustang onto Obsidian Road and scowled. "I took one of those aptitude tests on Facebook."

"You mean the kind that tells you what kind of pizza you'd be?"

"Exactly. It said I should be a shoe store manager."

"Ouch."

"Freaking Facebook."

Grayson laughed and fiddled with the door lock like an antsy little kid. "I don't follow. How did *that* lead into you getting a P.I. intern license?"

I shifted into third. "I was so pissed off after that Facebook test that I drank half a bottle of vodka. I woke up around three in the morning, still snockered. As fate would have it, the TV was blaring this late-night infomercial on how to 'Train at home in your spare time to become a private investigator.'"

"I see." Grayson pursed his lips and tapped his fingers on the door handle.

I bit my lip. "I know it sounds totally lame, but I was only pulling in ten bucks an hour as a mall cop. Barely enough to cover the gas to Gainesville and back."

"Wait a minute." Grayson stopped tapping his finger and turned to stare at me. "You were a *mall cop?*"

I pressed my molars together, wanting to curse myself out for letting that one slip.

Grayson laughed out loud, stifled himself, then burst out laughing again. He sucked in some air and blurted, "Did you have your own Segway?" Then he doubled over in the passenger seat.

I mashed the gas pedal to the floor. "Smartass."

"Sorry," he said, trying to compose himself. "It's just that ... well, most people who go into this line of work have a background in the military or law enforcement." He snickered, then recovered himself. "Though, I suppose mall cop could count as some branch of non-government counter-intelligence."

I shot him some major side-eye. "Ha. Ha. Ha."

Grayson pursed his lips. "Okay, okay. I'm done." He took a deep breath. "Tell me, from which prestigious school did you earn your intern certificate, Detective Drex?"

I glared at him. "The Forensic Academy, okay? It was just one of those wild-hair things. Like I said, I was half-lit when I called them. I put the tuition on a credit card. It was non-refundable. When I sobered up in the morning, I figured, the money's gone, so what the hell."

"Your insatiable passion for the profession is inspiring," Grayson said soberly.

I grinned despite myself. "Thanks."

"Where did you plan on getting your two years of on-the-job training?"

I scowled. "I didn't. I thought that once I passed the test for the Class CC intern license, I was good to go."

"I guess you should've done a better job investigating it before you shelled out the money."

I blew out a breath and rolled my eyes. "I guess. But half a pint of Stolli has a way of making me lose my train of thought."

"Apparently, so does tequila."

I winced, then pulled up in front of Vanderhoff's nondescript house in Cherry Manor. "We're here."

Grayson opened the side door and tipped his fedora at me. "Well, Ms. Graduate of the Forensic Academy. Time to show me what you've got."

Chapter Thirty-One

OLD LADY VANDERHOFF took a final drag off her Marlboro and stamped out the stub in the overflowing ashtray on her kidney-shaped coffee table. She sat back in the wingback chair and eyed Grayson and me. Perched on the chair above her left shoulder, a dead-eyed doll glared back at us like a graveyard demon.

"Beth-Ann put me under the dryer and went out for a smoke," the old woman said. "I was all by myself in her garage." She glanced over at me. "I mean, you know, *beauty parlor.*"

"Go on," Grayson said.

"Well, some guy all dressed up in a hat and an old-fashioned, double-breasted suit came in and asked me my name. I told him a lady don't just give out her personal details like that." She hocked a loogie and spit it into a napkin. "Then the fella asked for the time. I told him. But then, he said something weird."

"What?" I asked, trying not to look at her napkin.

Vanderhoff straightened her shoulders. "He said something like, 'Excuse me, but I meant to inquire after the *year.*' Just like that. Well, when I told him, he looked kind of surprised. He thanked me and then just up and left. When I got home, my phone was ringing. It was those damned beeping robots."

"You didn't mention the guy before," I said.

She shrugged. "Eh. I didn't think it was important. Well, truth is, I forgot. My memory ain't what it used to be."

"So have you gotten any more calls?" Grayson asked.

"Yeah. Last night, as a matter of fact. That robot bastard again. Now he wants me to meet him tonight at the Stop & Shoppe at nine-thirty. Well, I told him I couldn't go."

"Why not?" Grayson asked.

Vanderhoff looked surprised by his question. "Why, that's when *Matlock* is on!"

I stifled a smirk. "Was it the same voice that told you to go to A&P and steal the bananas?"

"I would assume so." Vanderhoff glanced over at Grayson and shook her head as if it were obvious I was some kind of nincompoop. "I mean, how many robots would get the idea to call *me* up? Right, Detective Grayson?"

"Good point," Grayson said. "Pardon me, but could I trouble you for a glass of water, Mrs. Vanderhoff?"

The old lady batted her gray eyelashes at him. "No trouble at all, for you, honey."

Vanderhoff heaved herself out of the chair and hobbled to the kitchen. I followed her in and stood in the doorway, serving as a lookout for Grayson's and my surreptitious plans to bug her telephone.

As Vanderhoff reached for a glass in a cabinet, I snuck a peek back into the living room. Grayson was fiddling with the phone jack on the wall. I don't know why, but I'd expected him to stick something into the receiver of the old rotary dial phone, like they always did in the black-and-white detective movies I'd seen.

I frowned and turned around. Vanderhoff had the glass in the sink, filling it from the tap. She turned off the faucet and took a step toward the living room.

"Uh ... wow," I said, sidestepping in front of her. "That's a lot of magnets." I pointed to her refrigerator.

Vanderhoff's head pivoted on her turkey neck. "Yeah. But I won't be getting no more. Mandy used to send 'em to me from all over the place."

"Oh." My eyes scanned the dozens of magnets littering the freezer door. Amongst the tacky display, I spotted my business card. It was half-covered with a round, brown magnet that looked suspiciously like a mound of dog poop.

Nice.

I glanced back into the living room. Grayson motioned he needed more time. I turned back and smiled at Vanderhoff. "I see you've stuck my card on the fridge there. That magnet ... where's it from?"

Vanderhoff hobbled closer to the refrigerator. While she squinted at the magnet, I shot a glance into the living room. Grayson was sticking the old-fashioned cell phone thingy under the sofa cushion.

"Grave Creek Mound," Vanderhoff said. She straightened up and sniffed. "That was the last one she sent, if I recall correctly."

I nodded solemnly. "I heard you reported her missing. I really am sorry."

"Thanks." Vanderhoff smiled. "Kids nowadays. Hopefully she'll turn up."

"I hope so."

Vanderhoff fetched the glass of water from the sink and took a step toward the living room. I sprinted ahead of her in an effort to warn Grayson she was coming. My gut flopped when I saw him fluffing the pillows on the sofa.

He winked at me and said, "And that, my little grasshopper, is how it's done."

"How what's done?" Vanderhoff asked.

I cringed. Grayson didn't even blink.

"Conducting an interview, ma'am," he said. "As you know, I'm here to help train our little Bobbie to become a bona fide private investigator. Don't you think she did a fine job today?"

Vanderhoff shrugged noncommittally. "I guess." She handed Grayson the glass of water. He drank it down in one, long gulp.

"We should be going," I said as he handed her back the empty glass.

"Thank you for your time. It's been lovely." Grayson kissed Mrs. Vanderhoff's hand. She beamed at him like a smitten, geriatric schoolgirl.

"Come back anytime, Detective Grayson," she said as we stepped onto the front porch. She followed us out and stood in the doorway, grinning and waving as we climbed into the Mustang.

"You seem to have a way with women," I said, and waved back at Vanderhoff. Her grin faded. Then she went inside and closed the door.

"She seemed nice enough," Grayson said.

"Sure. For a woman whose been known to spot the Virgin Mary in her French toast."

Grayson laughed. "It always pays to be polite—until it doesn't. That should be rule number one in the P.I. handbook."

I grimaced. "What does that even *mean?*"

Grayson grimaced, then burst into a grin. "Hey. I know! Let's get a picture of you standing in front of her place."

I eyed him suspiciously. "For what?"

Grayson pulled his cellphone from his pocket. "For your scrapbook, of course. *Detective's First Year.*" He snapped off a couple of shots of me with my mouth hanging open.

"I wasn't ready," I said.

"She's ready?" a woman asked excitedly. She was walking by on the sidewalk, towing a little white poodle on a leash beside her.

"What?" I asked.

The woman came over and bent down beside the driver's side window. She was Nellie Parker. I'd seen her at the beauty parlor a couple of times. Nosy Nellie was a bad tipper, according to Beth-Ann.

"Vanderhoff," Parker said. "Is she finally getting ready to sell her place?"

"No. Why would you think that?"

Parker's face collapsed with disappointment. "You're the second ones to stop and take a picture of her place today."

"Really?" I asked. "Who were the others?"

"I dunno. Just a guy I'd never seen before. I figured he was a realtor from Waldo or something." Parker glanced over at Vanderhoff's house and let out a big sigh. "Well, too bad, Doodles. We should get going." The little dog yipped. She turned back to face me. "Y'all have a nice day, now."

"You too," Grayson said.

"You thinking what I'm thinking?" I asked.

Grayson sighed wistfully. "Darn it. I guess I'm gonna miss Matlock tonight."

I fought back a grin, turned the key in the ignition, and fired up the Mustang.

"Let's do a test call," Grayson said as we cruised out of Cherry Manor and past the Stop & Shoppe. "See if mister tele-buggy's working."

"How?"

"Give Vanderhoff a ring."

I blanched. "Who? Me? What should I say?"

"Ask her if her refrigerator's running. Or if she's got Prince Albert in a can."

I rolled my eyes. "Don't you ever take *anything* seriously?"

"A few things. Sure. But this doesn't make the short list."

I pulled over and dialed Vanderhoff. The phone rang ten times before she answered it.

Grayson kept an eye on his own cell phone. When Vanderhoff finally picked up, a text message came up on his phone display. He tapped a button and stuck a pair of earbuds in his ears while I spoke with Vanderhoff.

"Mrs. Vanderhoff?" I asked.

"Oh. It's you, Bobbie. I wasn't gonna answer. I thought it might be that robot man again."

"No. Just me. I wanted to say thank you for your hospitality."

"Oh. You're welcome, honey."

"Have a good day, now, and let me know if you get any more weird calls."

"I will. Tell Detective Grayson it was a pleasure to meet him. He can come by any—"

"I will. Bye." I hung up and sneered at Grayson. "I think she's got a crush on you, lady-killer."

He grinned and pulled out the earbuds. "Jealous? I heard every word."

"So it's working?"

"Like a charm."

"Good. Speaking of charm, I need to call Paulson."

Grayson's eyebrows met in the middle of his forehead. "I fail to see the connection."

I smirked. "I need to give him an update on the case. But I don't know exactly what to say."

"Tell him Mothman's in town and is performing a one-night-only gig at the Stop & Shoppe tonight at nine-thirty."

I shot him a look. "You know, you're almost as bad as Earl."

Grayson grinned. "You said *almost*. I must be making progress."

Chapter Thirty-Two

"WHERE TO NOW, DETECTIVE Drex?" Grayson joked as we drove back toward Point Paradise.

"Well, I need to stop by the A&P."

"Let me guess. To check if Mothman's flitting around *Wool*worth's? Get it?"

"Ugh. Unfortunately, yes, I get it. And no. I need groceries. I'm out of coffee, milk, and pretty much everything else. I didn't think you'd want to go."

"Sure. Why not? But before we do that, I've got another idea."

"What?"

"Seeing as how we've got a stakeout coming up tonight, I thought we might work on your P.I. training some more."

"Okay. How?"

"I think it's high time you learned how to shoot a gun."

I raised an eyebrow. "That's not a bad idea, actually. I know a place we can fire off a few rounds. Why don't we swing by the garage and get your gun?"

"No need." Grayson patted his side. "I've got my trusty Glock right here."

"You've had it on you the whole time?"

"Of course. Never leave home without it. Don't worry. I've got a concealed carry license."

That wasn't *exactly* what I was concerned about. I'd been driving around with an armed stranger.

Whether Grayson was a friend or a fiend, the jury inside my brain was still in hot deliberation. If I was going to unload rounds with this guy, I needed to let someone else know, in case the guy turned out to be Dahmer and I turned out to be his next Happy Meal.

"Sure," I said. "Just going to check in with Earl. See if he needs anything."

I pulled the Mustang over and punched Earl on speed dial. I pasted on a smile and tried to sound casual. "Hey. I'm going with Grayson to do some target shooting. You need anything at the A&P?"

"Target shooting?" Earl laughed. "Is that what they're calling it nowadays? I thought it was 'Netflix and chill.'"

"Earl, we're going to test-fire his Glock. That's all."

"Here I am, gunning an engine, and you're gunning to get laid."

"Earl, you're fired."

I hung up the phone and looked over at Grayson. "Did you hear any of that?"

"Not a word. But since someone's expecting a 'happy ending,' I think it's only proper to buy you lunch first. What else has Waldo got to offer besides El Molino's?"

"Why?"

Grayson thumped his chest lightly with his fist. "I haven't quite fully recovered from last night's tacos yet."

FROM A PICNIC TABLE outside a small roadside attraction known as Randy's Rib Shack, I watched Grayson lick barbeque sauce off his fingers. Suddenly, I had a ghastly vision of it being blood instead of tomato sauce.

"How do you like Randy's special recipe?" I asked, trying to tame my willies.

"Not bad. Why aren't you eating?"

"I kind of lost my appetite."

"Is it me?" Grayson waggled his saucy fingers and grinned at me like a deranged demon. "Still think I might be after your lucky charms?"

"No." I smirked. "I've seen inside Randy's kitchen."

Grayson stopped mid-bite, grimaced, and set the pork rib back down on his plate.

I laughed. "You know, you keep mentioning this Mothman creature. What's the deal with that?"

Grayson wiped his fingers on a paper napkin. "It's supposed to be a true story. Like I said before, I'm here investigating reports of a red-eyed creature. Granted, that could be any number of cryptids—Bigfoot, the Boggy Creek Monster, even a wayward chupacabra. But since I've hooked up with you, I'm leaning more toward Mothman."

"Why?"

Grayson shrugged. "Sightings of a red-eyed, flying creature. Strange lights in the sky. And now, thanks to you and Vanderhoff, I know people are getting the same kind of weird phone calls the folks did back in the 1960s in Point Pleasant."

My nose crinkled at the prospect of a monster lurking nearby. "Did they ever catch this Mothman guy?"

"No. And after the tragedy, reported sightings of him dwindled to nothing."

I swallowed my spit. "Tragedy?"

Grayson shot me an incredulous look. "The Silver Bridge collapse. You never heard of it? The bridge spanning the Ohio River. It collapsed on December 15, 1967. It was full of rush-hour traffic. Forty-six people died."

"And they blamed that on Mothman?"

"Not exactly. They thought Mothman was some kind of omen. A sign. Haven't you ever heard of *The Mothman Prophecies?*"

"That movie with Richard Gere?"

"Yes. But also the book. It was a *New York Times* bestseller. It gives a sort of blow-by-blow diary of what happened in the town of Point Pleasant from 1966 to '67. The year of the Garuda."

Grayson picked up a little paper cup of barbeque sauce and downed it like a shot.

I grimaced. "Garuda?"

"That's what John Keel, the author of the book called it. The Garuda's a bird-like creature from Hindu and Buddhist mythology. People in Point Pleasant reported sightings of it all over the place. To some, it looked like a winged man. Others thought it was a giant bird. Some even thought it was a monster—a demon with bat wings. But they all agreed on two things. It had glowing red eyes, and it could fly."

A chill went down my spine. Maybe that *was* what I'd seen on the roof of the Stop & Shoppe the other night. "Did it kill people?"

"No. None that got reported, anyway. But it *did* seem to have a penchant for chasing people around and scaring the daylights out of them. Its favorite M.O. was to buzz by people in their cars. But it never actually caught anybody. Not that I know of, anyway. So it's hard to say what would've happened if it had."

I crinkled my nose. "Well, I don't want to be the first one to find out."

Grayson arched an eyebrow. "No?"

"So what exactly do you hope to achieve with this investigation of yours?"

"I'm hoping to find hard evidence to substantiate the creature's existence."

"Oh. Like what? A feather?"

"I don't think Mothman has feathers. Maybe a talon. Hair sample. Blood. I'd like to catch it, actually. But at this point, I'd even settle for scat."

I grimaced. "Moth poop? Who'd want that?"

"You'd be surprised. Lots of people think there's power in cryptic relics."

"Power for what?"

"For good or evil. Buddhists think the Garuda might hold the key to levitation and enlightenment. Others, well, who knows? Maybe they think it can turn them into Batman."

My eyebrows inched closer together. "So you really think this thing's real? That it's still alive?"

"I hope so. But nobody knows. After the bridge collapse, sightings of the creature pretty much disappeared from West Virginia. The reports around Waldo are the first in over fifty years."

My mind returned to my wallet. Maybe he'd pay me for my sighting story. "Are you offering any kind of ... reward?"

Grayson threw his sticky hands up. "Whoa. I answered your questions. Now it's your turn to answer one of mine."

I sighed. "Okay. What do you want to know?"

"Are you dating Paulson?"

I nearly choked on my iced tea. "That's none of your business," I hacked.

"I know. But he seemed a bit ... hmm ... *overzealous* yesterday at El Molino's."

"He's being protective. You *are* a stranger in town, after all."

Grayson shot me a perplexed look. "We're all strangers where we aren't known."

Okaay ....

"Speaking of Paulson, I still need to stop by his office," I said. "I promised him a report on Vanderhoff, but he didn't answer his phone this morning. Are you done eating?"

Grayson nodded. "Almost." He picked up the salt shaker, shook a generous portion of salt into his palm, and licked it.

What a weirdo.

"His office is here in Waldo," I said, pretending not to notice. "We might as well get it over with while we're here."

Chapter Thirty-Three

"ACCORDING TO THE ADDRESS, Paulson's office is a few miles on the other side of town," I said as we cruised down US 301 through the tiny, crumbling heart of Waldo.

"This place looked a lot better in the dark last night," Grayson said. "Oh. I take that back. I didn't see the big white horsey before."

He pointed to the sign for the Waldo Farmer's & Flea Market. Atop it stood a life-sized replica of a white horse. The stallion's jaunty expression seemed too dignified for the hodge-podge collection of nondescript buildings that made up Waldo Antiques Village.

"Let's stop," Grayson said. "I wonder what other curiosities they might have."

"They're closed on Mondays," I said, relieved for the excuse. "Besides, there's nothing there but junk disguised as antiques. After fifteen years in the business, I know the difference."

"I'll take your word on that."

Grayson watched the tiny town click by, its buildings standing not much more than a sidewalk's breadth away from the steaming asphalt of US 301.

"They like to stick close to the road here," he commented.

"Yeah. When they widened it to four lanes, they didn't leave the town much breathing room."

As we hit the center of Waldo, we passed City Hall, a white, boxy little structure no bigger than a coffee shop. Then, in quick succession, we passed the Waldo barber shop, Dixieland Music RV park, a junky place selling cypress-wood souvenirs, an Amtrak station, the

Tropix Inn motel, and a clot of dilapidated, corrugated-metal buildings tacked together with rusty nails and faded hopes.

As the scenery on both sides of the road was reclaimed by pinewoods and swamp, Grayson asked, "That's it? Where's Paulson's office?"

"He said it was out near Lake Alto Preserve. As you could see from your deluxe tour of Waldo, downtown office space is at a premium. Oh. There it is."

I shifted into second and took a left onto Alto Road. About a hundred yards up the rutted dirt lane, we came to a mailbox. A red clay driveway maybe twenty yards long led to a rustic wooden cabin tucked in among overgrown hedges.

"That must be it," I said.

The plain, metal mailbox next to the road had no name on it. It was mounted on an L-shaped post. A wooden, hand-painted sign hung below the mailbox. It read, "One nation under God."

That may have been so, but this place looked as godforsaken as any I'd ever seen.

"The place looks abandoned," Grayson said.

"Get used to it," I said. "Half the county looks that way. I don't see a car. He must be out on patrol."

"What kind of car does he drive?"

I frowned. "I dunno. A blue one?"

Grayson shook his head. "Blue? That's all you've got?"

"I don't pay much attention to that kind of thing. Today's cars all look alike to me."

"Drex, if you're going to be a P.I., you need to acquaint yourself with makes and models. You're going to spend half your time either tailing vehicles or trying to spot them. That's how people get around nowadays. You know, since that whole horse and buggy thing went by the wayside."

I blew out a breath. This whole P.I. thing was sounding like more work than I'd imagined it would be. My cellphone buzzed, saving me from having to come up with a snarky comeback. I looked at the display and groaned.

"You gonna get that?" Grayson asked.

"No. It's the hospital again. They keep calling. I don't know how I'm going to pay the bill."

"Huh." Grayson shot me a devious grin. "I've got just the thing to take your mind off thoughts of impending poverty."

"What?"

"Let's do something fun."

I frowned. "Like what?"

Grayson waggled his bushy eyebrows at me. "Let's go shoot something."

Chapter Thirty-Four

WITH NO OFFICER PAULSON to be found, we left the cabin in Lake Alto Preserve and drove back through Waldo. I turned onto Obsidian Road, then, a mile later, onto an unmarked dirt road. A quarter mile in, we reached the unofficial target-shooting spot known to gun-toting locals as Bullet Point.

I shifted into second and slowed down until I saw the fence posts. "That's it," I said, and shifted into park.

Grayson pulled out his Glock. A tinge of panic surged through me. If Grayson shot me, would Earl even bother to come find me? And if he did, would the vultures beat him to my remains?

I eyed Grayson's gun and forced a smile. "It won't take long to go through that magazine."

Grayson reached under the seat and pulled out a carton of ammo. "Good thing I brought more."

My eyebrows met my wig-line. "When did you put those under there?"

Grayson grinned. "When you weren't looking, obviously. Do you know you have a tendency to close your eyes when you're nervous?"

"Arggh!"

I flung open the car door and stomped over to the fence. Amongst the heap of battered tin cans and broken beer bottles, I found a few cans that weren't completely shot through with bullet holes. I set them up on fence posts and marched back over to Grayson.

"You go first," I said.

"No. Ladies first," he insisted. "Here, let me show you how to hold the gun."

"I know how!" I said.

"Sorry," Grayson said, handing me the gun. "Judging by your performance in my bedroom yesterday, I thought I could give you some pointers."

My mouth ached to deliver a devastating comeback, but I had nothing. Instead, I took my stance. Grayson sidled in close behind me, his chest nearly touching my back. As I inserted the earplugs he gave me, his arms encircled my shoulders.

My back arched from the electric twinge of his body heat.

I steadied myself. His forearms paralleled mine. His hands enveloped my fingers. As I held the polymer grip of the Glock in my hands, I could smell the musky maleness of him envelop me. I trembled.

"Hold your arms steady," he whispered.

I set my jaw. "You mean like *this?*"

I fired off five rounds in rapid succession. Five rusty Green Giant vegetable cans went flying off in all directions.

Grayson let go of me and stepped back. "Whoa!"

"Beginner's luck," I quipped, and headed over to the fence to reset the cans.

Grayson followed a step behind me. He picked up a freshly shot can. "Not bad," he said, holding it out for me to see. "But you're a little off center."

"Look closer," I said. "I was aiming for the giant's face."

Grayson examined the bullet hole above the Green Giant's neck. His mouth dropped open. "How'd you learn to shoot like that?"

"You forget. I was a boy until I was eleven. I got pretty good with a Daisy BB gun." I smirked. "I don't mean to brag or anything, but I can shoot out a baby doll's eye at a hundred paces."

Grayson whistled. "With one hand tied behind your back, I bet."

I grinned. "Should we set them up for you?"

Grayson nodded. "Sure."

Smug wallowed all over my face as I handed Grayson the Glock. I bent over and reached down for a can.

My heart nearly fell into my throat.

Staring back at me from the weeds was the raw, empty eye socket of a bloody skull.

I shot to standing. My brain went haywire. My ears throbbed with a strange, underwater-pulsing sound.

Something warm trickled down my leg.

Blood?

"You okay?" Grayson asked.

His voice sounded mere inches away. The hair on the back of my neck stood up.

OMG! That psycho's gone and stabbed me! He's lured me out here to .... Holy crap! This is Grayson's freaking killing field!

I screamed, ditched the green bean can, and made a mad scramble for the Mustang.

Grayson's footsteps crunched behind me. I could tell he was gaining on me.

Dear God! Will he rip my throat out, like he did the others?

Am I really going to die in this crappy hellhole of a place after all?

Chapter Thirty-Five

"DREX!" GRAYSON'S VOICE shouted out behind me. "Wait!"

I'd just flung myself into the Mustang, and was trying to get the key in the ignition. But my hands were shaking like I had ahold of a jackhammer.

Please, key! Please! Get in the freaking ignition!

I looked up. Grayson was ten feet from the car, his green eyes looked wild.

"What are you doing?" he yelled.

I jabbed the keys at the ignition hole. "Stay away from me!"

Grayson stopped in his tracks. "What's going on?"

The key slipped into the ignition. I turned it. The Mustang roared to life.

"I saw it. I know what you did!"

"What I did? What did I do?"

"The skull!" I screamed as I shifted into first.

Grayson blanched. "Skull? Where?"

"You know where!"

"What? Wait! Drex! You think I killed someone?" He took another step toward the car.

"Don't come any closer!" I shouted, and gunned the engine. The Mustang lurched forward, then stalled.

Damned air filter!

Grayson came a step closer and pulled out his Glock. My heart nearly stopped.

"Let me talk to you," he yelled. "Look, I'm dropping the weapon."

Suddenly, the gun fired, shooting out my left front tire.

I screamed and turned the ignition again. It caught. I slammed the Mustang into first and gently pressed the gas. The car moved forward a foot.

"Wait!" Grayson yelled.

But I didn't wait. What for? To get my brains blown out?

I shifted into second and mashed the pedal to the floor. Clouds of orange dust billowed up behind my squealing tires as the muscle car took off, fishtailing down the dirt road.

Grayson slowly disappeared in the dust behind me. I thought I was in the clear. But fifty yards out, I hit a huge pothole. The driver's side window disappeared into the door panel with a crunch of breaking glass.

Then, the tread on the blown tire peeled away like a strip of black alligator hide. The bare left front rim couldn't grip in the sand. The Mustang veered wildly to the left. It took all I had to keep it on the road as I hobbled along, the rim gouging and scraping and slinging up sand.

Without traction, the car inched along slowly—slower than I could run. I dared a glance in the rearview mirror. Grayson was about thirty feet behind me, and gaining fast.

Crap!

I scanned the car for a weapon.

Nothing.

I glanced in the rearview mirror and nearly swallowed my tongue. Grayson was almost to the car!

I grabbed the only thing I could find to defend myself—the green Tootsie Pop I'd licked once, then tossed in the ashtray. Grayson jogged up to my broken window. I hurled the sucker at him with all my might. It hit home, beaning him right below his left eye.

"Ow!" he yelled, rubbing the impact spot. "What'd you do that for? And why the hell are you running away from me?"

"You shot at me!" I screeched.

Grayson grimaced. "It was an accident. I swear!"

"No it wasn't. You're trying to kill me!"

"I am not!"

"Are too!"

"Am not!" Grayson rolled his eyes. "This is ridiculous. What are we? Three-year-olds?"

I stared at him sullenly. "How do I know you're not some serial killer living in that RV in the woods? What about that skull I saw!"

"What skull?" Grayson asked. "I don't know anything about a skull. Geez, Drex. I'm trying to *help* you!"

"*Help* me?"

"Yes. With your detective license, remember?"

My eyes narrowed. "Oh. In that case, thank you very much. I'll send Officer Paulson to pick you up."

I hit the gas. The Mustang's wheels spun in the sand.

"Come on, Drex," Grayson said, holding up his hands. "I don't want you to call the police."

I scowled. "You're in some kind of trouble with the law, aren't you? I *knew* it!"

Grayson shook his head. "No. I swear. I just ... I don't want my name in a public incident report, okay? Come on, I'm no killer. See? I'm too charming." He tried to wink his swollen eye, but only managed a flinch.

I sneered at him. "Lots of psychopaths can be charming when they need to be."

He shrugged. "Fair enough. But Drex, I could've killed you a dozen times already if that's what I wanted to do."

I jerked back in horror. "Is that supposed to be reassuring?"

He sighed. "It's the best I can come up with right now."

I stared at the strange man dressed in black. "Who are you really, Grayson?"

He touched the bruise on his cheek just below his swollen eye. "I'm a physicist."

Suddenly, the horror and fear clinching my gut evaporated. No one could make up a story like that. Not on the fly. Not with a Tootsie Pop freshly hurled into his eye.

"Prove it," I said.

Grayson smiled ingratiatingly. "Uh ... E equals MC squared?"

I laughed. I don't know why. Probably from sheer hysteria.

Grayson grinned. "Well, aren't we a pair. You think I'm Ted Bundy, and you look like John Wayne Gacy."

I shot a quick glance in the rearview mirror. My wig had flown off during the fracas, exposing my red, exceedingly receding hairline. Last night's mascara had melted into black rings around my eyes.

If that weren't bad enough, it wasn't blood that I'd felt earlier, when I'd first seen that skull.

It was urine.

I'd peed my pants.

Just when I think life can't get any crappier, it can.

I laid my hands over the steering wheel, rested my bullet-riddled forehead on my forearms, and laughed and laughed and laughed and laughed.

Chapter Thirty-Six

GRAYSON HELPED ME CHANGE the tire on the Mustang. Actually, he changed the tire while I fixed my wig and held him at gunpoint with his own Glock. This time, it wasn't so much because I didn't trust him, but because I had the upper hand. Besides, I needed the practice—for my P.I. license and all. This go around, however, I made sure the damned gun was loaded.

Changing the tire and handing over his gun to me were part of the deal Grayson had made in exchange for me giving him a ride back to civilization—and for not calling the cops.

The other part of the deal was that he had to come clean about who he was and what he was really up to out here in the middle of nowhere. He'd agreed to my terms without argument. Apparently, Grayson didn't feel like dying in a backwoods crap hole, either.

"So why'd you lie to me about being William Knickerbocker?" I asked, enjoying the weight of the Glock in my hand.

Grayson looked up from cranking the lug-nut wrench. "Because I didn't want to leave a trail. I'm kind of a big deal in some scientific circles. If the academic board found out I was chasing Mothman ... well, let's just say it could put a damper on my already fragile credibility, if you know what I mean."

"What about the whole private investigator malarkey?"

Grayson looked surprised. "That isn't malarkey. I am. A private investigator, I mean."

I sneered. "That seems highly implausible."

Grayson wagged his eyebrows. "Perhaps, yet it remains tantalizingly within the realms of theoretical possibility."

I gave him half an eye roll. "I guess being a physicist pays for your hobby hunting monsters?"

"More like the other way around. Physicists don't get paid jack. That's why I quit, kind of."

"So you really *can* make good money as a P.I.?"

Grayson shook his head. "It's always about the money with you."

I frowned. "I've got bills to pay. *Big* bills. *Hospital* bills."

"How much?"

I grimaced. "I don't know. I'm afraid to call them back."

Grayson frowned. "I detest doctors. No. I take that back. I detest the Western medical model."

"Why?"

"The whole thing is based on being dead."

My eyebrows converged below the crater in the middle of my forehead. "What?"

"Long story short, about four hundred years ago—"

"Hold on," I said, waving the gun. "You said 'short.'"

Grayson grinned and tightened the last lug nut. "Once upon a time, the Pope sanctioned this French guy named Descartes to dissect cadavers for scientific purposes. Now, thanks to his work, the entire Western medical model is based on the premise that we're nothing more than a biological machine made out of meat and bones."

"So?"

"Believe me, we're a lot more than that."

I sighed. "Are you saying that we have a soul? I thought you were a physicist, not a preacher."

"We don't *have* a soul, Drex. We *are* a soul. The body's merely a semi-material manifestation for our exploration and experimentation in third-dimension reality."

I crinkled my nose. "Okay. *Now* I believe you're a physicist. Can you repeat what you just said *in English?*"

"We need a body to maneuver this earthly plain. You can't drive a car without a foot on the gas pedal. No foot, no car, no go. See?"

"Sort of ...."

Grayson stood up and dusted off his knees. "Look, enough lessons for one day. What say we head over to the A&P, like you'd planned in the first place?"

"Okay. But I want to know more about—"

"Quantum physics?" Grayson asked hopefully.

"No. How you made your money as a P.I."

Grayson sighed. "You do have a persistently one-track mind, Drex. To the point of dogged determination, one might say."

I eyed him suspiciously. "When I'm interested in the subject, sure."

He smiled. "Good. *Your* motivation is money. *Mine* is mystery. Pursuing 'monsters' as you call them, takes persistence. And determination. And discretion. Extracting evidentiary material of the as-yet esoteric is a huge challenge."

I wasn't exactly sure what he was talking about, but didn't want to appear dumb. "Then why do it?"

"Simple. I want to be the first person to prove their existence beyond a shadow of a doubt."

I frowned. "Excuse me, but going back to that whole bell curve thingy you mentioned the other day. Do you think the *intellectual collective* is ready for the truth? About Mothman and bigfoot, I mean?"

Grayson's lip curled upward. "Well, that's just it, isn't it? I have to come up with a better version of the facts before it can become the new truth."

"Let me wrap my head around this," I said. "If your version becomes the new truth, it becomes the new reality? Or is it the other way around?"

Grayson grinned. "And I thought you were just a pretty face."

I smiled. No one had called me pretty since Grandma Selma passed away. I didn't like to think I was vain, but his compliment felt pretty damned good.

"So, should we gather some provisions before we head to your first stakeout?" Grayson asked.

I grinned. "Sure. What do you usually eat when you're tailing someone?"

"What most lovers of the unexplained eat, of course. Cheetos."

My nose crinkled. "Cheetos? Why?"

"Because no one's ever been able to scientifically prove what they're made of. Plus, they have the added bonus of glowing orange in the dark."

I shook my head. "Okay. To the A&P it is."

As I shifted into first, a thought hit me. I turned to Grayson. "What about the skull I saw in the woods? Shouldn't someone know about it?"

Grayson locked eyes with me. "I suspect *someone* already does."

I reached for my phone. "I'm going to call Paulson."

"Do what you want," Grayson said. "But if it were up to me, I'd wait until after our stakeout. It might not be safe for Paulson to go out into those woods alone. He's going to need backup."

"But shouldn't we at least warn him? We're out here goofing around looking for some Mothman freak when there could be a psycho killer on the loose."

Grayson locked eyes with me. "Who says the two things aren't interrelated?"

My mouth fell open. "You think they are?"

Grayson shrugged. "In the world of quantum physics, Drex, *everything's* interrelated."

Chapter Thirty-Seven

WHILE GRAYSON WANDERED the aisles of the A&P grocery store in Waldo, I snuck into the restroom to call Beth-Ann for a reality check.

"Hey, you got a minute?" I whispered into the phone.

"Just closing up shop. I swear I think I may be the only person on the planet still doing permanent waves."

"Listen, you were right about Knickerbocker. He *was* using that name as an alias. He said he did it to keep under the radar with his colleagues. His real name is Nick Grayson."

"Nick Grayson?" Beth-Ann's tired voice picked up a lilt. "Now *there's* a name I can work with. Still, too bad he's bald."

"He's not. His head's shaved. His hair's growing back."

"Does this mean you're calling dibs on him?"

"Geez! No. I was calling because ... well, I don't know whether to trust him or not. We went out to Bullet Point, you know, to shoot a few rounds. I found a skull in the grass—"

"What?" Beth-Ann nearly choked. "A *human* skull?"

"I don't know. I didn't get that good a look at it. I ... uh ... kind of freaked and ran. Then Grayson shot out my tire—"

"He *what?* Good grief! Are you okay?"

"Yeah. It was all a big misunderstanding. At least, I'm pretty sure it was."

"Now you listen here, Ms. Roberta Drex," Beth-Ann barked. "You stay out of the woods with that guy! He could be a madman. Like that Unabomber dude. He could have been living in the woods in that camper for years, getting crazier by the hour!"

"That's what I thought, too. At first. But if that were true, he could've killed me by now."

A toilet flushed. Nosy Nellie Parker emerged from a stall. I turned my back on her and cupped my hand over the phone.

"Maybe he's playing games," Beth-Ann said. "Building your trust."

"But why?" I whispered.

"Who knows? Blood sport? Why do psycho killers do anything they do?"

Parker washed her hands and hit the hand dryer.

"He says he's a physicist," I yelled over the noise.

"What? Like that pi-R-squared crap?"

"Yeah."

"Why are you yelling? Is this some kind of code? Has he got you at gunpoint?"

"What? No."

The hand dryer went off. Parker gave me the once-over and left the bathroom.

"Okay. Maybe you're right," Beth-Ann said. "If I were a serial killer, I'd have picked an easier cover. You know, like a restaurateur or janitor or something. Physicist seems like a weird choice for an alibi."

I bit my lip. "So maybe he's okay after all?"

"I dunno. Maybe. Either way, please tell me you'll be careful, okay?"

"I will. I'm going on a stakeout with him tonight at nine-thirty at the Stop & Shoppe."

"A stakeout at Artie's? You're kidding!"

"It's a long story. Have you ever heard of the Mothman?"

"The Mothman? Yeah. But what's that got to do—"

"I gotta go. Call me at ten tonight, would you? To make sure I'm still alive?"

"Absolutely. Be safe."

"I will," I said, then clicked off the phone, adjusted my wig in the mirror, and went off to find Grayson.

GRAYSON AND I WERE sitting in my Mustang by the side of the road in the dark, weeds up to the windows. On the opposite side of Obsidian Road, the fluorescent lights of the Stop & Shoppe gave off a bluish-white glow in the gloom, as if the place was some forlorn ghost of failed merchandising past.

"You're getting crumbs all over the seat," I grumbled at Grayson as he crunched on a handful of Cheetos. "You know, that isn't the healthiest stakeout food in the world—or the stealthiest. You're leaving a trail of orange goop all over the place."

"You're right." Grayson waggled his orange fingertips at me. "Could you imagine committing a murder with Cheetos fingers? No way to make a clean getaway."

I crinkled my nose. "Gross."

Grayson grinned. "Max Planck had it right when he said the world we perceive through our senses is only a tiny fragment of the vastness of Nature."

I rolled my eyes. "I doubt he was talking about Cheetos crumbs. Who's Max Planck, anyway?"

Grayson shot me a stunned look. "You don't know who Max—oh, how sad. Everybody knows Einstein. But poor Max Planck. Every bit as brilliant a physicist, yet cast to the second shelf of history."

I blew out a bored laugh. "Yeah, I hate when that happens. Poor Max. Was he another starving physicist, or did he become a P.I. like you, to pay the bills?"

"Neither. Max did all right for himself without a second job."

I sneered. "How nice for him. You know, you still haven't explained how you got all that cash in your glovebox."

Grayson shrugged. "Like they say, 'Do what you love and the money comes.' The pursuit of the mystical and unexplained is what makes me feel alive, Drex."

I shot him a sour look. "Yeah? Paying the rent makes *me* feel alive. Or, at least, it gives me the fleeting feeling I might survive for another month."

He laughed. "You're such a cynic. Okay. Let's just say I found something that was worth a lot of money to the right client."

I perked up. "What kind of client is the *right* client?"

"I only have one criteria. My client is always H.B."

"H.B.? You mean—*Halle Barry?*"

"No. Highest bidder."

"*Highest* bidder? You mean there's more than one nutcase out there interested in this stuff?"

Grayson sighed. "I'm glad to see you're keeping an open mind. You'd be surprised how many people want to get their hands on evidence that defies all conventional explanation. With rarity comes great value."

"So what was it you cashed in ... excuse me ... *collected evidence* on?"

Grayson glanced out the window. "Sorry. That's on a need-to-know basis."

"Come on, Grayson!"

Grayson went through the motions of locking his busted lip and throwing away the key.

I snorted. "You're such an idiot. Okay. I give. What does it take to be privy to this secret information of yours?"

"*Trusting* me, for one," Grayson said. "And being a partner."

"You have *partners?*"

He shrugged. "Had."

"What happened to them?"

"That's also on a need-to-know basis."

Jerk!

I turned and glared out the windshield, then held a pair of binoculars to my eyes so Grayson couldn't see how pissed off I was. I focused in on the Stop & Shoppe. After adjusting the viewfinder, I realized Artie was bending over the ice-cream freezer. I was staring right into his big, fat butt-crack. I groaned in disgust.

"What now?" Grayson asked.

"Nothing."

"Look, sorry about the Cheetos crumbs," he said. "But if you want to be a P.I., you're going to need a different car anyway. This one is way too conspicuous. You need some kind of gray, late-model, blend-into-the-scenery kind of vehicle."

"Oh. You mean like an old, algae-covered RV?"

"I'm on vacation."

"For how long? That thing looks like you've been camping in it since the Y2K scare."

Grayson sighed. "Okay. You have a point. But as far as RVs go, you have to admit, no one would ever suspect what I'm doing in it. Your Mustang here is the equivalent of me riding around in a shiny red bus with *Monster Hunter on Tour* emblazoned all over it."

Apparently, every single thing about my life is wrong. Even the stupid car I'm driving.

I was more than ready for a change of subject. "What time is it?" I asked.

"Nine twenty-six."

"Getting close to nine thirty. Let's concentrate on the Stop & Shoppe for now."

"Good idea."

We sat in silence, binoculars trained on the dilapidated old gas station. Not a damned thing happened—unless you counted Artie lifting up a butt cheek to fart.

I checked my phone. It was 9:57 p.m. "I think it's time we—"

Grayson's cellphone pinged. He glanced at it, then over at me. "It's Vanderhoff. She's getting a phone call."

I smirked. "Maybe it's Matlock."

Grayson grinned and put his phone on speaker.

"Penelope? Is that you?" a man's voice asked.

"Why, it sure is, tiger."

The voice was Vanderhoff's. In sexy mode.

Yuck.

"So nice of you to call," she said. "I was just thinking I'd have to go to bed all by my lonesome tonight."

The man laughed huskily. "Well, we wouldn't want that. Are you wearing those sexy little red panties of yours?"

"You know I am. And now they're getting all w—"

I reached over and clicked off the phone. "I don't want to hear any more. I already threw up in my mouth a little."

Grayson laughed. "Phone sex operators. Always the ones you'd never suspect, am I right?"

I grimaced, trying to block the vision my mind was trying to form. "Well, at least now I know how she supplements her Social Security check."

"What say we cruise through the Stop & Shoppe for a six-pack to celebrate?" Grayson said.

I frowned. "Celebrate *what?*"

"Your first stakeout."

"But it was a bust." I reached down to crank the engine.

"Yeah, but we sat in the car for over twenty minutes without killing each other. That should count for—" Grayson's eyes shifted to the Stop & Shoppe. "Hold on! What's that?"

Grayson lifted his binoculars to his eyes and trained them on something across the road.

"It's Artie," I deadpanned. "Wow. He actually got out of his chair."

"No," Grayson whispered. "Up on the roof."

I tipped my binoculars up slightly. There they were. Those red eyes again, just like two nights ago. "Oh, my—"

I never had a chance to finish my sentence.

Suddenly, the red eyes dipped, then headed right at us.

In the dim light of a quarter moon, a huge, bat-like creature swooped down over the car. As it passed over us, I stuck my head out the window and watched, slack-jawed, as it disappear over the tree-tops behind us.

Chapter Thirty-Eight

"WHAT WAS *that?*" I squealed.

"Mothman!" Grayson said, like a kid who just spotted Santa. "Come on! Let's see if it landed in the trees behind us!"

I winced. "Are you out of your freaking gourd?"

Grayson flung open the car door. "Depends on who you ask. Are you coming?"

I grabbed his arm. "Wait! It might've been a helicopter. You know, chasing an escaped convict."

Grayson grinned at me. "Sure. If the convict was flying."

My phone buzzed, scaring the bejeebers out of me. Grayson broke free of my grip and disappeared into the woods. I clicked on the phone.

"You still alive?" Beth-Ann whispered.

"Yes, I think so," I whispered back.

"Did you see Mothman?"

"Uh ... thanks for calling, Beth-Ann, but I gotta go."

I clicked off the phone and sat there, too stunned to move.

Had I? Had I really just seen Mothman?

Suddenly I realized I was alone. In the dark. With my car window open! I grabbed the crank and pumped it furiously. Nothing happened.

"What the—?"

Then I remembered the windowpane had broken at Bullet Point. My mind began to jump around like a squirrel on a hot stove.

Was that part of Grayson's plan all along?

I shot an arm across the passenger seat to roll up the other window. Something grabbed my shoulder from behind. I screamed, whirled around, and hurled a blind punch at whatever had a hold of me.

"Ouch!" Grayson yelled. "Drex, it's me!"

"You scared the crap out of me!" I screeched, wringing my painful knuckles.

Grayson opened his mouth to speak, but his cellphone pinged with another text alarm. He looked at the display. "Vanderhoff again," he said, and ran around the car. He jumped into the passenger seat and clicked his phone to speaker mode.

"Hello?" Vanderhoff said.

"*Beep. Beep. Beep.* You weren't there," a mechanical voice said. "Tell no one ... or you're next."

"Tell no one *what?*" Vanderhoff asked. Her voice sounded frail and shaky.

The line went dead.

"So she's not crazy after all," I whispered. I turned to Grayson. "What do you think this means?"

Grayson shook his head. "I don't know. But maybe we should do the same thing. For now, anyway."

"Do what?"

Grayson's green eyes locked onto mine.

"Don't tell anybody. You know. For Vanderhoff's sake."

Chapter Thirty-Nine

I WOKE UP THE NEXT morning shivering. I reached for Grandma Selma's afghan at the foot of my bed. It wasn't there. I sat up. In the pinkish-gray of twilight, I couldn't see it anywhere.

I crawled out of bed and looked around the room. It wasn't on the floor, either. I got on my hands and knees to look under the bed.

When I lifted the dust ruffle, two red, glowing eyes stared back at me.

I nearly swallowed my tonsils.

A squeaky, ghost of a scream made it halfway up my throat, then collapsed into a disgusted groan. The eyes weren't eyes. They were the reflectors on a pair of hand weights I wore back when I used to work out.

Geez. I hope this isn't going to be one of those crappy days that lasts a freaking week.

I put a hand on the bed for leverage and hauled myself up off my knees. Shivering from the cold, I slipped out of my sleeping sweats into work sweats, then climbed into my coveralls. As I padded to the kitchen in my stockinged feet to get the coffee going, a random brain cell fired.

I'd left Grandma Selma's afghan in her apartment the night I'd slept on the couch to keep an eye on Grayson.

Duh!

I dumped coffee into a filter and was contemplating taking a shower when I heard the sound of Earl banging around in the garage's service bay below. I turned on the pot, tugged on a jacket, stuck my feet into my father's boots, and made a quick clomp downstairs for a progress report on Grayson's RV.

To be honest, my motivation was more out of self-defense that curiosity. If I was going to face Grayson this morning, my poor, addled brain needed a topic of conversation a tad lighter than his screwy metaphysical philosophy.

"How's it going?" I asked Earl's backside. He was bent over the engine compartment of the old RV, tinkering with something or another.

"Not too bad. I need a couple more parts." Earl straightened up and handed me a list scrawled on a scrap of paper. "Be good if we could get 'em ordered this morning, boss man."

I glanced over the list. "Sure. Go ahead."

"How'd your date go with Grayson last night?" Earl teased as he stuffed the list back into his pocket.

"It wasn't a date. We just ... you know ... shot stuff."

Earl grinned. "Sure you did." He turned and stuck his head back under the hood of the RV.

I should've just turned around and gone back upstairs. Earl ate up conspiracy theories like Cheerios. But I had a burning question on my mind, and my smartphone was still too smart for me to figure out how to search the internet with it. That, and the bifocal demon had finally caught up with me. I needed glasses to read the damned cellphone screen. Glasses I couldn't afford—both financially and cosmetically.

I closed my eyes, took a deep breath, and said, "Hey Earl, you ever heard of Mothman?"

He popped up from under the hood. "Mothballs? Sure. I can't stand—"

"No. Mothman."

Earl's eyes lit up. "That critter what scared the daylights outta them people up in West Virginia? Sure, I heard of it."

"What did it turn out to be?"

"Turn out to be? It was the *Mothman*, Bobbie."

I suppressed a groan. "I mean in the official reports. What did they say it was?"

Earl raised an eyebrow, grabbed his stubbly chin, and rubbed beneath his nose with his index finger. "They never did say for sure. Some folks thought it came from outer space. Some thought it was a giant bat, all swoll-up and deformed by radioactive crap from that abandoned military place it hung around."

I cringed, but kept going. "Why would people think it was from outer space?"

"On account of seeing all kind of strange lights in the sky. And them weird phone calls."

My back stiffened. "What kind of phone calls?"

"Clicks. Beeps. Static. Stuff like that, mostly. Then these guys in black showed up and started tellin' everybody not to say nothing about what they saw. That's *really* why people think Mothman was the real deal, Bobbie. If it was a hoax, why would these guys come around and tell them folks to keep quiet about it?"

"What guys?"

"The weird dudes in black. That's where that whole 'men in black' thing came from, I think."

I frowned. "What were they like? These men in black?"

"Folks said they looked human, mostly. But something was always off about 'em. Some had real big, googly eyes. Like a bug. Some wore clothes that was out of style."

"Earl, that describes half of Alachua County."

Earl laughed. "I'm talking *really* old stuff. Like from the '40s and '50s. Or clothes that looked like they came from the future. They also spoke kind of stiff-like. Used old-fashioned words. A few of 'em didn't know basic stuff, either. Like it was the first time they'd ever set foot on Earth."

"What do you mean?"

"Well, I remember something about this one guy who tried to drink Jell-O."

I blew out an annoyed breath. "He was probably just drunk. You're full of it, Earl."

"Am not! You know, now that I think about it, when Knickerbocker come up in here, he was all dressed in black." He made googly eyes at me. "Maybe he's one of them M-I-B's. Think about it, Bobbie. He showed up here outta nowhere. And he's always wearing that funny old hat."

I scowled. "He wears that hat because his head is cold." I blew out a frustrated sigh. "How much longer before the RV is fixed?"

Earl shrugged. "Might have it ready for a test run tomorrow. Why?"

"I need to give Grayson a progress report this morning."

"Where is he?"

"Upstairs."

Earl's face took on a mischievous look. "Well, while he's not here, let me show you something I found in his RV. Maybe you'll change your mind about your boyfriend being one of them M-I-B weirdos."

The part of me that wanted to tell Earl to mind his own business got kicked to the curb by the part of me dying to know what he'd uncovered. I followed my cousin over to the RV's side door, and then crept inside with him.

I was expecting Earl to show me a baby alien in a pickle jar. Instead, he pointed to the kitchen and said, "Look."

My nose crinkled in disappointment. "What?"

"All them cabinets is locked."

I stared at the small padlocks on the kitchen cabinets. "So?"

"Why would he lock up his cabinets?"

"So stuff doesn't fall out when he's traveling? Or so nosy jerks like you don't go through them?"

Earl shrugged. "All right. But why would he have eight deadbolts on his *bedroom door?*"

"How should I know? Same reason? To keep you out?"

"I'm telling you, Bobbie. Something ain't kosher with that feller. Why you asking me about the Mothman anyway?" Earl grinned. "Wait. Don't tell me. That's what Knickerbocker calls his little man, ain't it? Did you get a look at it last night?"

"No!" I growled. "He's a *customer.* That's all. Now get back to work."

I turned to go. Earl called after me.

"Hey Bobbie, you ever smelled mothballs?"

I turned back around. "Yeah. Why?"

"How'd you get your big nose between his tiny legs?"

"Earl, you're fired."

I turned and stomped out of the garage. My cousin had aggravated the stew out of me for the millionth time. But he'd also gotten me thinking.

Why *hadn't* Grayson mentioned anything about men in black when he told me about the Mothman case?

Chapter Forty

AS I REACHED THE TOP of the stairs, Grayson came out of Grandma Selma's apartment. I couldn't help but notice he was dressed all in black, including that old fedora.

Could he really be an MIB like Earl said?

"Good morning," Grayson said pleasantly. "Coffee ready?"

"Yeah. Sure. Come on in."

As he followed me into my apartment, my mind raced around like a rat on a greased Hot Wheels track. Earl was right. Grayson *did* come out of nowhere. He wore black clothes. Yesterday, he drank barbeque sauce like it was a shot of whisky, and licked salt like a Jersey cow. He claimed to be a physicist ....

Oh my word! A man from outer space would be well acquainted with physics, wouldn't he? It was the perfect foil!

"You call Paulson?" Grayson asked.

I whirled around. Grayson was putting a dash of salt in his coffee mug. I stared, open-mouthed.

"What?" he said. "It cuts the bitterness."

My cellphone buzzed. I looked at the display. "It's the hospital again."

"Answer it, Drex. They're not going to go away."

I groaned and picked up the phone. "Hello?"

"Roberta Drex?" a woman's voice asked.

"Yes."

"I'm calling for Dr. Brown. He'd like for you to come in for an appointment."

"What for?"

"He'd like to discuss your MRI results."

I cringed. "Can't you tell me over the phone?"

"No, I'm afraid not. Please. He says it's imperative that you come in as soon as possible."

"Tomorrow?"

"I had a cancellation. The doctor's got an opening in an hour if you can make it."

I sighed. "Okay. I'll be there." I clicked off the phone.

"What's the deal?" Grayson asked.

"I dunno. Dr. Brown wants to see me right away. It can't be good. Unless .... Maybe this whole thing is a trap to shake me down for the bill."

Grayson's lip twisted. "I wouldn't put it past them. Blasted doctors. Speaking of jerks, did you call Paulson yet?"

I shot Grayson a look. "Yes. I told him about finding the skull out at Bullet Point."

"What did he say?"

"That he'd check it out. And I should get some rest. He thinks I could've had another post-concussion hallucination."

"Huh." Grayson took a sip of coffee. "So he thinks the skull could be another false sighting? Besides the dead guy in the orange jumpsuit and the dead guy who shot you?"

"Yeah."

Greyson tapped his upper lip with an index finger. "Spooky action at a distance."

"What?"

"Quantum physics theory. You see—"

My mind glazed over. "Save it. Maybe Paulson's right. Maybe I *am* imagining things. I haven't felt like myself since the accident." I glanced at the clock. "Crap. I've got to be at the hospital in Gainesville in an hour. I better get going."

Grayson followed me toward the door. "Can I catch a ride with you into town?"

"I guess. But first, tell me where you got your physics degree."

"The University of Hard Knocks."

I turned, suddenly angry. "I'm serious, Grayson!"

Grayson held his hands up. "MIT. Geez! Don't shoot."

I scowled. "Sorry. I'm just nervous."

"Understandable. Nothing good ever came from an MRI."

"Or an MIT," I muttered to myself, then I stumbled down the stairs toward the garage, Grayson hot on my heels.

When we got to the service bay, Earl was hunched over the RV's engine again, singing along with Madonna to *Material Girl*.

I suddenly felt all alone in the world.

I turned to Grayson. "Will you come to the hospital with me to see Dr. Brown?"

Grayson's left eyebrow shot up. "*Me?* Why?"

"Who else am I going to take? *Him?*"

Grayson glanced over at Earl and blew out a breath. "You have a point. Okay. I guess I owe you one."

Chapter Forty-One

"YOU COULD BE SUFFERING from a coup contrecoup concussion," Grayson said as we climbed into the Mustang.

"A coo-coo what?"

"Coup contrecoup. It's a kind of brain injury. A coup injury happens when your head's struck by a moving object. A contrecoup injury occurs when your head is moving and hits a stationary object. You said the bullet hit you, then you hit the sidewalk. You could've sustained a kind of 'rebound' injury to both sides of your brain. Both a coup and a contrecoup."

"Oh."

"That might explain the strange visions," Grayson continued. "You may be having flashbacks, or memories mixed together."

"You mean my brain may be scrambled?" I turned the key in the ignition. The Mustang roared to life. I scowled at the dashboard.

Yeah, sure. Now *you're working just fine. Stupid car.*

"Eh ... not exactly," Grayson said. "The effects of a coup contrecoup injury are usually temporary. But, then again, they can last a long time, too."

I steered the car out onto Obsidian Road. "How do you know all this stuff?"

"Head injuries can change people. They can cause your personality to shift—your brain function to shift. In some cases, even your brain *capabilities* to shift. That's how I got my eidetic memory."

"I have an idiotic memory, too," I said. "Why is it that I can only remember totally useless stuff?"

"Not idiotic. *Eidetic.* I have total recall of stuff I've seen for just a few seconds. My memory's like a photo album. I can kind of go in and view memories like they're photographs."

"You're saying you have a photographic memory?"

"Yes and no. With a photographic memory, you can recall pages of text, lists of numbers, that kind of thing. But a true photographic memory has never been proven to exist."

I shot Grayson some sarcastic side-eye. "Tell that to anyone who's ever walked in on their parents in bed together."

Grayson laughed. "Fair enough."

"So you got your great memory from an accident," I said. "Should I believe you, or is this another cover story? Maybe you're really some super-brained alien from another planet."

Grayson's lip curled sinisterly. "I'd tell you, Drex, but then I'd have to erase your memory."

I nearly steered into the ditch. "You can *do* that?"

"Your question is irrelevant," he said in a strange, robotic tone.

I thought about punching the jerk in the arm. Instead, I decided to take the bait. "Why?" I asked.

Grayson smiled at me, then spoke in his normal voice. "Because, Drex. If I could erase your memory, how would you ever know?"

"DR. BROWN WILL SEE you now," the nurse said. The look on her face made me feel as if she'd read my charts and knew I shouldn't be buying any green bananas.

"Come in with me," I pleaded with Grayson, and took his hand. I still had serious doubts about the guy, but if some stranger in a lab coat was going to walk into a room that smelled like disinfectant and tell me I only had hours to live, I didn't want to be alone when I heard the news.

Any port in a storm.

"Ms. Drex," Dr. Brown said as I entered his office. He looked surprised when Grayson followed me in. "Who's this?"

"My fiancé," I said. I smiled and squeezed Grayson's hand. He surprised me by squeezing back. My already pounding heart thumped a beat faster.

"Have a seat," Dr. Brown said. "I'll come to the point. We found an anomaly on your MRI."

My shoulders slumped. "What kind of anomaly? Am I going to die?"

"First of all, it's not life-threatening at this point. At least, not as far as we can tell."

I stared at the stranger in the lab coat. "What do you mean? What's wrong with me?"

Dr. Brown stabbed a finger at the MRI scan on his desk. "See this mass here next to your pineal gland? It's vestigial."

"I'm going to be a vegetable?" I squeaked.

"*Vestigial*. It's the remnants of your *twin*, Ms. Drex."

My mouth fell open. "My *twin*? How is that possible? I didn't have a twin."

"But you *did*," the doctor said. "It just didn't wholly survive gestation. You see, early in your mother's pregnancy, your fetus absorbed the embryonic mass that was supposed to become your twin brother. He vanished, if you will. Except for this small mass of tissue here."

"How do you know the twin was a male?" Grayson asked.

The doctor looked up from the scan. "Well, a vestigial twin can be completely formed, or it can be a random clump of cells or body parts. An arm, teeth, that kind of thing. Given the shape and density of the mass, the vestigial twin in Ms. Drex's brain appears to be made entirely of ... ahem ... *gonadal* tissue."

"*What!*" I shot a glance at Grayson. He was pursing his lips. Whether it was from concern over my health or he was trying not to laugh, I couldn't tell. My head was too busy swimming against a tsunami of unexpected, unwanted thoughts ....

"What's the prognosis?" I heard Grayson ask.

His voice sounded dull, as if he were underwater. Too stunned to react, I sat still and passive as the two men spoke to each other about me as if I weren't there.

"The mass is at the center of her brain," Dr. Brown said. "It would be extremely difficult to remove surgically. But as long as she's not displaying adverse symptoms and the mass doesn't enlarge, I believe the best course of action is to leave it as it is and monitor it every few months."

"Keep an eye on it. Make sure it doesn't sprout limbs." Grayson said, his voice echoing in my clogged ears.

Dr. Brown's eyes widened. "Well, in a manner of speaking, yes."

"I'd like to take the scans with me," Grayson said.

"These are part of Ms. Drex's confidential medical files."

Grayson stood up. "She paid for them, didn't she?"

Dr. Brown shrunk back in his chair. "Well, technically, no. Not until she settles her bill."

"How much is it?" Grayson asked.

"I ... I don't know. I don't handle such things."

"Of course not. A doctor never sullies himself by talking about money." Grayson turned to me. "Drex, wait here. I'll be right back."

"Where's he going?" Dr. Brown asked as Grayson disappeared out the door.

"I have no idea. Am I going to be all right, doctor?"

"Ms. Drex, I'm a doctor, not God. Only *he* knows for sure."

A hot flare of indignation thawed my frozen state. "Typical," I muttered to myself. "Of course God has to be a *man*."

"What?" Dr. Brown asked.

"Nothing. Doctor, what will happen if this thing ... this twin ... *gets bigger?*"

"If it begins to exert pressure on your brain, any manner of symptoms could occur."

"Like hallucinations?"

"Well, yes. I suppose. Why? Have you had any?"

"I ... uh ...."

Grayson burst back into the office. He shoved a receipt in front of Dr. Brown's face. "Bill's paid in full." He grabbed the MRI and my file from the doctor's desk and turned to face me. I was speechless.

"Ready to go, dear fiancé?" he asked.

I bolted to my feet like a conspirator in a prison break. "Absolutely."

"She should be under the care of a physician," Dr. Brown said.

"She will be," Grayson replied. "I'm a doctor."

Dr. Brown's expression was as stunned as mine.

"I'll be sending for the rest of her records," Grayson said. "In the meantime, thank you, Doctor, and have a good day."

Grayson locked his arm around mine and led me out the door. I wanted to press him for details about paying my bill, but was distracted by an orderly pushing a patient on a gurney. Her head was wrapped like a mummy.

"I don't want that to happen to me," I whimpered.

"What?"

"The patient who just went by. She just had brain surgery or something."

"Don't worry," Grayson said. "I don't think you'll need it. I think I know what's going on here."

I looked up into his eyes. "What? It's not that coup contraband thing, is it?"

He smiled sourly. "You really should pay more attention, Drex. No. It's not that."

"What, then?"

"I'll explain on the ride home."

I winced. "Will you have to erase my memory afterward?"

Grayson kept his eyes ahead. "We'll see. But at this rate, I don't think it'll be necessary. You don't seem capable of holding a straight thought in your head."

Chapter Forty-Two

"THANK GOD I DIDN'T take Earl with me," I said, sucking in a lungful of fresh air as we headed toward the Mustang in the hospital parking lot. "He already thinks I'm half guy. Now I've got the gonad to prove it."

Grayson shot me a look. "Having a gonad doesn't make you half a guy, Drex."

"It doesn't?"

"No. It makes you a hermaphrodite."

I scowled. "If you're trying to cheer me up, you should work on your bedside manner, Dr. Grayson. What kind of doctor are you, anyway? Or was that just another lie?"

Grayson looked offended. "What do you mean *another* lie?"

"Are you a brain surgeon, or what?"

"I'm a certified holistic practitioner."

"Holistic medicine? Isn't that curing people with rocks and crystals and psychic crapola?"

"Don't forget needles and potions and poultices," Grayson said sourly.

"Oh, great." I fumbled for the keys.

"I think I should drive, Drex. You're in no shape to be behind the wheel. In your state, you might mistake a red light for a black hole."

After just finding out I had my twin's gonad kicking me in the pineal, I didn't bother to argue his point. I handed Grayson the keys. He opened the passenger door for me, waited until I was buckled in, and handed me my medical scans.

As he closed the door and walked around to the driver's seat, an odd numbness overtook me. I felt out of my element—as if I'd fallen down a hole and landed in someone else's life ... in someone else's reality.

This can't be happening. A man is actually treating me with concern and respect ....

Grayson scooted into the driver's seat. I turned to face him. "Grayson, I don't know how to thank you. I'll pay you back—"

"Forget it." He closed the driver's door and reached for the ignition. "That was a lot for you to take in. We should do an energy clearing on you when we get back to your place."

I crinkled my nose. "Energy clearing? Couldn't I just get a chocolate milkshake instead? Now that I'm gonna die, who cares about my thighs?"

Grayson shook his head. "You're not dying, Drex. Look, I know you don't believe it, but alternative healing modalities have been around for thousands of years. Why would people keep using them if they didn't work?"

I shot him a look. "Because they didn't have *real* medicine back then?"

"Oh. So sawing open your skull, digging out parts of it and hoping for the best is *real* medicine?"

I shrunk back in my seat. This wasn't happening. The scans had to be wrong. My nose grew hot. I fought back tears. I glanced over at Grayson. "You said you think you know what's wrong with me. So, what is it?"

"It's just a theory. I need to run some tests on you first." He reached to put the key in the ignition.

"Tests? What, are you going to do? Read my aura? Fix a hole in my psychic energy field?"

"No." He cranked the engine.

"Come on," I said. "Have you ever seen any of that holistic crap work?"

Grayson put his hand on the gear shaft, then stopped. "Yes. I absolutely have. I don't know why you're so skeptical, Drex. There've been at least a hundred scientifically run clinical trials demonstrating the effectiveness of all sorts of things that, according to Western medicine, shouldn't work."

I sniffed back a tear. "Like what?"

"Well, take *the placebo effect*, for one. In tons of pharmaceutical trials, people given a sugar pill got results as good as those taking the actual medicine. Stuff like *that* drives doctors nuts. But it kind of proves the whole tenet behind the holistic approach."

"What? That everything's a crapshoot?"

Grayson sighed and shook his head. "No. Just the opposite. Everything's a *placebo*, Drex. If you *believe* whatever it is you're doing will heal you, it will. Holistic medicine taps into our inner capacity to heal ourselves."

"So you think I can get rid of this twin thing by wishing it away?"

Grayson shrugged. "Maybe. But then again, why would you want to? You're unique, Drex. And I think that's why you've been seeing things."

I leaned over, closer to him. "Why?"

"You heard the doctor. The vestigial twin. The impact of the bullet must've dislodged it. Shaken it loose somehow. Now it's pushing up against your pineal gland."

"So? What's that got to do with seeing things?"

Grayson studied me for a moment, his green eyes locked on mine. "Some ancient cultures called the pineal the 'third eye.'"

"You mean, like a cyclops?"

"No. The third eye is the *spiritual* eye. The seat of enlightenment. It's the gateway to other worlds ... other *dimensions*, if you will."

"Bull crap, Grayson! We've all got pineal glands. If that were true, we'd *all* be seeing stuff."

Grayson shrugged. "Maybe we do—but mostly when we're kids, before our pineal glands calcify over."

I shot him a look. "What are you talking about?"

"Remember how you were when you were a kid? Carefree. Joyful. Full of imagination and wonder? Anything seemed possible—even creating your own special world."

I frowned. "Sort of, I guess."

"That's what it's like to have a fully-functioning pineal gland." He shifted into reverse and pulled out of the parking space.

I chewed my lip. "So what happens? Why does it quit working?"

Grayson sighed. "Lots of reasons. Adulthood, mainly. Changes in our hormones and diet cause it to calcify. Most people lose function by the time they're seven or eight. Getting it back is what the life work of most mystics and shamans is all about. Some say it's the true goal of yogis, and why yoga was developed in the first place."

I studied the windshield as we pulled into traffic. "I thought yoga was an exercise."

"Here in the States, maybe. Power yoga. Swing yoga. They've lost the whole point."

"If it's not to fight flab, what *is* the point of yoga?"

"To awaken the kundalini energy and experience cosmic consciousness and union with the divine. To reconnect with the life force that brings bliss."

I sneered. "Well, I hate to break it to you, but my pineal gland must still be calcified. I'm not feeling anything even *close* to bliss."

Grayson laughed. "Drex, you're either the luckiest person on Earth or the *un*luckiest. I guess we'll find out soon enough. Mind if we stop at that medical supply place over there?"

"Why?"

"I need some Ten20 conductive paste. I'd like to give you an electroencephalogram."

My eyebrows raised an inch. "Electric shock treatment? No way!"

"No," Grayson said. "An electroencephalogram. To measure your brain waves."

My nose crinkled. "Will it hurt?"

"Not physically, no."

I bit my lip and weighed my options. It didn't take long, given I had exactly zero. I owed Grayson big time for paying my hospital bill.

"If I let you do this, you promise you won't tell Earl a word about it?"

Grayson raised his hand in a Boy Scout pledge. "As your physician, it's my sworn pledge to maintain your confidentiality. Your medical records are on a need-to-know basis."

I grimaced. "That's what scares me about you, Grayson. Who do you think needs to know?"

WHILE GRAYSON WAS IN the medical supply store, I had just enough time to increase my paranoia to psychosis level.

Why has this strange guy paid my hospital bill? What's in it for him? Am I his human Guinea pig now?

Grayson returned to the car carrying a paper bag. "Have electrode paste, will travel," he quipped.

"So what am I? Some new lab rat for you to experiment on?"

He smiled and climbed in. "I have to admit, your case *is* most intriguing."

"What if I don't want to take your electro-polygraph thing?"

"Electroencephalogram." He handed me the paper bag. "Come on. Like I said, it won't hurt. I do it to myself all the time."

"Wait. Is that why your head's shaved, and you have those tentacle marks all over your skull?"

"Yep." Grayson turned to me and smiled. "Very nice deduction, by the way, future P.I."

Grayson glanced at a point above my eyes. "And, seeing as how your head is already shaved, now's the perfect opportunity to get an initial electroencephalogram of your alpha brain waves. We'll need a baseline for comparison. You see, with your pineal gland reactivation you—"

"Sorry, Grayson," I said, cutting him off. "I'm not so sure about this. Things with you keep getting weirder and weirder. Enough with this baloney!"

Grayson looked taken aback. "It's not *baloney*, Drex. You have a unique opportunity here. I don't want to see you waste it."

"An *opportunity?*" I grumbled. "For what? Seeing things? Going crazy?"

"No," Grayson said calmly. "For seeing things and *not* going crazy."

Chapter Forty-Three

THE MUSTANG FLEW PAST the pinewoods and wide-open pasturelands between Gainesville and Waldo. An early autumn frost had turned the wiry grasses endless shades of gray. They echoed my mood precisely.

"So how's this electro whatever-agram going to keep me from going crazy?" I asked Grayson as he swerved to miss an already flattened armadillo.

"It's not. It's simply a measuring tool. An EEG displays your alpha brainwave activity. The more alpha waves you produce, the more relaxed your nervous system is."

"So what's the point? Will this thing tell if I'm having hallucinations?"

"No."

"Will it help me to not have them anymore?"

"Highly doubtful."

"Then what's in it for *me?*"

"Quite a lot." Grayson glanced over at me. "I'm offering you a chance to learn to control your body's subconscious reactions with your conscious mind. Think about it, Drex. Whether you're having hallucinations or what you saw was real, if you can train yourself to override your innate fight-or-flight response, you can remain calm in any situation. That's a pretty good skill for a P.I. to have."

I looked over at him. "Is that why you do it? The test, I mean?"

"Yes," Grayson said. "I can't tell you if what you're seeing is real or not. Only you can decide that. The real question is, do you want to be scared out of your wits every time you see something, or do you want to learn to control your reaction?"

I frowned. "Are those my only two options?"

Grayson grinned. "I'm afraid so. What do you say? You ready to let me run an EEG on you?"

"I dunno."

Grayson shot me a boyish grin. "It comes with free tacos from El Molino."

I blew out a breath. "*And* a chocolate shake?"

"You drive a hard bargain, Drex. But okay. Deal."

GRAYSON CRUNCHED A tortilla chip. Shards scattered over the same greasy table in the same greasy booth we'd sat at last time we were in El Molino.

Grayson wiped up the crumbs. "Just think, Drex. You could be sitting on a mountaintop that yogis work their entire lives to climb."

"What are you talking about?" I dawdled with the corn chip in my hand, unable to commit to a bite.

"Yogis practice all kinds of strange things for decades, trying to stimulate their pineal glands. But you might've done it with one shot."

I crinkled my nose. "Why would they want to stimulate their pineal glands?"

"For enlightenment. For bliss. Take the Khechari Mudra."

"The ketchup what?" I dredged the tortilla chip in the little bowl of salsa. An image of my skull being cut open turned my stomach.

"The Khechari Mudra," Grayson said. "It's a special technique master yogis use. They train their tongues to be flexible enough to access their nasal passages from inside their throats."

My stomach turned some more. "Are you saying they pick their noses from the inside with their tongues?" I glanced at my salsa-covered chip and cringed. "Gross!"

"No. The pineal gland is located—"

"Listen, Grayson," I said, cutting him off. "I'm trying to eat here. Could we stop with all this for right now?"

Grayson shrugged. "Sure. You're not into bliss. I get it."

"I didn't say *that*. It's just ... well, it's a bit too much to ask for, isn't it? I mean, what is *bliss* anyway?"

"Yogis describe the feeling of bliss as being like the climax point of orgasm."

I nearly choked on my iced tea. "Excuse me?"

Grayson laughed. "For people stuck in lower consciousness, when it comes to bliss, the best they can hope for is the fleeting sensation of orgasm. That's why sex is such a big deal to people trapped in mundane states of existence. They can only get a tiny, transitory glimpse of the never-ending cosmic bliss attained by some yogis."

"A mundane existence doesn't sound so bad to me," I said. "Sorry, but I don't think I could stand being in a never-ending state of orgasm."

Grayson stifled a grin and locked eyes with me. "Me either. But once in a while wouldn't be so bad now, would it?"

I shifted my eyes down to the bowl of salsa. "No. I suppose it wouldn't."

Chapter Forty-Four

"I HOPE YOU ENJOY THIS particular selection from my whine cellar," Grayson quipped in an attempt to lessen my nervousness. He waggled his eyebrows and said, "I call this one *Nightmare on Over-wh'Elm Street*. Get it?"

I made a sour face and laid back on my bed. I blew out a breath and chewed my lip as Grayson fiddled with the controls on some weird-looking monitoring machine he'd dragged out of his RV.

The sticky electrodes pasted all over my skull itched and tugged at my scalp. I shook my head softly, chiding myself for being such a gullible doofus.

What the hell have I gotten myself into? Grayson's either a quack or a genius, and I'm either a guinea pig or a fool. Will I be able to figure out which before it's too late?

"Relax and breathe," Grayson said.

He'd taken off his fedora and rolled up his sleeves—neither of which did anything to enhance his credibility with me. He looked like a bald politician running for county pallbearer.

"I've established your resting alpha wave pattern, see?" Grayson pointed at a graph on the machine.

I gave him a tentative nod. *Whatever, you weirdo.*

"Now I'm going to show you some pictures." He set his open laptop on a TV tray at the side of my bed. "Watch the blue screen."

I did as instructed. I smiled at the first image that popped onto the display. It was a basket of basset hound puppies in a field of daisies. The second image popped up and I nearly swallowed my tongue.

It was a pile of mangled zombie corpses.

"What the hell, Grayson!" I yelled. "No wonder you keep this crap in a padlocked cabinet!"

"Hmmm," Grayson said, keeping his eyes on the machine. He pointed to the graph displayed on the monitor. "See how your activity changed here?"

"What? Whose wouldn't? Where'd you get pictures like that, anyway?"

"Lie back, breathe. A picture can't harm you, and neither can a ghost."

I sneered. "How do *you* know?"

"Well, theoretically, ectoplasmic anomalies—"

I rolled my eyes. "Never mind. I know what this *really* is. It's desensitization training."

Grayson's eyebrow shot up. "Yes, in a way, you're right. A person can get used to anything after a while. Even bombs dropping in warzones. But when it comes to other-worldly and other-dimensional beings, it requires a conscious effort to remain centered, even for seasoned professionals."

I locked eyes with him. "Can you? You know, control your *own* reactions?"

"*Now*, yes. But I couldn't at first."

I studied Grayson. He seemed sincere. "Really?"

"Really," he said. "There's some truly scary, as yet unexplainable crap out there, Drex. To do my job, I've got to rise above the fear."

He turned a knob on the machine. "I want you to look at each image and breathe. You control how you feel about each one. Remember, they have no power other than what you give them."

I breathed in deeply. The needle on the machine jumped up, indicating my alpha waves had increased. "Hey, I'm doing it," I said, surprised.

"Yes, you are." Grayson's smile took a subtle slant toward the sadistic. A new image popped on the screen. A greenish, pus-bloated face screamed at me from the black, rotten hole that used to be its mouth. Maggots tumbled out.

My alpha waves crashed. "Holy crap!"

"Breathe," Grayson coaxed. "You're in control. Find your safe space. Your grounding center."

"My grounding center?"

"Your favorite teddy bear. A pet bunny. Whatever makes you feel safe and at peace."

I grimaced. "It sure isn't pus face."

"*Practice*, Drex. It works. And if you're seeing what I think you might be seeing, you're going to need this as your first line of defense."

"What?" I nearly choked. "What do you *think* I'm seeing?"

"What you most fear, Drex. The guy who shot you. An escaped convict from Starke. A woman needing brain surgery."

Something clicked inside my mind. "Geez! You're right. I fear all of those things. The images ... they seemed so real."

Grayson nodded. "Maybe they were, maybe they weren't."

I chewed my lip. "So what's this 'first line of defense' you mentioned?"

"Breathing."

"*Breathing?* Really? Uh ... hello. I've been doing that all my life."

"And doing it wrong, I might add," Grayson said. "Use your breath to calm and center yourself, like I showed you. Now, I'm going to leave you here to complete the program on your own."

Grayson turned and walked toward my bedroom door.

"Wait!" I called out. "What's the *second* line of defense? In case they get past the first?"

Grayson laughed. "These are just images. They can't harm you. They'll come up and disappear automatically. When the program's done, it'll shut off. Your challenge is to find your calm center before each new image emerges."

I frowned. "Where are you going?"

Grayson cocked his head at me. "You said I could borrow your car."

"Yes, but—"

"You didn't say I needed to tell you where I was going. I promise I'll take good care of it. And I'll be back before dawn. Tell you what—I'll even fill the tank."

"But," I started to get up.

"Don't move. If you pull out an electrode, you'll have to start over."

I fell back onto the bed. "Ugh. How many times have you done this yourself?"

"More times than I can remember."

"By yourself?"

"Yes." Grayson grabbed his fedora off the bureau. "But don't worry. You're not alone. Your Grandma Selma's standing by your bedside. She says, 'Hi,' by the way."

I turned to look. No one was there.

I looked back. Grayson was gone.

Sneaky bastard.

Chapter Forty-Five

WHETHER IT WAS THE power of suggestion or Grandma Selma really *was* by my side, I thought I smelled White Shoulders, her signature perfume. Unsettled, I stuck with my task, and tried out different "happy places" until I found one that seemed to work somewhat consistently, no matter what vile images Grayson's horrible training program threw at me.

After exhausting its repertoire of bloated corpses, devilish beings, and alien autopsies, the program ended. The screen on Grayson's computer went blue, and a yellow smiley face emoji popped up. Under it flashed the words, "Have a Nice Day!" The computer beeped and shut itself off.

I sat up and checked the clock. It was 8:36 p.m. Grayson had left me alone with his computer, and he wouldn't be back for hours.

Perfect time to brush up on my computer skills ....

I hit the power button. The laptop's screen blinked back to life. A flashing message on the display read, "Are you sure you want to do this?"

Startled, I jerked my hand away from the screen. My face grew hot. I cautiously reached over and whacked the power button. The computer shut down again. I closed it, carried it over to the bureau, and set it down.

"No," I said aloud, in case the computer was somehow recording me. "I'm *not* sure I want to do this. I'm not sure at all."

AFTER SCRUBBING THE electrode paste from my stubbly scalp, I took a shower, pulled on some sweatpants and a T-shirt, and brushed my teeth. After all those gory test images, I was too wired to sleep. I couldn't even concentrate enough to follow the plot of *Matlock*.

I switched off the TV and slumped onto the couch.

I missed my Grandma Selma. She'd been the only person I could count on to give me a woman's perspective in the messed-up man's world we lived in. She'd passed away two years before my father. I'd lost my mother way before that—first to bourbon, then to parts unknown with Mr. Applewhite. With no one else springing to mind for a friendly chat, I called Beth-Ann.

"I still don't know if Grayson is a genius or a psycho," I said when she picked up.

"Don't tell me you went out on another date with him," she said, not missing a beat.

"No. And it wasn't a date. He hooked me up to electrodes."

"Ooooh. Kinky. What else did he do?"

"Argh! It wasn't like that. He was measuring my alpha waves. He's into all this yoga and kundalini crap."

"It's not crap, Bobbie."

"You're into it, too? Why didn't you tell me?"

"Around here, people already think I'm weird enough."

I blew out a breath. "Beth-Ann, I need to know if this guy's for real, or if he's some kind of nut job. Have you got any helpful hints on how to do that?"

"Isn't there anything in your detective handbook?"

"It doesn't cover Mothman kooks."

"Then do a Google search on Grayson. Check out his Facebook profile."

"I don't want to be a busybody, Beth-Ann. This town's got enough of them already."

"Oh. So *that's* why you wanted to become a private investigator. So you could *stay out of* other peoples' business. *Now* I get it."

"Ugh. You're right. But there's so much more to being a P.I. than I thought."

"Like what?"

"Like *this*. I mean, how can you tell the good guys from the bad guys?"

"Uh ... you never saw that problem coming?"

My gut sunk four inches. "I'm an idiot."

"No, you're not, Bobbie. You're just naïve when it comes to men. Give me his full name and everything you've got on him, and I'll do the search. That way, you can keep your hands clean."

"Thanks, Beth-Ann. You're a lifesaver."

Beth-Ann laughed. "I hope you don't mean that literally."

Geez. So do I.

Chapter Forty-Six

I WAS COZIED UP ON the couch with a vodka cocktail. Okay, it was a glass of vodka. But it was a small glass.

It was nearly midnight, and Grayson still hadn't returned. I'd switched on the TV half an hour ago. A beautiful woman in a cocktail dress and diamond earrings was busy convincing me to buy a contraption that could clean my drapes and give me a facial.

But not at the same time.

I was reaching for my cellphone to order the blasted thing when the landline for Robert's Mechanics rang. It was exactly midnight. I picked up the receiver, thinking it might be Grayson with a flat tire or something.

"Hello?"

"*Beep beep beep.*"

The hair on the back of my neck stood up.

"Who are you?" I demanded. I was pretty sure the faltering squeak in my voice did nothing to persuade these robots that I meant business.

"*Beep beep beep.*"

"What do you want?" I hissed, barely able to squeeze the words from my tight lungs.

A mechanical voice buzzed over the line. "Bring a large pepperoni pizza to 387 Obsidian Road. Pronto."

Air whooshed back into my lungs.

"Earl, you're fired," I screeched.

I heard him howl with laughter as I clicked off the phone. I flopped back onto the couch, totally pissed. Then a thought made my back straighten.

Crap! I forgot to check on Vanderhoff today!

I couldn't now. It was too late. Besides, Grayson had my car. I'd have to wait until morning. I sighed and turned my attention back to the TV. Just my luck. I'd missed the limited-time offer to order one VaccuFacial and get a second one free.

I scowled and clicked the "off" button on the TV remote.

After draining my vodka glass, I hauled myself off the couch and padded down the hall to my bedroom. Pulling back the curtains, I stared out at the thin slice of silvery moon, wondering where Grayson was. I didn't want to be a nag by calling him. He was a grown man, after all.

As I pulled down the bedcovers, I shivered.

Crap.

I'd left Grandma's afghan in Grayson's apartment. I couldn't go get it now. Not without invading his privacy. I climbed into bed and lay down. A beam of moonlight shone in my eye. I'd forgotten to close the curtains.

Double crap.

I hauled myself out of bed, grabbed a handful of curtain, and totally freaked.

Inches from the windowpane, two glowing, red orbs hovered at eye level with me. I closed my eyes, shook my head, and took a deep, calming breath.

It's just my imagination.

I opened my eyes.

The glowing red orbs were still there.

But now they weren't orbs.

They were *eyes*.

Burning, ember-like eyes—set deep inside the skull of a hideous, insect-like face!

As a blood-curdling scream ripped from my lungs, I caught a glimpse of something on its back. It was a cape.

No.

It was Grandma Selma's afghan.

Icy spiders crawled up my back.

That horrible thing's been inside my house!

My knees gave out.

I crumpled to the floor.

The safe little world I once knew went bye-bye.

Chapter Forty-Seven

I WAS IN A TUG OF WAR with Mothman over Grandma Selma's afghan. Through my bedroom window, I slapped his ugly insect face with a flyswatter and grabbed the corner of the blanket. I gave it a huge tug, but bug-man held on with his spindly, lobster-claw hands.

He wasn't letting go.

Well, neither was I.

I dug my heels into the shag carpet and tugged for all I was worth. But a sudden, swift yank by Mothman pulled me out the second-story window.

I was dangling in midair!

As I hung onto the tail-end of Grandma Selma's blanket for dear life, Mothman buzzed above the pathetically small metropolis of Point Paradise, trying to shake me loose.

I saw the roof over my parent's garage ... the flashing light at the intersection of nowhere and oblivion ... the sagging awning of the Stop & Shoppe. As we flew over Cherry Manor, I spotted old lady Vanderhoff's house. I took my chance and let go of Grandma's afghan. I tumbled, butt-first, into old lady Vanderhoff's swimming pool.

She heard my cannonball splash and came running out of the house. Vanderhoff was naked except for a pair of red, lace panties and that green avocado mask. My poor eyes didn't know where to look.

"You're going to electrocute yourself!" she yelled, and handed me a mirror. My bald head was covered in electrodes.

She shook her avocado-smeared head at me. "Drex! What's wrong with you?"

Wait a minute. This has to be a dream. Mrs. Vanderhoff always called me Bobbie. Never Drex.

I snorted myself awake.

I was on the floor of my bedroom, my right cheek stuck to the pages of a *Good Housekeeping* magazine. A beam of morning sun filtered its way through the dust circling in the air. I blinked against the glare, then I nearly peed my pants.

Mothman was standing right over me.

I jolted awake like Frankenstein in a nuclear reactor.

I screamed, scooted backward across the floor on my butt, and kicked at the creature like a deranged donkey.

"I know I have morning breath," Mothman said, "but I think that's a bit of an overreaction."

I blinked again, then blushed. With the light no longer stabbing my eyes, Mothman had melted into Grayson.

"What are you doing in my bedroom?" I yelled.

"Checking on you. Your front door was open, so I came in. Why are you on the floor?" He wagged a shaming finger at me. "Don't tell me you got into the vodka again."

"Shut up! Where were you last night?"

"Excuse me? I wasn't aware I owed you an explanation. Or are you my warden now?"

"You should've been here!" I screeched. "Mothman was here! He tried to get in my bedroom window!"

Grayson's eyes nearly doubled in size. "What? Damn! Did you get a good look at it?"

"Yes," I grumbled. "And I'm okay, in case you're interested."

Grayson grimaced. "Oh. Yes. Good. I'm glad." He smiled at me for a moment, then said, "So? What did it look like?"

"Like a moth ... man. Sort of." I hesitated as I tried to read Grayson's expression. He had the best poker face I'd ever seen. "And he—" I began, then changed my mind.

"He what?" Grayson coaxed.

"He...." I stopped and shook my head. "No. You'll laugh at me."

He slapped on a solemn face. "I won't. I promise."

"He ... he stole Grandma Selma's afghan."

I had to hand it to him. Grayson's effort to suppress a grin was truly valiant. He nearly swallowed his lips.

"This afghan," he asked with one raised eyebrow, "it wasn't made of *wool*, was it?"

"You're such a jerk!" I yelled. I picked up a pillow from the floor and threw it at him.

"Come on, Drex. I'm just trying to get you to lighten up."

"How can you joke about *this* of all things?"

"Because it helps. Especially when you know the things I know."

I stared at him, red-faced, unable to decide if I was angry, mortified, or just plain embarrassed. "What do you know?"

Grayson bent down and offered me a hand. "How about *I* fix the coffee this morning? You get cleaned up. And when you're ready, we can talk."

Chapter Forty-Eight

IF I'D LEARNED ONE thing in life, it was that caffeine could solve a myriad of problems. Abject terror over Mothman, however, wasn't one of them.

On that score, Grayson was no help, either.

"Hope you don't mind. I put some clothes in the wash," he said as I hobbled into the kitchen. My knees were still wobbly from my encounter with the insectoid peeping Tom, whether it was real or I'd just imagined it.

"Sure. No worries." I shuffled to the counter and made myself a cup of coffee. "Why in the world would Mothman be after *me?*" I grumbled, and took a giant gulp.

Grayson was sitting at the round oak table. He glanced over at the portrait of Jesus my parents had hanging on the wall. "God doesn't send you anything that you're not ready for, Drex. That which does not kill us makes us stronger."

I sneered. "Thank you, oh great Pez dispenser full of stupid clichés."

"Come on, Drex. You didn't get a degree in Art Appreciation to end up managing a grease pit in the middle of nowhere. You're ready for something bigger."

I looked down at my coffee. A fly was doing the backstroke in it. "Sure I am," I said as I poured the coffee down the sink. "Because I'm smart, I'm pretty, and gosh-darn it, people like me."

Grayson snickered. "You've already told me more than once that you want out of this place. So, here it is, your big break, and you act all surprised. *Hurt*, even. I'm telling you now, you might as well embrace the situation like you personally ordered it, and dive in. Because you did. And you can."

Anger flared up inside me like a Duraflame starter packet. "*Ordered* this? Are you talking about Mothman, or *you?* Right now, if I had to choose, I'd pick Mothman. He's a whole hell of a lot less irritating."

Grayson smirked. "Be careful what you wish for. You just might get it."

"Pez hack," I spat.

Grayson shot me a grin I wanted to erase with an Uzi. "When the student is ready, the teacher appears, Drex. And I do believe it's time for another lesson for the unruly pupil."

"What lesson?"

I glared at him, then rolled my eyes. Did it matter? What else did I have going on?

"I need more coffee first," I growled.

Grayson nodded. "Then pour yourself a gallon and come with me."

GRAYSON'S LATEST P.I. "lesson" had me kicking around outside in the cold mist of morning, checking the ground under my bedroom window for evidence of Mothman's visitation last night.

"What are we looking for?" I grumbled. "There's no footprints. I told you, the thing was flying."

"Look for hairs. Detritus. Anything that looks out of place."

"Like what?"

"Like *that.*"

Grayson pointed upward to the boughs of a small crepe myrtle tree. Hanging about ten feet off the ground was a piece of yarn.

My heart soared. I wasn't crazy. "Grandma's afghan! See? I *didn't* imagine it!"

"Hold your horses. It's a piece of yarn in a tree, Drex. It could've gotten there a hundred different ways. *You* could have put it there, for all I know."

"Me?" I said with righteous indignation.

"Sure. You could've tossed the blanket out the window last night in the middle of some weird, somnambulistic dream."

"Dirty mind!"

"That means *sleepwalking*, gutter girl."

I scowled, folded my arms across my chest, and festered in self-recrimination. Meanwhile, Grayson found a hook-shaped stick and used it to bend the crepe myrtle branch downward to retrieve the evidence. He stuck the foot-long piece of blue yarn in a plastic baggie. Then, to my surprise, he held the baggie open, stuck his nose in, and sniffed.

What a sicko.

"It's wool, all right," Grayson said. "I can smell the difference."

I marched over to him and grabbed for the baggie. "Give me that!"

"No can do." He raised the baggie up and out of my reach. "I need to test it for DNA. Does it look like it might have come from your granny's blanket?"

"Maybe," I grumbled. "It's a bunch of colors. Now what?"

Grayson didn't answer. He was looking right at me, but his eyes were far away. I hoped he was pondering a solution to this whole crazy mess. Or, even better, how to get his ass out of town.

"Interesting," he said at last.

"Interesting? That's all you've got to say?"

"I thought maybe this was all a coincidence. But now, well, let's just say I've never been a big believer in coincidences."

I shot him a sour look. "What are you talking about?"

"What's your safe space, Drex? You know, from the test yesterday. What do you envision to keep the monsters at bay?"

My back stiffened. "None of your business."

"I disagree. I wouldn't be asking if it wasn't important."

I'd envisioned myself balled up in my grandma's lap, sucking my thumb. Thinking about it now, my cheeks flared with heat. "It's personal."

"*Fine*." Grayson blew out an aggravated breath. "I think I know, anyway. I'd like to test you again. To hone your skills some more."

"You might think you know me, Grayson, but you don't know sh—" My phone rang. It was Paulson. "I better get this."

I turned my back to Grayson. "Hello? Paulson? Listen, I'm sorry I didn't get by Vanderhoff's yesterday. I was—"

"Save it, Bobbie," Paulson said curtly. "There's no need for you to give me a case update. Vanderhoff's dead."

"Oh, my word! What happened?"

"Someone broke in through a window. Ripped her throat out in the middle of the night."

I glanced at Grayson. He was looking away, but I got the feeling he'd been listening in. He'd been gone all night. His clothes were in the washing machine. A knife-blade of fear stabbed me in the back.

"Bobbie? Are you there?" Paulson asked.

I took a step away from Grayson and whispered, "Yes. Should I come by?"

"No. The FBI's been called. Stay where you are. Is that lodger of yours still around?"

Cold wind swept down my spine. "Yes."

"Be careful, Bobbie."

"I will." I hung up the phone.

"What's up?" Grayson asked.

I turned to face him and tried to smile, but it wouldn't stick. "Nothing. Beth-Ann's cat had kittens is all. I'm going to go over there to, you know, help out with the delivery."

"I love kittens. Can I come?"

Grayson took a step toward me. I took a step back.

"Well," I fumbled, "I'm gonna get my eyebrows tweezed, too. So why don't you hang around here? Talk to Earl. He told me your RV should be ready soon. Maybe today, even."

Grayson eyed me like he wasn't buying it. "What's really going on?"

I looked away. "Nothing. I just need some girl time, okay?"

Grayson shot me a dubious look. "Okay."

I wanted to run, to get the hell away from Grayson. But I willed myself not to. Instead, I channeled my fear into enough energy to march back up the stairs to my apartment without falling on my face.

As I headed down the hall to my bedroom, the sound of the washing machine made me stop in my tracks. I looked around to make sure Grayson wasn't behind me, then I carefully opened the bi-fold doors to the closet housing the washer and dryer. I lifted the lid on the washing machine and peeked inside. The water around the clothes in the drum was tinged dark pink.

"What are you doing?" Grayson's voice rang out behind me. I dropped the lid on my finger.

"Ah ... uh ... nothing," I said, my finger pulsing with pain. I tried the lame smile again, but even *I* wasn't buying it. "I just wanted to see if there was room in the washer for, you know, a few of my unmentionables."

Grayson smiled. "Sure."

"Thanks."

"Don't *mention* it," he quipped. "Get it?"

I laughed, but this time his humor was totally lost on me.

Chapter Forty-Nine

AS I PULLED OUT OF the parking lot, I caught Grayson eyeing me from the upstairs window of my grandmother's apartment. Something creepy crawled down my neck and over my shoulders.

Great. Thanks to him, not even my own home *feels safe anymore.*

I hit the gas and headed in the direction of Cherry Manor. Despite Officer Paulson's instructions to stay clear, I felt compelled to check on Mrs. Vanderhoff. I'd known her since I was a kid.

Suddenly, I had an epiphany. I was driving my dead father's car, wearing his coveralls and boots, and atop my head was some random stranger's wig Beth-Ann had fished out of an Amazon box.

Is any part of my life something I actually chose for myself?

I did a mental inventory and couldn't come up with a single thing. I was working a hand-me-down job, living a hand-me-down life. My grandmother was gone. My father was gone. My mother was gone. And now, Mrs. Vanderhoff was gone. Point Paradise was slipping away, despite my attempt to resurrect it.

Maybe it's time to just let it go ....

The pine trees ticked by on either side of the road. Never again would I be a little tomboy stalking dolls in the woods with a BB gun. Never again would I get another warm, White Shoulders-scented hug from my Grandma Selma. Never again would I help my dad change an oil filter. Or hear my mother chide me about how dirty I'd gotten my clothes.

Clothes.

Grayson's bloody laundry was churning in my washing machine. Was he getting rid of evidence, or just skid marks?

He might be a murderer. He might be a saint. But either way, Grayson had been right. I *had* wished for change. *Big* change. A *whole new life* kind of change.

I'd yearned for something more interesting—more exciting than changing dead spark plugs. But tracking down Mothman? Had someone upstairs heard my prayers wrong?

Again?

I blew out a sigh. As aggravating as he was, at least I still had Earl. *Yippee.*

I hit the gas, wishing I could outrun a past I no longer wanted. But what else was out there? Only a future I couldn't see. Still, one thing was for sure. Wherever I ended up, that stupid twin inside my head was along for the ride.

Thanks to it, my life was never going to be the same.

Grayson was right. I should've been a lot more careful about what I'd wished for.

Chapter Fifty

I PULLED UP IN FRONT of Vanderhoff's modest little block home. It had been plain before. But somehow, today it seemed even plainer, now that her life had gone out of it.

Paulson's car was out front. A blue Toyota Corolla. I made a mental note of it, then walked up to the front door and rapped my knuckles on the wood paneling. Paulson's face appeared in the small window.

"What are you doing here?" he asked as he opened the front door a crack.

"I thought I might be able to help."

"It's pretty gruesome."

"Where is she?"

"In her bed."

Paulson opened the door wider. His hands had blood on them. He noticed that I noticed.

"It's awful, Bobbie." He turned, and I followed him into Vanderhoff's kitchen. "I covered her with the bedsheets. I couldn't bear for someone to see her like that...all exposed and everything."

Paulson's voice cracked as he washed his hands in the sink. I noticed my business card on the refrigerator. My heart pinged.

Poor Mrs. Vanderhoff. Oh, geez! Poor ME! If the FBI finds my bogus P.I. card, I'm toast!

While Paulson had his back to me, I peeled my business card from the fridge. The magnet came to, glued to the card by some sticky substance I didn't have the time or desire to discern at the moment. I jammed them both in my pocket right before Paulson turned around.

He reached for the dishtowel hanging off the refrigerator door. His eyes were filled with tears. I patted him on the back. He nearly broke down. "How could something like this happen?" he asked.

"I don't know."

"Maybe you were right about seeing that convict in the woods after all." Paulson sniffed back tears. "Thanks for coming by, but you should go now. This may be the work of a serial killer. Like I told you before. The FBI's been notified. They should be here any minute now. I don't want you to get hung up in all this. I had no idea it would turn out like ...." His voice trailed off.

I winced. He looked devastated. "Okay," I said, and patted him on the shoulder. "You sure you're all right?"

"Yes." Paulson looked me in the eyes, an apologetic expression twisting his handsome face. "I know it's unprofessional to cry. But I've just never seen anything like this."

"I understand. Nobody expects much to happen here in Point Paradise."

As Paulson ushered me to the door, a thought crossed my mind. Should I retrieve the tele-bug device Grayson had stashed under Vanderhoff's couch cushion? For a second, I considered telling Paulson about it. But with Vanderhoff dead in the next room and the FBI on their way, every fiber of my being wanted to get the hell out of there. This whole thing was way out of my league. Besides, who was *I* to point the finger at Grayson? What if it really *was* the Mothman who did it?

Mothman? Cripes! I really do *need a shrink.*

I decided to keep my trap shut and let the FBI do their own investigation. They'd find the tele-bug soon enough. And if Grayson was guilty, he'd be found out. To borrow one of Grayson's pez-hack clichés, let the chips fall where they may.

Paulson ushered me out the front door. "I guess that means our little wager is off."

"Wager?" I asked.

"Twenty bucks or dinner. For figuring out the phone calls."

"Oh. Right," I said absently. "Yes. You're off the hook."

"That's too bad." Paulson gave me a sad smile and closed the door.

I walked to the Mustang and climbed in. As I turned the ignition, something about Paulson and men in general got under my skin like a swarm of chiggers.

Guys. Do they ever *stop thinking about sex?*

A tap on the passenger door window made me flinch. It was Nellie Parker, the dog-walking neighbor lady I'd seen last time I was here with Grayson.

"What's happening at Mrs. Vanderhoff's?" she asked. "Did she find a buyer?"

"I don't think she's looking for one, Mrs. Parker. She's dead."

"Dead?" Parker's face registered delight for a second, then shifted into the furrowed-brow concern of a decent, law-abiding citizen. "That's too bad." She looked down at her dog. "Well, Doodles, I guess we won't be seeing any more of Popeye."

"Who's Popeye?" I asked.

Parker made a sour face. "Vanderhoff's mangy, one-eyed mutt. He's the terror of the neighborhood. Always digging out from under the fence and trying to do his business with my poor Doodles. I can't say I'll miss him."

"*Or* poor Mrs. Vanderhoff?" I asked sarcastically.

"Well, to be honest, no."

For the umpteenth time, I tried to roll up my broken driver's side window, and for the umpteenth time, I grimaced at my own stupidity. I shifted into first, and, just to prove I was honest as well, I did what I told Grayson I was going to do.

I headed to Waldo to see Beth-Ann.

"IF GRAYSON ASKS, YOUR cat had kittens," I said as I walked into Beth-Ann's converted beauty-shop garage.

"I don't have a cat. And why would Grayson call *me?*"

"I don't know. But I want to have a plan, just in case he does."

"You sound paranoid, Bobbie."

"Maybe I am. Vanderhoff died last night."

"Dang it!" Beth-Ann hollered. "I just ordered a whole case of that blue rinse she uses."

I shot her some side-eye. "Somebody *murdered* her, Beth-Ann."

Beth-Ann did a double take. "What?"

"They ripped her throat out. Just like the corpse I saw in the woods."

"What corpse? Don't tell me there's a serial killer on the loose and you didn't even bother to tell me!"

"I'm telling you now."

"And you think Grayson's the killer?"

I studied her face. "Maybe. Why would you say that?"

"I did that Google search, like you asked. He's got kind of a shady past."

"And *you* didn't bother to tell *me?* He could have killed me, for crying out loud, Beth-Ann! Do you know he was gone all last night? And this morning ... his laundry ... it was all bloody."

"Criminy!"

I winced. "What did you find out about him?"

"That he was telling the truth, mostly. Grayson *was* a physicist, like he said. But he got discredited and lost his position at MIT."

"Why?"

"The grounds were kind of vague. Unethical behavior."

"That could mean anything from stealing paperclips to creating mutants in a lab." I wrung my hands. "What are we going to do?"

"I know what *I'm* gonna do."

Beth-Ann marched over to a cabinet and opened a drawer. She pulled out a pistol and pointed the barrel toward the sky. "Watch out Mothman, and any other kind of man who gets in my way."

I eyed her enviously. "You wouldn't happen to have another one of those, would you?"

Beth-Ann bit her lip. "Well, I was saving it for your birthday, but I think I'd rather give it to you now, so you live to turn thirty-seven." She reached into the drawer and pulled out a wrapped gift.

"Here, Detective Drex. Happy Birthday."

Chapter Fifty-One

I RETURNED TO ROBERT'S Mechanics feeling like a new woman. I was invigorated, supercharged, and packing heat.

With my very own, no-hand-me-down Glock tucked away in the right hip pocket of my coveralls, I was prepared to handle whatever Grayson threw at me. And I figured he wouldn't cross me. He knew firsthand what a good shot I was.

I pulled into the parking lot. Grayson's RV was out of the service bay. Earl's coverall-covered butt was bent over the open hood.

"How much longer?" I asked as I shut off the Mustang's coughing engine.

"Just took it for a test drive." Earl wiped a socket wrench with an oily rag. "Needs a few adjustments and she's ready to roll."

"Good, because I'm ready for Grayson to leave."

Earl's eyebrows disappeared under his shaggy bangs. "Lover's quarrel?"

"Har har har. I think he's outstayed his welcome. And what gives? I thought you said you'd have that thing ready by now."

"I would've," he argued, "but these two fellas stopped by asking for directions to Alto Lake. I told 'em to find Waldo and—"

My eyebrows shot up. "What did they look like?"

"Like them men-in-black fellas. Only they was men in *blue*. Probably FBI." Earl looked up to the sky and scratched his stubbly chin. "I wonder if a UFO crashed somewheres around here."

"What makes you think they were FBI? Did they say so?"

"No. But I watch *The X-Files*, Bobbie. I know the difference."

"Earl, they *were* the FBI. Paulson called them. Vanderhoff's been killed."

"Kilt? As in dead?"

"Yes. Murdered."

"How? Who done it?"

"I don't know. Where's Grayson?"

"Upstairs packing."

For his getaway, no doubt.

"Okay. Listen, Earl. If he tries to leave, don't let him."

Earl smiled slyly. "Lookin' for one more roll in the hay first?"

"No!" I hissed. "He owes us a hundred and eighty-eight dollars."

I turned and stomped up the stairs, my bravado fading with each step.

Should I call Paulson? Should I confront Grayson on my own? Should I just get the money from him and let him go?

I tapped on the door to Grandma Selma's apartment. Grayson called out, "Come in."

I crept in cautiously, my pistol drawn at my side. Grayson was sitting at the kitchen table. He looked up from his laptop and smiled. Beside him on the table were two stacks of pink T-shirts and boxers, neatly folded and stacked with the kind of precision that made me further question his mental state.

Yep. Totally OCD.

I eyed him suspiciously. "Funny. I pictured you as the tidy-whitey type."

Grayson shrugged. "That's what I get for buying cheap red handkerchiefs. I tried out that biker, do-rag look. But I think the fedora is more me." He held a red kerchief to his forehead. "What do you think?"

You've got a sketchy answer for everything, that's what I think.

I tightened my grip on the Glock hidden from his view. "You going somewhere?"

Grayson shrugged. "Thought I'd rob a liquor store and go to Disneyland. You in?"

"Cut the crap, Grayson. You're a liar. You told me you're a physicist."

Grayson's brow furrowed. "I *am*."

"You were discredited."

"So? Once a physicist, always a physicist. How did you find that out, anyway? Did you use my computer?" Grayson smiled in a way that made me squirm inside.

"No."

"Why not? Couldn't get past the question on the screen?"

I frowned. "I didn't try. I guess I really *didn't* want to find out what would happen if I tried to use it. What do you do to people who mess with your computer anyway? Rip their throats out?"

"It's a *joke*, Drex." Grayson laughed and shook his head. "You really *are* uptight. Look." He turned the laptop around on the table until the screen faced me. The same question from last night was flashing on the display: "Are you sure you want to do this?"

He pressed the button. The computer opened to a menu. "See? It's not even locked. The only password required is a conscience. Looks like you've got one. Congratulations."

"My personal integrity is important to me," I said in a way I hoped implied that I didn't think *his* was.

Grayson eyed me silently for a moment. "I want to show you something."

I hesitated. "If it's your lizard, I'm not interested."

Grayson laughed. "Keep Gizzard out of this."

He got up and walked past me, out of my grandmother's apartment, down the breezeway, and into my apartment.

Flabbergasted, I tagged along after him. "Where are we going?" I asked.

"To your bed."

"Forget it!" I yelled. He turned around. I hid the gun behind my back.

"I want to show you some important evidence I found, Drex. And I want you to be hooked up to the alpha wave monitor when you see it. I need to see how you react subconsciously."

"Why?" I asked angrily. "What difference does it make?"

"It makes *all* the difference, Drex. Trust me on this."

"*Trust* you? Why *should* I?"

Grayson shrugged. "I guess that's a valid question. But good grief? If you don't by now, will you ever?"

I stared at Grayson until he sighed.

"Would it help if I asked nicely?" he said.

I didn't answer.

"Would you *please* do this for me, Drex? Cherry on top? People's lives could be at stake. Including yours."

I know. That's what I'm afraid of.

Chapter Fifty-Two

I WAS LYING IN MY BED, my hand tucked inside the pocket of my coveralls. Unbeknownst to Grayson, my fingers were wrapped tightly around the grip of my sleek, new subcompact Glock. The barrel was pointed at Grayson's heart as he leaned over me and stuck electrodes on my stubbly scalp.

"Calm your mind," he said softly.

Clearing my head was oddly difficult to do with him so near. Just inches from me, I found the animal warmth of his body teasing me in places long left unteased. Grayson was a man of mystery. Dangerous. Provocative. Strangely alluring. Possibly insane.

If I wasn't careful, he could be the death of me.

"Try to keep your concentration," he said, "Find your inner balance."

His eyes were bright with excitement—the sparkling, wide-open, intense eyes of a madman. Was he going to shock me senseless and try to rip my throat out? I didn't know. But I'd found myself too curious to refuse him. He'd promised to show me something that would change my world as I knew it.

For better or worse, I was ready for the change.

And, thanks to Beth-Ann, I was also ready with my Glock.

"Brace yourself," Grayson said, and took a step back. He began to fiddle with the controls on the machine. "What I'm about to show you isn't for sissies."

"Okay. I'm ready."

"Here goes." Grayson pushed a button. An image came on his laptop screen. But this time, it wasn't a series of static pictures. It was a video.

Shaky and amateurish, it appeared to have been made with someone's cellphone as they walked around inside a small ship or submarine. Everything was gray and slick. The hand holding the camera was trembling so badly that after a few seconds of watching, I began to feel nauseated.

I swallowed against the bile rising in my throat. On the screen, the cameraman entered a small, black, oval doorway. What happened next made me forget all about being sick.

I was too astounded.

Beyond the doorway, three gray, human-like alien creatures looked up from what appeared to be control panels. Despite having no eyelids, no discernable nose, and only a slit for a mouth, I could still clearly read the panic on their faces.

Suddenly, a cacophony of human voices rang out in confusion, like the drug raids I'd seen on detective shows. A man in military fatigues ran in front of the camera. He yelled at the creatures. "Stop what you're doing. *Now!* Release them!"

The shaky camera panned to the right. Three columnar, aquarium-like tubes glowed eerily in the dim light. Inside each one was a human child no older than ten.

I gasped.

"Steady," Grayson said. "Think of your happy place."

In my mind, I climbed into Grandma's lap as the man with the automatic weapon fired at the top of the first glass tube. It shattered. The child inside tumbled out and cried, "Daddy!"

I wrapped Grandma's imaginary afghan around me as the guy in fatigues fired at the other tubes. They blew apart. The children held captive inside screamed and cried out for their parents.

The camera panned left. The three gray aliens were in a state of sheer horror, clumped together in a corner like frightened rats.

Then a man screamed.

It was a horrific, unforgettable howl. Off camera, the automatic weapon fired repeatedly. The phone taking the video fell to the ground.

Screams and shrieks and unearthly wails echoed into each other, but whatever was emitting them wasn't captured by the phone. The device lay still on the floor, its camera focused on the ceiling of what surely must have been some kind of alien spacecraft.

I hugged Grandma and started sucking my thumb. Hard.

Suddenly, the decapitated head of a gray alien flew into view. It hit the ceiling above the camera, then fell on top of the cellphone with a sickening thump. The image went black.

"Excellent," Grayson said.

"Excellent?" I screeched. "You think *that's* excellent?"

"Not the video. *You*. Drex, you were able to maintain your alpha waves better than anyone I've ever seen."

He showed me the graph. My alpha waves looked like a roller-coaster ride that fell into a ravine. "That doesn't look that impressive to me."

"Believe me, compared to the others, this is phenomenal."

"What others?"

Grayson shrugged.

"Is this just another made-up test, Grayson?" I wished and hoped and prayed he'd say yes.

"Depends." Grayson stared at me with the least readable expression I'd ever seen on a human face. "Do you want it to be fake?"

"Hell, yes!" I bellowed.

Grayson nodded.

I bit my lip. "But it's not, is it?"

"That information is on a need-to-know basis, Drex."

Aggravation climbed up my neck and clenched my jaws like a vise. "Why are you showing me this, Grayson?"

"Because I think you've got a gift."

I scowled. "This pineal twin thing?"

"That's part of it."

I locked eyes with him. "What do you want to use my so-called *gift* for?"

"I can't tell you—unless you're all in."

"What do you mean?"

"I was discredited by MIT because of my pursuit of unexplained phenomena. I believe there's more out there than what we currently understand, Drex."

"Like what?"

"Mothman. Bigfoot. Skin Walkers. Who knows? There's a whole gamut of things that exist beyond the ability for the rational mind to accept. I'm obsessed with proving that they're real. And I want you to help me."

"*Me?* Help *you?*"

"Yes. Be my partner."

"Partner?" I muttered, too stunned to do anything but parrot Grayson's words back at him.

Grayson nodded. "It's dangerous. But it's also the adventure of a lifetime. But Drex, if you take this step, there's no going back to life as you now know it."

I think I've already crossed that threshold.

Someone banged on the front door, making me jump off the bed and rip half my electrodes out.

"Hey boss man," Earl called out. "We're almost out of Fritos!"

I pressed my molars together and looked Grayson square in the face.

"So how much does this partner thing pay?"

Chapter Fifty-Three

"WHERE'D YOU GET THE film?" I asked Grayson as I pulled the rest of the pasty electrodes off my scalp.

He smiled thoughtfully. "I have friends in low places. *Now* do you believe me? At least about the *possibility* of Mothman being real?"

I shook my head. "I don't know. To me, the two don't seem related."

Grayson frowned. "What would it take to convince you? I've *seen* him, Drex. You saw him yourself last night."

"I saw something fly over my head, and I saw something at my window. In both instances, it was dark. I'm not exactly prepared to say there's a mutant cryptid on the loose."

"Your skepticism is appreciated ... up to a point," Grayson said. "As for me, the only question remaining is why Mothman would choose to turn up *here*, in Point Paradise."

"I think I might know the answer to that."

Grayson looked at me, surprised. "You do?"

I pulled the dog-poo shaped magnet from my pocket. "I got this off Vanderhoff's refrigerator. She said it was the last thing her niece Mandy sent her from her travels."

"So?"

"Mandy's been missing for two weeks."

Grayson studied the magnet. "Grave Creek Mound?"

"Yeah. I Google searched it."

Grayson looked up at me and smiled. "You did, did you?"

I shot him a sour look. "Save it." I nodded at the magnet. "The place is an old Indian burial mound. It's in West Virginia, not that far from that Point Pleasant place where they had—"

"The original sightings of Mothman," Grayson said, finishing my sentence. He set the magnet down and flipped open his laptop. "Interesting."

"It's just a burial mound of a chief or something."

Grayson shook his head. "Then why would it warrant an entry by Lewis & Clarke in 1803?" He stared at the screen. "Drex, this is the biggest burial mound in the United States."

"Okay. So it's big. I only brought it up because I think it might've been possible for—"

"This mound is over two thousand years old," Grayson said, paying me no mind. His eyes were glued to the screen. "Good grief. It's over sixty feet tall and as big around as a football field."

"So?"

"Says here it was excavated in 1838. They found two burial chambers and three bodies inside."

"And let me guess. You think one of them was Mothman?"

"Drex, why would Stone Age people bust their butts moving sixty thousand tons of dirt just to cover three bodies? They didn't have backhoes back then, remember."

"I know that."

"They didn't even have horses or the wheel." Grayson studied the screen again. "Huh. It says the original structure had a forty-foot-wide moat around it, too."

I blew out a breath. "Okay. It had a moat. What's that got to do with Mothman?"

"It seems to me like these people wanted to make damned sure those bodies didn't get unburied. But why?"

I shrugged. "I dunno. Why did *any* ancient culture build monuments?"

Grayson shot me a knowing glance. "Precisely."

I rolled my eyes. "Argh!"

Ignoring me, Grayson returned to his computer screen. "Huh. It says during the excavation, they noticed the soil around the bodies had turned blue."

"Blue? What could cause that?"

"Copper. Toxins. Radioactivity."

Radioactivity?

"Okay, Grayson. Suppose you're right. What if they *did* bury Mothman monsters in there? How could they have gotten out of the mound?"

"Any number of ways. Through excavations. Earthquakes. Coal mining. Injection of industrial waste. Any of those could have unsettled the soil and created an escape pathway. Look."

I glanced at the computer screen. The giant earthen heap comprising Grave Creek Mound was dotted with huge trees that appeared to be a hundred years old or better.

"These trees growing on the mound could've disturbed a protective talisman or penetrated a protective barrier," Grayson said. "Even time itself could've done the deed. It's had a couple of thousand years to crack it."

I shrugged. "I guess."

Grayson punched a few keys on his computer. A map of the town of Moundsville, West Virginia appeared. "Huh. Take a look at this."

"What?"

"Look what's just a few blocks away from the burial mound."

I glanced at the map. "The Roller Derby?"

"No."

"Dairy Queen?"

"No. The West Virginia State Penitentiary."

"Aha! That's what I've been trying to tell you, Grayson. About how Mothman got here, I mean."

"What? You think Mandy gave Mothman a lift on her way home to Point Paradise?"

"Well ... not exactly. Maybe Mandy got involved with a conman in Moundsville. Or maybe he spotted her in town and marked her as a target. It's the last place she's been seen in weeks."

"Hmm," Grayson said, rubbing his chin.

"I mean, it's plausible, isn't it?" I asked. "Maybe a criminal type followed Mandy back here to Point Paradise. You said yourself that everything's interrelated."

Grayson's lip twitched. "Sure. But why would Mothman need a ride when he can fly?"

I groaned. "Not Mothman. A *convict*."

Grayson shot me a *why don't you believe* look.

"Okay," I said. "For the sake of argument, let's say it's Mothman. You said Mothman liked to chase cars. Maybe he followed her car here. Or maybe he likes to chase women, too, and the combo was irresistible."

Grayson appeared to be mulling over my idea. "Well, it's the best theory we've got to work with right now. Speaking of work, will you give my partner offer a serious think?"

I smiled. "Yes. I will."

"Good. No pressure or anything, but I'm considering leaving in the morning, so I'll need an answer then. With the Feds around, I don't want to tangle you up in anything you don't want to be part of. I can continue my investigation alone from the RV, no worries."

I let out a bitter laugh. "That's rich. I'm already tangled up in this, Grayson. And what about the wiretap contraption you left at Vanderhoff's? You going to take that with you, too?"

"No. I bought the tele-bug on the black market. No one can trace it back to me. Besides, she won't be getting any more calls."

My internal alarm began clanging again. I hadn't mentioned Vanderhoff's death to Grayson. "How do you know?"

"Because I—"

The phone rang. Grayson clammed up mid-confession. Somehow, he knew Vanderhoff was dead without me telling him. Had he killed her after all? I grabbed the phone like it was the governor offering a stay of execution.

"Hello?"

"Bobbie, it's Paulson."

"Hi—"

"Listen very carefully," he whispered. "I'm trapped in my office out at Alto Lake. I didn't want to tell you, but two convicts escaped from Starke Prison ten days ago. Two FBI agents came out to help me apprehend them, but something in the woods out here killed them." His voice cracked. "Bobbie, whatever it is, it's after *me* now! I need help—"

The line went dead.

I looked at Grayson. "Paulson's in trouble. The nearest help is all the way in Gainesville. I gotta go."

Grayson stood. "Not without me."

I shook my head. "No. You need to stay here."

"Not happening."

Whoever or whatever was after Paulson, I knew it wasn't Grayson. He had an airtight alibi. He was standing right beside me, pointing his Glock in my ribs.

Chapter Fifty-Four

I WAS DRIVING MY FATHER'S Mustang like a hostage on a desperate, life-or-death mission.

Mainly because I *was*.

Grayson was in the passenger seat beside me, his Glock pointed at my vital organs.

"What are you doing?" I hissed at him. "You ask me to be your partner, then you pull a gun on me? Are you working undercover? FBI? CIA? MIB?"

I was too afraid to say what I really thought. It might set Grayson off enough to pull the trigger. Was he a deranged physicist? A throat-ripping serial killer? A crazy UFO chaser? An alien with two navels? A real-life *Dr. Jekyll, Mr. Hyde?*

Or maybe it was even worse than that. Maybe he was telling the truth.

"No offense, but I just didn't have time to argue with you," Grayson said. "Is this the fastest this thing will go?"

I stomped the gas pedal. "Vanderhoff's throat was ripped out. Did you do it?"

"No."

I eyed him angrily. "But you practically *confessed*. You said she wouldn't be getting any more calls. You *knew* she was dead!"

Grayson eyed the road ahead. "I didn't know she was dead. And I didn't know her throat had been ripped out."

"Then how did you know she wouldn't get any more calls? Wait. *You* made all those weird calls, didn't you?"

"Geez! No, I didn't make those calls, Drex. I know because when I tried to test the battery on the tele-bug, it told me her phone line had been disconnected."

"Oh." My gut flopped. I slunk back in my seat, more confused than ever. Grayson stared straight ahead, unnerving me. At this point, I had nothing left to lose. I went for broke.

"How do I know *you're* not the killer, Grayson?" I asked. "How can I be sure you're not some kind of monster trying to save yourself?"

Grayson turned and looked me in the eye. He shook his head softly and said, "Aren't we *all*, Drex?"

We drove along in the fading daylight until the darkness and tension were both thick enough to cut with a hacksaw. I blew through Waldo without another word to Grayson. Only when I pulled onto the road leading to Paulson's office cabin by Lake Alto Preserve did Grayson break the silence between us.

"Listen, Drex. I didn't mean to scare you. But I wasn't going to let you come out here alone, and I knew you'd put up a fight. We would've wasted time pissing and moaning at each other while this Mothman creature ripped Paulson's throat out."

"Fine," I said, and got out of the car. I was too angry and scared to say anything more. Grayson had a point. Still, lots of serial killers came across as rational people, didn't they?

As Grayson and I approached the driveway to Paulson's cabin, we saw a gray sedan blocking the dirt road.

"I had a feeling," Grayson said. "Good thing you've got a gun."

What? How did he know about my Glock?

"Had a feeling about what?" I asked.

"Things not being what they seem. They rarely are. Is that Paulson's car?"

"No."

"Then he's got company."

"Mothman?" I asked.

Grayson shook his head. "No. Most likely the FBI. Like I said before, Mothman prefers to fly."

Chapter Fifty-Five

GRAYSON CAUTIOUSLY climbed out of the Mustang, his Glock firmly in his grasp. He waved it slightly, motioning for me to follow his lead.

We skirted past the gray sedan and stalked, hunch-backed, the twenty yards to Paulson's cabin. Our only cover was the darkness of a crescent moon. As we approached the front door, the yellowish light on the front porch flickered.

The shower-scene music from *Psycho* jarred through my head.

"What's the plan?" I asked, hoping it didn't include me getting killed.

"We'll have to play it by ear," Grayson whispered. "Keep your voice down."

He pulled me next to him, our backs against the outside wall of the cabin. Then he leaned over, reached out, and turned the knob on the front door. He waited a beat, then pushed it open with a kick of his heel.

After about thirty seconds of listening to crickets, Grayson took a cautious peek inside. He waved me in.

Paulson's place was a sty. It was literally covered in spider webs, pizza boxes, and crushed beer cans.

"Geez," I whispered. "This guy's a pig."

"Help," a weak voice called out from behind a ratty sofa. It didn't sound like Paulson.

I gripped my Glock and inched over until I saw a pair of legs. Nice dress pants and Gucci loafers. Definitely not Paulson. Not on a cop's salary.

I whipped around the sofa and pointed my Glock at the guy. "Who are you?" I demanded with a harsh whisper. "What's going on here?"

A second later, Grayson was at my side.

"FBI," the man gurgled. Only then did I see the blood oozing out from beneath his jacket. "Agent Johnson. Officer ... down ... Terry Paulson ...." He hacked up blood.

"We'll find him," I said. "I know what he looks like."

"She ... she." Johnson fumbled for his jacket pocket, then lost consciousness.

I reached inside his jacket and pulled out a photo of a red-headed woman in a police uniform. "Terry Paulson's a woman?"

"*Was* a woman," Grayson said.

"I like redheads," Paulson's voice sounded behind us. "So sue me."

I jerked my head around. Paulson was standing with a semi-automatic weapon trained on Grayson.

My life flashed before my eyes. It didn't take long. I took a deep breath and went to my happy place. For a split second, Grandma Selma's sweet face replaced Paulson's angry one.

"Drop your guns," Paulson demanded.

"Do it," Grayson said.

I followed his lead, and bent down and laid my Glock on the floor beside his. As we started to rise, the blast of a gunshot sounded. I nearly fell to my knees. Then I realized it had come from outside the cabin.

Another blast sounded. The dim, yellow porch light shattered.

The room blinked out to black.

I dove behind the couch and crouched beside the fallen FBI agent. In the darkness, someone grabbed my hand and yanked it.

Hard.

I hoped it wasn't Paulson.

Whoever it was, he had the strength of a bear. I couldn't get free.

He pulled me across the room and we stumbled out the cabin door. In the faint starlight, I saw it was Grayson. Relief flooded through me. I finally knew who the good guy was.

"Let's get the hell out of here!" I whispered.

"You read my mind," Grayson quipped. "I knew you were talented, but really ...."

I punched his arm and giggled from sheer, scared-witless hysteria.

A twig snapped behind us. A shot ricocheted off a pine tree, showering us with splinters. Grayson grabbed my arm again, and we took off running for the car.

We were about thirty feet from the Mustang when another car's headlights came on, illuminating our backs and the road ahead of us.

"He's gotten to his car first," Grayson yelled. "We've got to get out of here fast."

"Who's driving?" I panted, out of breath.

"I call shotgun," Grayson answered, climbing into the passenger seat. "Get in, Drex, and drive like hell!"

I cranked the engine. When it caught on the first try, I wanted to kiss the dashboard. I slammed the Mustang into first and sideswiped the parked sedan as I made a wild attempt to turn it around on the narrow dirt road.

While I shifted and lurched, Grayson grabbed my phone and tried to call 9-1-1. There was no signal.

"I need to report that injured FBI agent," he said.

I shifted into reverse and made the last point on a ten-point turn. "Try again when we get nearer to Waldo. They've got better reception there."

"Right. But you may have to slow down when we find a signal. I'll need a minute to make the call."

I bit my lip and nodded, shifting into second gear. "I'll try to get some distance between us."

I stomped the gas pedal to the floor.

The tires spun dirt like a buzz-saw through soft pine all the way until we hit the pavement of US 301. I took the turn on two wheels. Soon, the blinking, pink-and-green neon sign of the Tropix Inn motel came into view. "Check your signal strength," I said, and let my foot off the gas.

"Three bars," he said, and punched 9-1-1. "FBI agent down at Lake Alto Preserve," he shouted into the phone. "Send an ambulance, quick."

"Could you repeat that, sir?" I heard the operator say. I looked in the rearview mirror. Paulson's headlights were barreling toward us.

"FBI agent. Shot. Lake Alto Preserve," Grayson repeated as he flailed his arm at me to get going.

I hit the gas, but not soon enough. Paulson's blue Toyota slammed into the back of the Mustang with a sickening crunch.

I got a close-up look at the steering wheel, but avoided slamming my face into it. With my phone in his hand, Grayson didn't have time to brace for impact. He groaned as his already cracked clavicle hit the dashboard.

"You okay?" I asked as I stomped the gas.

"Yes. Cut the lights."

I did as instructed, and blew through the rest of Waldo in the dark, steering half blind.

As the forest and swamp retook both sides of the road, so did the darkness. Using the dim light of Paulson's headlights behind us and gut instinct, I managed to jerk the steering wheel sharply to the right and onto Obsidian Road.

I looked back. "Crap! Paulson's still behind us."

I'd hoped Paulson would miss the poorly marked turn, but the Mustang's back bumper had come loose and was dragging on the road, spewing a shower of sparks like a homing beacon for him to follow.

We were about three miles from Point Paradise when the Mustang coughed and skipped a beat. The tank was on empty.

I glanced in the rearview mirror. Paulson was about thirty yards away and gaining on us. I swore I could see his eyes glowing red behind the windshield like two evil reflectors.

The Mustang's engine sputtered and died.

"Crap!" I screamed as we began to roll silently along in the darkness. "We're out of gas!"

Grayson shot a glance in the side view mirror. "Oh, shit. Brace yourself—"

Paulson rammed the back of us again. The rear of the Mustang tilted up like a bucking bronco.

I tried to keep the car on the road, but with no power steering, the wheel locked down tight. The muscle car jackknifed, then rammed into the metal guardrail of the small bridge over Wimbly Creek.

Paulson's Toyota buzzed by us. Twenty yards past, his brakes squealed. His taillights flared.

He was coming back for us.

"We've gotta run for it!" I said.

"Excellent idea," Grayson said.

As I reached to unlock my seatbelt, a brilliant beam of white light shot out of the woods about eight feet off the ground. It honed in on us, blinding us as we sat in the Mustang.

I shook my head and squinted against the piercing glare.

Saved by alien abduction? Never saw that one coming.

I watched, dumbfounded, as the blazing white light split into two beams that bore down on us like huge, twin lasers. Unable to move my legs, I hazarded a glance down the road at Paulson. To my surprise, he'd turned his car around again and was hightailing it out of here.

Lucky him, I thought as his taillights flashed, then grew fainter against the powerful white lights engulfing and overpowering Grayson and me.

"What kind of aliens are they?" I asked Grayson. My sphincter puckered involuntarily in anticipation of being probed ....

"What in blue blazes are you two doing out here?" Earl's voice thundered from somewhere behind the twin laser beams.

The roof-mounted strobe lights on Bessie went out. In between the dark spots cratering my retinas, Earl and his gigantic black monster truck slowly came into view.

I never thought I'd be *that* glad to see my annoying cousin.

"You won't believe this," Grayson began.

I poked an elbow in his ribs to silence him. "We had a little car trouble, Earl," I said. "Give us a tow back home."

Earl gave the Mustang a once-over and whistled long and low. "Geez Louise. Looks like you backed over the Loch Ness Monster, Bobbie."

"Women drivers," Grayson said, leaving me with nothing to do but slap on a sheepish smile and save my payback for another day.

"Lemme hook her up. Good thing I was out coon hunting tonight." Earl climbed back in the truck, shifted gears, and began turning Bessie around.

While Earl hooked up the tow on the Mustang, I climbed into Bessie's cab beside Grayson and whispered, "Do me a favor. Keep quiet about this whole Mothman business. Earl already thinks I'm an idiot, and I just don't feel like getting into it with him tonight. We'll tell him everything tomorrow. Okay?"

"Tell who what?" Earl's head poked in the driver's side window. "Wait a minute." He shot us a sly grin. "Are y'all engaged?"

Grayson nearly snorted. "Well, it's a funny story ...."

"No!" I yelled. "We're not engaged. Are we ready to go?"

"Yes, ma'am. Party pooper." Earl got in, hit the gas, and pulled the Mustang out of the ditch. As we hobbled down the road dragging it behind us, I did my best to ignore Earl as he grilled us about our honeymoon plans.

We were about half a mile from home and an inch from me punching Earl in the face when we spotted taillights in the ditch off to the right side of the road.

"Look at that," Earl said, slowing Bessie to a crawl. "Another careless driver. Must be something in the air tonight."

From our vantage point six feet up in the air, we could see the undamaged back end of Paulson's vehicle. It was still running, but Paulson was nowhere to be seen.

"That looks like Paulson's car," Earl said. "Why in tarnation would he go off and leave his vehicle running like that?"

Before I could stop him, Grayson cracked, "Like I keep telling Drex here, Mothman doesn't need wheels. He prefers to fly."

I shot Grayson a dirty look. "I asked you not to mention 'the M-man.'"

"I think it's time Earl knew," Grayson said. "Because if my hunch is right, we haven't seen the last of the M-man tonight."

Chapter Fifty-Six

"YOU DON'T HAVE ANY proof that the guy pretending to be Paulson is the Mothman," I said to Grayson as Earl maneuvered Bessie around and backed the wrecked Mustang into the service bay.

"You don't have any proof he's *not*," Grayson argued.

"Is *that* what this is about?" Earl laughed. "I thought y'all was having a lover's quarrel." He waggled his eyebrows at me. "You afraid the little ol' Mothman's gonna get you, Bobbie?"

"Or maybe the Feds," Grayson said.

Earl winked at me. "The men in blue are after you!"

"Argh! You guys suck!" I clambered over Grayson's lap, yanked open the truck door, and tumbled onto my knees in the parking lot.

I got up and dusted myself off. "While you two joke around like a couple of jerks, whoever's after us could be hiding in the bushes getting ready to blow our heads off! The stupid Mothman has nothing to do with this!"

"But why'd the FBI show up if they wasn't chasing Mothman?" Earl asked.

I adjusted my wig. "The guy pretending to be Officer Paulson called them."

Earl climbed out of the cab. "But if Paulson's the killer, Bobbie, why would he call the FBI?"

Crap. He had me there. I scowled. "How the hell should I know?"

"The FBI doesn't usually get involved in simple homicide cases," Grayson said.

"I don't think ripping people's throats out is simple homicide," I argued. "But Earl's got a point. If this fake Paulson guy was guilty, why would he call the FBI? Why would he call *me* for backup?"

"Wait!" Earl's eyes grew wide—probably from the strain of using his noodle. "Maybe this *fake* Paulson's working undercover with the FBI, and he thinks one of *you* is the Mothman."

I rolled my eyes. "Then why would he shoot his own team?"

Grayson shut the cab door behind him. "Maybe this fake Paulson guy *didn't* call the FBI at all. He might've gotten a heads up somehow that the FBI was on the way, so he used it to his advantage. He could've been monitoring Terry Paulson's phone or radio or something. When he found out the FBI was coming, he played you along, Drex."

I grimaced. Grayson could be right. "He told me two prisoners escaped from Starke prison ten days ago."

"He might've known that because he was one of them," Grayson said.

I shook my head. "He didn't seem like the criminal type to me."

"Too good looking?" Grayson asked.

He struck a nerve. "No! The guy was *crying* at the scene of Vanderhoff's murder. He seemed genuinely unnerved. And he told me not to trust you, Grayson. Maybe when he saw us at his cabin, he thought you were holding me hostage. You *did* have a gun on me."

For once, Grayson finally lost his cool. "This guy's *an imposter*, Drex! He made us drop our weapons. He held us at gunpoint. He fired at us and tried to run us off the road! What more proof do you need that *he's* the bad guy here?"

I shrunk back. "Okay, okay. He's not who he says he is. I'll give you that. But that doesn't prove the guy's some ridiculous Mothman from outer space!"

I stomped my father's boots over to the office and flipped on the service bay lights for Earl. Grayson trailed after me.

"What about all those spider webs in his cabin?" Grayson argued. "They could've been the makings of a cocoon."

I made a sour face. "He doesn't clean up after himself. If that were a crime, every guy on the planet would be in jail."

"Okay. But if he's human, why did he abandon his vehicle? It was still running when we drove by."

I shrugged angrily. "Maybe he was afraid of being spotted, Grayson. He could've seen you on the phone. He might've thought you were calling the cops to report him."

Grayson grabbed my arm. "I don't think so, Drex. He left his car in the ditch because he didn't need it. He can fly."

I looked Grayson in the eye. "Don't you see how crazy that sounds?"

Grayson looked indignant. "No. Not really."

I shook my head. "Look. Whether Paulson's the Mothman or not, he's out there on the loose. We need to get inside and lock the doors. And call the Sheriff's Department!"

Grayson's face lost its tension. "You're right, Drex. He's nearby. And he's after us. We need to prepare ourselves."

A cold streak made my back arch. I suddenly became aware again of an uncomfortable dampness in my coveralls. For the second time since ditching diapers at age two, I'd peed my damned pants.

"Listen," I said. "I need a shower and a stiff drink. Stay here with Earl. He's exposed all alone out here in the service bay. When he's done unhooking the Mustang, both of you come upstairs and lock up behind you."

Grayson looked me over intently, as if trying to ascertain not only my plan, but my state of mind as well. Finally, he nodded. "Okay."

I turned and headed up the stairs to my apartment, each step harder and heavier than the last. Inside my bedroom, I kicked my father's burdensome old boots off into a corner. They seemed to stare at me accusingly as I unzipped my soiled coveralls. I dropped them on top of the boots and stared at the crumpled heap.

I peeled off my urine-soaked panties. Getting shot at had scared the piss out of me. Did that prove I wasn't fit to be a private eye? I added the wet panties to the heap in the corner, along with my sweaty bra. I put my wig on the bureau and padded to the bathroom, as bald and naked and vulnerable as a newborn chick.

As I stepped into the shower and the hot water trickled over my shaved head, I wondered how, in just under a week, my life could have gotten so far off track. One lousy, unlucky shot from some bike-thieving punk at the mall had changed the trajectory of my entire life.

A week ago, my daily routine had been simple. Mundane. Predictable. Now, it felt as if I'd been yanked out of line at Walmart and forced to star in a low-budget horror flick.

Mothman: The Redneck Years.

I stepped out of the shower, dried off, and wrapped myself in a towel. It was going to be a long night. I padded over to the closet to get a clean T-shirt. As I opened the closet door, my mouth fell open. My hairbrush dropped from my hand.

Staring at me, eyeball-to-eyeball, was the same creature I'd seen outside my bedroom window last night. The same hairy, human-like face. The same glowing, red eyes.

Mothman was finally coming out of the closet—and heading right for me!

I screamed. Mothman pounced on top of me. I guess I was going to die in Point Paradise after all.

Crap.

Chapter Fifty-Seven

I WAS IN A STRUGGLE for my life.

Mothman was real.

The creature came at me from its hiding place inside my closet. The sound of my own scream broke my paralytic shock. Running on instinct and adrenaline, I smashed my right fist into the monster's ugly, insectoid face.

He flew backward into my hanging clothes, then bounced back at me like a ricocheting bullet. I grimaced as his horrible, hairy face head-butted into mine.

His stiff, nasty whiskers scratched at my cheeks as I grabbed him by the torso and tried to throw him off balance. But I tripped on a flip-flop, lost my footing, and took him with me as I fell sideways onto the floor.

With the air nearly knocked out of me, I wrestled the creature on the shag carpet. Sometime during the struggle, Mothman ripped the towel from my body.

Naked as a jaybird, I scrambled on top of him, straddled his belly, and walloped him good with a one-two punch to the face. He tried to roll over onto his stomach, but I pinned him with my thighs. Then I set out delivering a set of kidneys jabs to his torso until he let out a weird, squeaky, fart-like sound.

Suddenly, the bedroom door flew open. Grayson burst in, holding Earl's shotgun. As he scrambled to my rescue, his face broke into a grin. Then the jerk burst out laughing.

I was ready to punch *him* in the face, too. "Uh ... a little help here?" I yelled.

Grayson shook his head. "What are you *doing*, Drex?"

I stared at Grayson, then down at my assailant. My adrenaline rush over, my thumping heart nearly stopped in my chest.

Mothman wasn't real.

He was a blow-up sex doll in a cheap monster mask.

I glared up at Grayson. My vision went red.

"Very funny, you smartass!" I shrieked. I yanked Grandma Selma's blanket off the inflatable doll's back and hastily covered myself with it.

Grayson pursed his lips in a poor attempt to hide his amusement. "Drex," he guffawed, "I promise, I had nothing to do with this."

"Sure you didn't!" I hissed. "Tell me, jackass. How'd you get that stupid thing to fly outside my bedroom window last night?"

"With one of them drones," Earl said, appearing in the doorway. He shot me a sadistic wink. "Ha ha, Bobbie! Looks like I got you good!"

Chapter Fifty-Eight

IT WAS NEARLY MIDNIGHT. The three of us were sitting vigil around the kitchen table, waiting for who-knew-what to come dragging up out of the darkness. I got up and poured Grayson and Earl some coffee, mainly because I didn't have any arsenic on hand.

"How could you do this to me?" I muttered angrily.

"Aww, don't take it so hard," Earl said. "Beth-Ann told me about how you and Grayson was gonna do a stakeout by the Stop & Shoppe. I figured I'd have me a little fun."

I shot Earl a scathing look. My whole life was nothing but a joke to him. "So Mothman was *you* the whole time."

Earl grinned proudly. "Yeppers."

"No." Grayson said, shaking his head. "It couldn't have been you in the woods the night of my accident. I didn't even know you then."

Earl looked over at Grayson. "What you talking about?"

"The night my RV broke down. I saw it. *Oculi rubere.*"

"The red octopus," Earl whispered, his eyes as big as plums.

"Red *eyes*," Grayson corrected. "The night I broke down, I saw glowing red eyes in the woods. I tried to roll up the window, then I felt this pain in my shoulder. I passed out. I couldn't remember anything else."

"That's when the Mothman bit you," Earl said.

"It was his seatbelt!" I yelled.

Grayson scooted his chair away from the table. "I can't say for sure if it was Mothman or not. But if it *was*, it wouldn't be the first time something like this has happened to me. I guess it's time I showed you two something."

"What?" Earl asked. "You got a tattoo of him?"

I thought Grayson was going to show us his two navels. But then he stood up and said, "Not here. Follow me."

We tromped down the stairs behind Grayson and out to the parking lot. Since we'd lost our guns at Alto Lake, Earl kept a wary watch for fake Paulson with his trusty Mossberg shotgun. After ascertaining the coast was clear, the three of us crossed the lot and climbed inside Grayson's RV.

"You might've noticed I've got padlocks on the cabinets and bedroom door," Grayson said as he pointed them out.

"Nope," Earl said. "Hadn't noticed at all."

I shot my cousin a dirty look.

"Well, there's a good reason for it." Grayson took out a jumble of keys and opened the padlock on one of the cabinets. It was full of brown bottles with eyedropper lids.

"You must really be into aromatherapy," I said dryly.

"Something like that." Grayson padlocked the cabinet again and shuffled down the small hallway, past the tiny bathroom to the bedroom. He unlocked deadbolt after deadbolt on the bedroom door. After unlocking the eighth one, he opened the door and stepped aside for Earl and me to have a look inside.

Cautiously, we peered into the room. The walls were padded with a thick, gray, quilted fabric that reminded me of the back of an insulated potholder. Heavy-gauge wire mesh covered the windows. It was the perfect lair for a psycho killer to keep his hostages.

Earl grunted. "Darn. I thought there was gonna be some kind a critter in here."

I turned to Grayson. "What is it?"

"It's an electromagnetic holding cell."

"Is that like a toaster oven?" Earl asked.

Grayson sighed. "In layman terms, it's a monster trap."

Earl's eyes lit up. "Woohoo!"

Grayson nodded. "And it's time we set this trap to catch the Mothman."

"You're kidding," I said.

Grayson shook his head. "No. I'm dead serious." His eyes scanned the ceiling of the RV above his head. "He's out there. I can feel him. But we're going to need the right bait."

Grayson shot a glance at Earl, raised an eyebrow, and tilted his head toward me.

Both men turned their heads, locked eyes with me, and smiled.

I scowled. "What?"

Then I figured out what, and ran for my life.

Chapter Fifty-Nine

"COME ON, DREX! WHAT do moths find irresistible?" Grayson's voice sounded muffled as he tried to reason with me from the other side of my locked bedroom door.

"I dunno," I yelled through the door. "You're the genius here. *Mothballs?*" I looked around for something to barricade the door.

"No. *Flames.*"

"So what? What's the pyro-maniacal leanings of a deranged insect got to do with *me?*"

"Think about it, Drex. I think he's attracted to your flaming red hair. He said he liked redheads, remember?"

I stopped shoving the chest of drawers toward the door. "That was fake Paulson, not Mothman."

"Po-*tay*-to, po-*tah*-to."

I groaned. "Okay. So what if he *does* like redheads? I'm bald, remember?"

"That's only a temporary setback. When he met you at the mall, you had all your hair, right?"

I frowned begrudgingly. "Yeah."

"Listen," Grayson said. "I think we have a chance of luring him into the RV if you could persuade him."

"Me? *Persuade* him? How?"

"With your feminine, redhead wiles."

My face puckered. "Right. And then what? Let him kill me in your rundown RV deathtrap? Uh...*no thanks!*" I tugged on the chest of drawers again.

"No. If I'm right about this, he'll be powerless around you."

I stopped and put an ear to the door. "What do you mean, powerless?"

"It's hard to explain. I'm going to have to show you. You're going to have to open the door."

I laughed bitterly. "No way, Grayson. I'm not falling for any more of you guys' stupid pranks."

"Don't you find it interesting that Mothman appeared to you in your Grandma's afghan? Your *security blanket?*"

I thought about it for a second. "No. That was Earl's doing."

"Oh. Right. Well, still, what if this Mothman creature feeds on your fears? What if he's able to lure his victims with a false sense of security?"

My brow furrowed. "What do you mean?"

"What if Mothman can somehow read minds, Drex? Know his victims' safe places? Then, he uses that knowledge to lure his victims. You know, make them feel like they have nothing to fear. It would explain how he's been able to overwhelm them without an apparent struggle."

"Or maybe he's just a smooth talker," I said through the door. "Like somebody else I know."

"What?" Grayson said.

Suddenly, I remembered something. "Grayson, in the cabin tonight, right before somebody shot out the lights, I saw an image of Grandma Selma's face over Paulson's. Was that a hallucination?"

"I don't think so, Drex. I think your vision was the work of the Mothman. He must be able to project images into your mind. He knew you wouldn't shoot your grandmother, right?"

My gut flopped at the thought.

"This creature knew your safe space," Grayson said. "It's your Grandma Selma, isn't it?"

I frowned. "Yes."

"He tricked you, if only for a moment. Now it's our job to figure out how to trick him back."

"How?"

"I'm going to need your wig."

I winced. "My wig? But I'll be bald! What do you need it for?"

"You'll see."

I cracked open my bedroom door and peeked out. Grayson was in the hall alone.

"Where's Earl?" I asked.

"He said he's making booby traps."

Aww, geez.

"You don't know him like I do," I said. "He shouldn't be left alone out there unsupervised."

Grayson nodded. "Okay. Then let's go back down to the service bay."

I grabbed Earl's Lucky Red ball cap to cover my bald head and handed over my *Woody Woodpecker* wig to Grayson. He and I tromped downstairs to the parking lot. While he walked over to his RV with my wig, I went into the service bay to see what Earl was up to.

As anticipated, I was neither surprised nor impressed by Earl's redneck ingenuity.

In a masterwork only he could have concocted, my brilliant cousin had taped together sections of cardboard boxes until they'd formed the basic size and shape of a refrigerator. Then he'd covered the whole Frankenstein mess with duct tape, sticky side out.

As usual, disaster had struck. Somehow the boy genius had managed to get the whole contraption stuck to his back. As I walked up, he was flailing around like Quasimodo stuck to a roach motel.

"Gimme a hand here, Bobbie!"

I smirked. "If I did, then I'd only have one left."

"Come on, Cuz."

"What *is* that thing, anyway?"

"What the heck's it look like?"

I smirked. "A redneck's worst nightmare?"

"It's a Mothman trap, you dingdong. Help me get it set up."

"How'd you get it stuck on your back?"

"I was gonna tote it out to the RV and ... uh ... I kinda forgot it was sticky."

I rolled my eyes and sighed. "Fabulous. Follow me."

"What's the plan?" I asked as Earl shuffled along behind me, hunched over with the trap stuck to his back.

"We make this thing look like a moth cocoon," Earl said as we made our way across the parking lot. "Grayson said that might be the creature's safe space."

Before I could come up with anything more stupid than that, Grayson emerged from his RV with a Windex bottle in one hand, my wig in the other.

"What's that?" I nodded at the Windex bottle half-full of brownish liquid.

Grayson beamed. "My proprietary blend of moth pheromones. I took the liberty of spraying your wig with them." He handed me the soggy mass of red hair. "Now, put it back on and I'll spray you down."

I stared at him. "Not in this lifetime."

Grayson blanched. "What? I've left the bedroom door in the RV unlocked. The plan is, you get all pheremoned up and wait for him in there. Earl and I will hide nearby. When Mothman goes inside, we'll run in and stick that cocoon thing over him."

Grayson took a glance at Earl's convoluted duct-tape trap and his confidence evaporated. "Earl, I told you to put the duct tape on the *inside*."

I stared at the two men. I was supposed to entrust my life to *these* two idiots? *Grizzly Adams* caught in his own moth trap, and Professor Pheromones with a Windex bottle full of happy hormone juice?

I don't think so.

"Hold on, gentlemen," I said. "I've got a better idea."

Chapter Sixty

TYPICAL ACADEMIC.

Grayson's moth-trap idea might've seemed good in theory, but it didn't translate in the real world—at least, not in *my* real world. If all went according to *my* plan, however, Mothman would soon be buzzing around us again, and into Grayson's monster trap.

I set my jaw to Wonder Woman mode and got to work.

I ripped Earl's sticky, cardboard box from the back of his flannel shirt and tossed it on the ground.

"Grab your duct tape and follow me," I commanded. "And you, Grayson. Spray down your monster trap bedroom with that pheromone stuff of yours. But be sure and save some for me. Come on, Earl."

My burly cousin shot me a look, but then tromped up the stairs behind me. He followed me into my apartment and down the hall to my bedroom.

I pointed at the floor. "Fix Mothman so he can fly again."

Earl grinned as he contemplated the deflated remains of his blow-up-doll creation. "Looks like he put up a good fight, Cuz."

"Get to work," I barked. "And don't use Grandma's afghan this time. Use *this* instead."

Earl caught what I threw at him and grinned. "Yes, boss man." He ripped off a piece of duct tape with his teeth, got down on his knees, and went to work.

While Earl doctored up the Mothman sex doll, I fished through my closet for the perfect outfit for our flying bait. I re-dressed the re-inflated body while Earl patched leaks and tested out the drone.

"Does it still work?" I asked.

"Ain't too much worse for wear, Bobbie. You never were good with a punch."

"Har har. Grab that stupid thing and let's roll."

When Earl and I emerged downstairs a few minutes later, the flying drone had been transformed. With the help of an old nightie of mine, fuzzy high-heeled slippers, and one of Grayson's pink T-shirts for a cape, Mothman had become Moth*woman*.

Grayson's jaw fell open.

"Spray her down, professor," I said. "Earl, tape that wig to her head, then let her fly."

"Yes, boss man."

"All right, men," I said, crossing my arms. "Let's get that pheromone scent up in the air, shall we?"

WITH EARL AT THE HELM of the remote control, Mothwoman worked like an insect's wet dream. She buzzed her way around the vicinity of the garage and bordering woods, advertising her wares like a mothy harlot.

Unfortunately, about ten minutes into it, things went a little off plan.

Earl emerged unexpectedly from the bushes and stepped under the light of a lamp post in the parking lot.

His hands were in the air.

Behind him was a man holding a gun to Earl's ribcage.

And it wasn't Paulson.

Chapter Sixty-One

"FBI SPECIAL AGENT TOM Hicks," the guy announced. "Come out now. And if you've got any weapons, lay them down."

Grayson and I glanced at each other from behind the RV. He nodded and laid Earl's Mossberg shotgun on the asphalt. I followed suit with my Daisy BB gun.

"What's going on here?" Hicks demanded.

"We're on your side, Agent Hicks," I called out from across the lot. "We're trying to apprehend Paulson ... I mean the guy who's pretending to be Terry Paulson."

The FBI agent poked his gun in Earl's ribs. "Is this him? I found him crouched in the bushes, giggling like a moron."

"No," I said, taking a cautious step toward them. "I know he looks abnormal, but he's just my cousin, Earl Shankles."

Suddenly, a large, pinkish, bird-like creature buzzed over us, mere feet from our heads. We all looked up.

"What the?" Agent Hicks yelled. He pointed his weapon toward the sky and fired twice.

Shards of plastic rained down on the parking lot. A moment later, Mothwoman smacked into the asphalt between us. She squealed and deflated with a long, flappy, whine.

I glanced up at Agent Hicks. His face was impossible to describe. He pointed his gun at Mothwoman, then Earl, then me; then just let it drop to his side. "Can somebody please explain what the hell is going on here?"

"It's a decoy," I said. "We're using it to lure Paulson in."

"With a flying blow-up doll?" Hicks eyed me like I was crazy. I couldn't blame him.

"It's a long story," I began, but Grayson cut me off.

"We don't have time for long explanations. Agent Hicks, whoever this guy is who shot your partner, he ditched his car nearby. He's out there somewhere ... he could be aiming a gun at us right now."

Agent Hicks nodded toward our Mothman trap. "Who's in the RV?"

Grayson fumbled. "Uh ... no one. It's part of the lure. I put on some soft music and lit a candle."

I smirked. "Nice touch."

Hicks jaw went tense. He pointed his gun at us again. "Shut up! I need some straight answers. Why is there a blow-up doll here wearing a monster mask and a red wig?"

I grimaced. "This Paulson imposter is ... uh ... partial to redheads."

"And monster ladies," Earl added, as if that explained everything else Agent Hicks needed to know.

I was preparing myself for being cuffed and led to a psych ward when Grayson stepped forward.

"Agent Hicks, I'm Nick Grayson, Private Investigator." He flashed his badge. "I'm working on a case for Chief Warren Engles."

Agent Hicks' eyes grew wide. But not as wide as mine.

"I'm here investigating reports of Mothman sightings in the vicinity. The apparatus you shot down was, as my assistant said, a pheromone decoy."

Agent Hicks appeared incredulous. "I thought Mothman was just an urban legend."

"That's what I'm here trying to determine."

Agent Hicks shook his head. "I've heard some ridiculous crap in my day, but this takes the prize." He chewed his lip for a moment, blew out a breath, and looked Grayson in the eye. "Okay. What's the plan?"

Grayson turned my way. All of a sudden, all eyes were on me. Again.

Chapter Sixty-Two

"TERRY PAULSON WAS REPORTED missing by her family five days ago," Agent Hicks said as the four of us crammed into the small banquet in Grayson's RV. "I ran the plates on the Corolla in the ditch. They were stolen. The number's registered to a Mandy Vanderhoff."

I wanted to kick myself in the head. The blue Corolla. There were millions of them out there. Mandy drove one. I hadn't made the connection.

"This guy must've abducted Mandy," I said. "She has red hair. Terry Paulson has red hair. I've got ... I shot a glance around at the men's faces. I *had* red hair."

Agent Hicks nodded. "Interesting observation. Officially, Terry Paulson was last seen ten days ago, when she left Starke prison driving a police transport vehicle. Her passenger was a murder suspect named Eugene Hollister."

I gasped. "The guy pretending to be Terry Paulson must be Eugene Hollister! The dead body in the woods ... with the orange jumpsuit. Hollister killed her and switched clothes. He messed up her face, so no one could identify her."

"You could be right, young lady," Agent Hicks said. "Yesterday, we found Terry Paulson's body in a shallow grave about two and a half miles south of here."

"I told Paulson—I mean Hollister that I'd found a body," I said. "He must've gone back and hid it, then made me go back to the scene to show me it wasn't there." I shook my head. "He wanted me to think I'd imagined it. Then he must've gone back later that day and buried it. The rain would've washed away his trail."

"But why hadn't anyone reported Ms. Paulson missing until now?" Grayson asked.

"Apparently, the guy assumed Terry Paulson's identity," Agent Hicks said. "She was filling in as interim officer for Jack Barker. Nobody knew her in Waldo. Hollister could've reported in to the Alachua Sherriff's Department online. Or used a device to change his voice to sound like a woman over the phone."

My back stiffened. "They make devices like that?"

"Sure," Grayson said. "Hollister might've been able to fool department employees with it, but he couldn't fool Terry Paulson's family."

I shook my head. "That's why he didn't want to go to Vanderhoff's himself. Paulson ... I mean Hollister. He gave me that assignment because he was afraid old lady Vanderhoff would recognize Mandy's car. She must've made the connection anyway, and so he had to kill her."

"What's this Hollister fella look like?" Earl asked.

Agent Hicks pulled out a photo. "Kind of like Paul Newman, some say. I, personally, don't see it. Reports say he's got a way with the ladies, though."

Earl and Grayson both shot me *told you so* looks. I grimaced. As Agent Hicks passed the photo to Earl, I snatched it from his grubby hand and stared into the handsome, irritatingly attractive face.

I didn't recognize it.

"That's not him," I said, shaking my head. "That's not the guy who was pretending to be Terry Paulson."

I handed the photo to Grayson. He agreed. "You're right. It's not."

Hicks stared at us both. "Then who the hell are you trying to catch?"

I bit down on my lip. Hard. "I guess we'd better reset that trap and find out."

Chapter Sixty-Three

PHASE TWO OF "OPERATION Moth Trap" was well underway.

The door to the RV's monster-trap bedroom was open for business. A few feet down the hall, Grayson and Agent Hicks were holed up inside the miniscule bathroom. I didn't even want to know how two grown men were making that work. The soft music was playing again, and because Grayson insisted, a candle was left burning on the kitchen table to offer Mothman a symbolic "flame."

Our comrade in arms, the dearly deflated Mothwoman, was duct-taped to the RV's open doorway. She was wearing my wig, my sexiest lingerie, and a nylon rope around her waist.

I was positioned upstairs in my bedroom above the garage. My role was to flick on a lighter when I saw anyone approaching. The light, in turn, would signal Earl. He was hiding inside a smelly trash can beside the RV.

I smiled to myself. That had been my idea. Being in charge of the plan had its privileges.

Once I signaled Earl, his job was to pop up out of the trash can and tap on the bathroom window to alert Grayson and Hicks that our prey was approaching the RV door. They, in turn, would then tug on the rope and yank Mothwoman inside.

Once the perpetrator stepped inside the RV, Earl was supposed to run around and close the door, then make sure it stayed closed until Agent Hicks and Grayson gave the all clear.

I looked down at the RV in the parking lot and shook my head. I wasn't kidding myself. This was a foolish plan devised by foolish people. Still, as I stood by the window and kept watch, I prayed with all

266

my might that God would keep his promise to take care of children and fools.

Because if this didn't work, Earl and Grayson would never let me live it down.

Never.

Chapter Sixty-Four

ABOUT A QUARTER PAST two, I was about to call the whole thing off when a shadowy figure appeared out of nowhere. I blinked, unsure if I was just seeing things. In a split second, the dark figure somehow managed to traverse the parking lot. He was nearly to the RV door.

"Damn!" I hissed, and fumbled with the lighter. It faltered.

I tried again. The lighter shot out a flame. I pressed my nose against the windowpane, trying to see if Earl had seen my signal. My breath fogged up the glass. When I wiped it with my sleeve, the figure was gone.

So was Mothwoman.

Suddenly, a loud ruckus arose from the RV. It began to rock to and fro like it was in a Cat-4 hurricane. I opened the window and stuck my head out for a better view. That's when I saw Earl run into the RV toting a baseball bat.

The door slammed closed. An electric buzz stung the frosty air. Suddenly, all the lights in the house and parking lot went out, plunging everything into pitch-black darkness.

My heart lurched in my chest. I stood still as a stone, waiting, grinding my teeth in the inky night.

What in the hell's going on in there?

After what seemed like an hour, one lone flashlight emerged from the RV. Whoever had a hold of it pointed it up to my darkened bedroom window. The glare blinded me instantly.

"Argh!" I fumbled backward as footsteps crunched across the parking lot toward my open window. I tiptoed back to the windowsill, and strained to see beyond the stars dancing in my eyes.

"Who is it?" I cried out, hoping Mothman wasn't going to fly through my window again.

I was about to need another change of underwear when a second flashlight appeared. Then a third.

Then Earl's voice rang out from the gloom.

"Woohoo! Bobbie! We caught us a Mothman!"

Chapter Sixty-Five

"SO, WHO'S IN THE TRAP?" I yelled down from the bedroom window.

All three men were huffing and puffing, leaning against the wall of the garage looking like they'd just survived Walmart's Black Friday door-buster sale.

"Eugene ... Hollister," Agent Hicks said between gasping lungfuls of air.

Earl grabbed his side and wheezed, "Boy howdy, I sure could use me a beer."

Grayson looked up at me. "How about you, Drex?"

"Me?" I called down. "I sure could use me a new life."

I WENT DOWNSTAIRS, and after the guys finally caught their breath, the four of us crammed into Grayson's RV.

"I don't get it," I said as Agent Hicks squeezed into the banquette across from me. "Why would Hollister be after *us*?"

"You saw him out at Lake Alto. He shot a federal agent out there. My partner Rick Tomlinson."

"Is he okay?"

"I can't say for sure. I waited until the ambulance arrived. He was hit pretty bad, but still alive when I left. You can bet Hollister was trying to eliminate you all as witnesses."

I chewed my lip. "But it wasn't Hollister I saw at the cabin. It was the guy impersonating Paulson."

Hicks looked me in the eye. "You absolutely sure about that?"

"It was dark, Drex," Grayson said. "We only saw him for a second. Hollister and the guy impersonating Officer Paulson look a lot alike. It could've been Hollister who ambushed us in the cabin, then chased us back here with Vanderhoff's stolen car."

How could I argue with Grayson? I thought I'd seen Grandma Selma out at that cabin, too. What kind of reliable witness did *I* make? With that stupid gonad stuck in my brain, I couldn't be sure that *anything* I saw was real. There was a real possibility I could've gotten Hollister and the other guy mixed up.

I blew out a breath. "I guess you're right, Grayson. But even if Hollister *was* the shooter, this other guy pretending to be Paulson ... he has to be tangled up with Hollister somehow. Why else would they have both known about that cabin at Alto Lake?"

Earl whistled and shook his head. "Is that coffee ready yet? All this figurin' is starting to give me a headache."

Grayson leaned over and checked the pot of coffee perking on his propane stove. It was our only option for an early-morning cup of joe. It was only five-thirty. The Stop & Shoppe didn't open until eight o'clock, and I didn't have any electricity.

I'd checked the electric meter. Hollister hadn't cut off my power. The electric company had. They weren't likely to turn it on any time soon, either. I owed them more than my entire net worth.

"You may be right, Ms. Drex," Agent Hicks said. "The two men might be working together. But right now, *your* mystery man's not on our radar. In fact, we don't have any data on him whatsoever. As far as we're concerned, he doesn't exist. But you come up with picture or a name for him, and I'll be the first to help you out."

Grayson poured the coffee while we waited on the good folks of Alachua County Sheriff's Department to provide luxury armed transportation for Eugene Hollister back to whatever dark holding cell they had waiting for him. From the sounds emanating from the bedroom of the RV, Hollister was none too happy about it, either.

"What about Mandy and Mildred Vanderhoff?" I asked Agent Hicks. "Who'll be working on their cases?"

"The Sheriff's Department, I suspect. But right now, they're both missing persons. I hate to say it, but thousands of people go missing every day, Ms. Drex. Cases with bodies take precedent."

"But Vanderhoff ... she was killed in her house. Her body was there."

Hicks took a sip from his mug. "Did you see it?"

I shook my head. "No. I saw blood, but no body."

"Neither did anyone else." Hicks took a peek out the small window beside the banquette. "Looks like my ride is here. Thanks for helping me capture Hollister, but we'll need y'all to clear out of the RV while we get him loaded."

We tumbled out of the RV. Earl headed for the bathroom in the service bay. Grayson walked toward the woods that lined the parking lot. I followed him over there.

"You've been awfully quiet, Grayson."

He sighed. "There goes a cool million, easy. Nothing I can do to stop it, either."

"Wait. You *still* think Eugene Hollister's the Mothman?"

"Not *the* Mothman. *A* Mothman. I think there's more than one out there, Drex."

I grimaced. "Really?"

"The guy we knew as Paulson. Where is *he? Who* is he? I agree with you. He and Hollister were working together."

"Okay. But why?"

"Lots of species join forces for survival. Safety in numbers, you know. But they especially gather together during mating season."

My nose crinkled. "Mating season?"

"Consider this, Drex. What if our Paulson impersonator had chosen Mandy Vanderhoff as his mate, and you were supposed to be Hollister's?"

I nearly choked. "What! That's crazy, even for you, Grayson! And why me and Mandy?" I shot him a look. "And don't say it's because they like redheads."

Grayson's lip twisted. "Only half of one percent of all the people on the planet are redheads, Drex. Why would these guys have gone to all the trouble to find you and Mandy unless there was something about you two that set you apart? What if redheads possess certain unique genetic traits that allow Mothmen to produce offspring with them?"

"Geez! If that were true, why didn't they take Terry Paulson when they had the chance?"

Grayson shrugged. "Maybe they tried. She could've been killed in the struggle to abduct her. Maybe she was sterile. Or had a hysterectomy. Or maybe there were three Mothmen, not just two."

I shook my head in exasperation. "Or maybe there were none. You never give up, do you, Grayson?"

He smiled thoughtfully. "Now what would be the fun in that?"

Chapter Sixty-Six

AFTER GIVING OUR STATEMENTS to the Sheriff's Department officers on the scene, we were summoned by the deputy in charge of the transport detail.

"You must be Detective Drex," he said as I approached his vehicle. He laughed and shook his head. "Hicks said you were a looker."

Considering the bald dome I was sporting under Lucky Red, I didn't know if I'd just been complimented or insulted.

The man held up two Glocks. "Which one of these belongs to you?"

"The nineteen, thanks." I took my gun and stepped back from the window of his vehicle.

"And this one's yours, I presume, Detective Grayson. By the way, Chief Engles sends his regards."

"Thanks." Grayson grabbed his Glock and headed toward the garage. I followed, hot on his heels.

"What's this business with Chief Engles?" I called out behind him.

Grayson turned to face me. "That's on a need-to-know basis, Drex."

I bit down so hard the tendons in my neck stood out. "You know, Grayson, this Paulson imposter we've been chasing? He's not a Mothman. He's probably just like *you*—another weirdo chasing down imaginary monsters."

Grayson's face was unreadable. "Why would he pretend to be Terry Paulson?"

I gave him half an eye roll. "Don't try to tell me you've never pretended to be someone you're not."

Grayson smiled softly. "Fair enough. But for the record, I think you're wrong. I think he's another Mothman."

I grimaced. "But that would mean ...."

"He's still out there."

I thought of my happy place. Grandma Selma. Then something clicked in my mind.

Grandma Selma. At the cabin. Was Grayson right? Did Hollister project her image into my mind? If so, he could've easily done the same with the image of the man I knew as Paulson. Hollister could've been both men.

I cleared my throat. "Maybe he's *not*, Grayson. What if Eugene Hollister is actually a shapeshifter? What if he and the man who pretended to be Paulson are the same guy? Then there'd be only one Mothman, and he's in federal custody."

Grayson's right eyebrow ticked up. "Well, I didn't see *that one* coming from you, Drex." He rubbed his chin. "Huh. I suppose it's possible. If Hollister can turn into a moth and fly, putting on a different human face should be child's play."

The sun was just beginning to peek over the horizon, and I shivered as we walked together back to the service bay. Earl was busy surveying the RV for damages caused by our stakeout last night, and I was still searching for a normal, pedestrian answer to the bizarre events of the past week.

"Something still bugs me," I said to Grayson. "Those weird phone calls to Mildred Vanderhoff. What reason would a creature like the Mothman have for following her around and asking her dumb stuff like what year it was?"

"I think he went there to see if Vanderhoff would recognize him or his voice. You know, to see if he needed to eliminate her as a witness."

I frowned. "Maybe."

Grayson poked me in the ribs. "Or the phone calls could've been little green men pulling a couple of cosmic fast ones."

I stopped in my tracks. "Little green men? Gimme a break, Grayson! Why would beings from outer space dress in old-fashioned clothes? Or use outdated landline phones to communicate with us? It doesn't make any sense!"

Grayson raised an eyebrow playfully. "Who knows, Drex? Maybe they were using an outdated issue of *Travel Guide to the Galaxies*. Or maybe their time machine was on the fritz and screwed up the dates. Like you said, the guy *did* ask what year it was."

I shot Grayson a look that made him wince. "He was probably just trying to make Vanderhoff look crazy. Like he tried to do with me."

"That's one theory," Grayson conceded. "But how about this? Just suppose for a minute that we're dealing with a couple of juvenile delinquent aliens who stole daddy's flying saucer, and are out on a joy ride. Why not prank a few humans along the way? You know, like you did to Vanderhoff when you were a kid."

I shot him a scowl. "Ugh."

Grayson grinned. "Or, think about this. What if this whole thing was some superior beings' attempt to blow our squirrelly little minds and leave us to ponder the exact questions you're asking right now?"

I shook my head. "Come on, Grayson. There's got to be a logical explanation for this. What did that guy say happened? The one who wrote *The Mothman Prophecies*?"

Grayson smiled. "John Keel. He concluded his investigation by citing Socrates. 'The more I learn, the less I know.'"

"That's real helpful," I said sourly.

"In the end, Keel decided that the whole Mothman debacle had been some kind of game."

I scowled. "A *game?*"

"Yeah. Keel realized that as soon as he figured out some element of the game, the other side changed the rules. You know, you chase a red-eyed, flying creature, they replace it with lights in the sky. You chase the lights, they send strange men door-to-door asking inane questions."

"Who is *they?*"

"Superior intelligences. Perhaps even the universal mind itself."

I shook my head. "That's crazy."

Grayson shrugged. "Perhaps. But as my personal hero, Charles Fort, speculated, 'If there is a universal mind, must it be sane?'"

My jaw came unhinged. "Even if all this *has* all been a game, why Point Paradise? Why now?"

Grayson shrugged. "This kind of thing is nothing new, Drex. Or even that uncommon. Since recorded history, mankind has been plagued by the unexplained. Monsters, magical beings, visitors from the stars."

"That's true," Earl said, emerging from the RV. "I found a two-headed turtle in Wimbly Swamp last year. Remember, Bobbie?"

Grayson laughed. "A two-headed turtle here, a Wendigo there. A mermaid in the ocean. A reptilian humanoid in an underground tunnel. What if all of these things were sent here to shake us up? To boggle our minds? Simply for the amusement of some higher intelligence who gets off on making us squirm?"

I grimaced. "Geez. That's a dismal prospect."

Grayson grinned. "Or maybe they do it to spark our imaginations. To see what we're capable of as a species. To keep things interesting for them *and* us. Either way, I, for one, want to keep on playing."

I studied Grayson. "Why? It's a game for lunatics!"

Grayson straightened his shoulders. "Because one day, I want to win a round. How about you, Drex? Don't you want to play along?"

I pressed my molars together and sighed in contemplation.

Grayson and me versus the quite possibly insane cosmic consciousness.

I've played worse odds.

Chapter Sixty-Seven

THE LIGHTS BLINKED back on in my apartment. Grayson had placed a phone call half an hour ago. That's all he would tell me.

"You thinking what I'm thinking?" Grayson asked me.

I groaned. "God, I certainly hope not."

"*Tacos*, Drex. I think we need one more run to El Molino before I blow this Popsicle stand."

I smirked. "Point Paradise isn't big enough to have a Popsicle stand. But okay. I'll borrow Bessie from Earl. We need to pick up the last few parts for your RV anyway. I don't know how you got them delivered in two hours ... and right now, I don't want to know."

Grayson grinned. "You're learning. It's better not to ask."

"IT'S TIME TO FISH OR cut bait," Grayson said as he dragged a chip through a bowl of El Molino's famous salsa. "Are you going to join my little traveling sideshow or not?"

I winced with indecision. "I'm not sure."

"Well, what *are* you sure of in this little slice of heaven we call life?"

Really?

I shot Grayson some side-eye. "I know I don't want to stay in Point Paradise."

Grayson frowned. His voice took on an unfamiliar, serious, business-like tone. "Sorry, Drex. That's not a good enough reason to join me. I want a partner with a burning desire to explore the unknown. Not someone simply looking to escape their current circumstances."

My brow furrowed. "I understand. Can you give me another hour or two to think it over?"

The waitress delivered a huge plate of tacos. Grayson and I eyed them greedily. He reached for one and I grabbed his hand.

"Well? Can I have just a little more time to let you know?"

Grayson locked eyes with me. "Why? What's the hesitation?"

"I have obligations here."

Grayson nodded and grabbed a taco. "I tell you what. You can have until the first signs of indigestion kick in. Fair enough?"

I smiled faintly and nodded. "Fair enough."

AFTER THE HUMONGOUS amount of tacos Grayson and I put away, I knew my time was running short. Sure enough, as soon as the flashing yellow light that marked Point Paradise came into view, Grayson belched.

"Excuse me," he said. "Well, looks like your time's up. Are we going to be partners or not?"

From the driver's seat of my cousin's monster truck, I spotted Earl working away in the service bay. My Southern guilt took over.

"Listen. I want to, Grayson. But I can't leave Earl in this financial mess."

Grayson looked at me wistfully. "I understand."

As I maneuvered Bessie's huge tractor tires into the parking lot, Earl came out toting a paper bag.

I rolled down the window. "What's that?"

Earl grinned. "Your trade for the tacos."

My face scrunched warily. I handed my cousin his lunch, and grabbed the paper bag he offered in exchange. I opened it cautiously and took a peek inside. My nose was assaulted by the stench of half a dozen balls of poop.

"Argh!" I smashed the bag closed and looked over at Earl.

He grinned and laughed like a redneck hyena. "Hahaha! Gotcha, Bobbie!"

"Earl, for the last time, *you're fired!*"

"What is it?" Grayson asked. "What's in the bag?"

I shoved the paper sack across the bench seat at Grayson. "See for yourself."

Grayson opened it and yelped. "Where'd you get this, Earl?"

My cousin grinned. "Compliments of one Mr. Eugene Hollister."

Grayson stuck his nose in the bag and sniffed.

Yep. Total sicko. And to think I was seriously thinking about entrusting my life to this guy ....

Grayson let out a whoop of delight. "Earl, you're not fired. Drex! Get out and come with me."

"What for?"

Grayson didn't answer. He just made a beeline for the RV.

I climbed down out of the cab and followed him.

"What's going on?" I asked, watching Grayson fiddle with a piece of wood paneling on the wall above the RV's banquette. He peeled away a section of paneling. I nearly fainted. Row upon row of dollar bills were stacked between the joists in the wall like insulation. He grabbed a six-inch thick bundle and handed it to me.

"Is this enough to buy your freedom?"

I blanched. "What? Why would you do that for me?"

"I'm not doing anything *for* you, Drex. It's payday. You and Earl *earned* this money. You wouldn't believe how much Mothman scat goes for on the black market."

My mouth fell open. "You mean ... I could be free?"

"Sure. As long as money's the only thing holding you back."

I chewed my lip. "Well, I also need to get my full P.I. license."

Grayson grinned. "I think I can help with that. What do you say? You ready to play the game?"

"The game?"

"Yes. The game for lunatics, as you put it."

I smiled up at Grayson. "Yeah. I'm ready to play. But unlike you, I don't care about winning. I just want to find the jerks who're running the show and rip 'em a new one."

Grayson laughed. "Hey. To each his own."

AFTER THE SHOCK OF seeing more cash than I knew existed on Earth wore off and my legs were able to hold my weight again, Grayson and I emerged from the RV to find Earl pacing around the wrecked chassis of my father's vintage Mustang.

He wagged a finger at me. "You sure did a number on your dad's car, Bobbie. It's gonna take me ages to fix it."

I shot him a wry smile. "Yeah. You might want to check the air filter while you're at it."

Grayson laughed.

Earl opened his mouth to speak, but I cut him off.

"Listen, Earl. The parts to finish off the RV are on the front seat of Bessie. Grayson wants to leave tonight, so I suggest you work on his vehicle first."

"Yes, boss man." Earl surveyed the massive damage to the Mustang and let out a low whistle. "Looks like I'm gonna need me a bigger bag of Fritos, Bobbie."

I shrugged. "Is that so? Well, you're gonna have to go to the A&P all by yourself, Earl. I quit."

My cousin's eyes grew wide beneath his shaggy bangs. "What? You can't quit on me, Bobbie. You're the *boss man*."

"Watch me." I handed him a paper sack.

He took it absently. "But you're a born grease monkey, like me."

"No, Earl. I thought I was. But turns out, I am so totally *not*."

Earl pouted. "You just gonna up and leave me here all alone, holding this sack of poop?"

"Look inside, Earl."

He shot me a wary glance, then opened the sack. One peek inside and his face turned as green as the stacks of money filing the bag. He looked up at me, his mouth hanging open like a screen door off its hinges.

My heart pinged.

Man, I thought it would feel better to finally win a round with him.

I scowled. "Earl, just finish up the repairs on Grayson's RV. And you can have Dad's Mustang. I won't be needing it anymore. I'm going with Grayson."

Earl took a long look at Grayson, then at me. "You sure about this, Cuz?"

"Yeah. I'm sure. I'm a lousy mechanic. And a lousy boss. Dad was right to pick you over me. I'm going upstairs to finish up some stuff."

"But—"

I whirled around, suddenly angry as wet hen. "Don't you *get it* Earl? You *won*. You can have this whole stinking place!"

"Win?" Earl asked. "Wait, Bobbie. You got this all wrong. Your dad didn't pick *me* over *you*."

"Yes he did. Dad always wanted a son. I turned out to be a lousy girl. So he picked you instead."

Earl shook his head. "Your dad didn't kick you outta the garage because you were a *girl*, Bobbie. Don't you think he kinda figured that one out the day you were born?"

I scowled. "Then *why*? Why else would he turn his back on me the day I hit puberty?"

Earl scratched his head. "I thought you *knew* why."

"Because I turned into a girl."

"*No*, Bobbie. That ain't it at all. On your eleventh birthday, your mom got drunk as a skunk and finally told your dad the truth."

I frowned. "The truth?"

"That your daddy ain't your daddy. Your real dad's a man named David Applewhite."

Chapter Sixty-Eight

"YOU AIN'T NEVER COMING back, are you?" Earl asked as he handed me another tissue.

"Why should I? This whole place ... my whole *family* is nothing but a *lie*, Earl." I honked into a Kleenex.

"Not all of it, Bobbie. *I'm* still your cousin, blood or not."

I smiled. "You're right." I stood up and gave him a hug. "Never is a long time. I'll stay in touch. I promise."

Earl nodded. "Good. All right, then. I suggest you get your fat butt in gear before Grayson changes his mind."

I laughed. "Had to get the last zinger in, didn't you?"

Earl winked. "Who says it's the last?"

As I turned to head up the stairs, Earl called after me. "Hey Cuz, don't forget to turn out the lights when you leave. I'm the new boss man, you know."

"Right," I said, saluting. "I know."

AFTER CALLING BETH-Ann to give her the news, I glanced around the bedroom I'd inhabited for the past six months. Unlike the ghostly memories of my parents, I hadn't made enough of an impression for it to linger here after I was gone. And for that, I was glad.

On the nightstand, the picture of my unhappy family glared at me, frozen in a time better off forgotten.

I picked up the framed photo and studied it. Dad was still frowning in his shiny, new Mustang. Mom still offered up her dour, distant countenance. And Grandma Selma still held me in her arms, her eyes glazed-over with a faraway stare.

I blew out a breath. Then something caught my eye I hadn't noticed before.

Me.

The baby in the photo. Her lips were curled, ever so slightly. She was *smiling*.

Had the picture itself changed, or just the way I *perceived* it? I shook my head.

Grayson's crazy ideas must be contagious.

I set the photo back on the nightstand. From under the bed, I grabbed a duffle bag and stuffed in a few clothes. On top of them, I placed Grandma Selma's afghan.

I stripped off my father's shoes and mechanic coveralls for the last time. Carrying them across the room, I realized just how heavy they actually were.

Suddenly, a devious smile worked its way onto my lips. I marched across the room and flung the boots and coveralls out the window. As they hit the asphalt of the parking lot below, the thud made me grin.

Naked, I stepped into the shower, and let the warm, soapy water wash me clean.

IT WAS DUSK WHEN I climbed into the passenger seat next to Grayson. Earl waved at us from the service bay as the old RV rumbled out of the parking lot. I waved back at him.

"You're going to miss him, aren't you?" Grayson asked.

I smiled. "Yep. Every chance I get."

Grayson laughed and tipped his fedora to Earl.

I looked over at Grayson. "So, Mister Private Investigator, what now?"

Grayson shot me a thoughtful smile. "Mothman may be played out for now. I think it's time we look for a new game."

"Sounds good. Any ideas?"

"I've heard reports of something strange going on in Plant City."

I laughed. "What? A killer weevil infestation?"

"Close. Possible alien invasion."

"Huh. And it's not even strawberry-picking season yet."

Grayson grinned. He shifted gears and steered the RV out of the parking lot and into the southbound lane of Obsidian Road.

I reached over and touched Grayson's arm. "Wait. I forgot something."

Grayson hit the brakes. "What?"

"This."

I rolled down my window, pulled the Glock from my purse, aimed, and fired. The flashing yellow light between oblivion and nowhere shattered into a million pieces.

Grayson flinched. "What'd you do that for?"

I smiled and faced the road ahead. "Just putting out the lights, like the boss man said. Okay, Grayson. I'm ready. Let's roll."

THE END—OF THE BEGINNING ....

Ready for More *Freaky Florida adventures?*
Find out where Bobbie and Grayson go from here. Check out episode 2, Dr. Prepper!
https://www.amazon.com/dp/B07RCG6SHX

I HOPE YOU ENJOYED Moth Busters! If you did, it would be freaking fantastic if you would post a review on Amazon, Goodreads and/or BookBub. You'll be helping me keep the series going! Thanks in advance for being so awesome!

https://www.amazon.com/dp/B07RC7HVD2#customerReviews

Get a Free Gift!

DON'T MISS ANOTHER sneak preview, sale, or new release of *Freaky Florida Mystery Adventures!* Sign up for my newsletter for insider tips. I'll send you a free copy of the *Chronicles of Florida Woman* as a welcome gift!

https://dl.bookfunnel.com/ikfes8er75

For more laughs and discussions with fellow fans, follow me on Facebook, Amazon and BookBub:

Facebook:
https://www.facebook.com/valandpalspage/

Amazon:
https://www.amazon.com/-/e/B06XKJ3YD8

BookBub:
https://www.bookbub.com/search/authors?search=margaret%20lashley

Also, please enjoy the following excerpt from:
Dr. Prepper, Freaky Florida Mystery Book 2!

Dr. Prepper Excerpt:

Prologue

LAST WEEK, I GOT SHOT in the head.

The doctor said I didn't have brain damage. But the things I did afterward make me question whether I should've gotten a second opinion.

First, I let a complete stranger stay in my Grandma Selma's apartment.

Okay, that's not *so* crazy.

But then I spent a week with that same stranger, rambling around Alachua County chasing after Mothman.

Yes, Mothman.

When I finally realized the guy might be a raving lunatic, I did the only sensible thing I could think of.

I ditched my entire life, climbed into his dumpy RV, and headed off to Plant City to help him save the world from an alien invasion.

You're welcome.

Chapter One

I woke up and smelled the coffee.

I cracked open a crusty eye. What I saw in the dim light sent memories of yesterday slamming into my brain like a saltwater tsunami.

Less than twenty-four hours ago, my cousin Earl Shankles had hit me with a family secret that turned my life into a complete dumpster fire.

My father who'd died six months ago wasn't my father. And my mother had run off with Mr. Applewhite, the postman. According to Earl, 37 years ago, I was Mr. Applewhite's "special delivery."

Funny. I didn't feel special.

So, with no one around to point my bastard-child finger at, I did something that a mere week ago I'd have considered totally irrational.

Insane, even.

I ran off and joined the circus.

To be more specific, I joined a monster-chasing, freak-show of a circus led by a man I'd known for all of six days.

From what he'd told me, Nick Grayson was a private investigator, an amateur entomologist, an alternative healer, and a noted—albeit somewhat disgraced—physicist.

If *any* part of what he claimed was true, his credentials blew mine out of the water.

All I brought to the table was a bachelor's degree in art appreciation, a fairly limited knowledge of antiques, and a fairly *un*limited distrust of ... well, pretty much anything that talked.

But I could shoot a gun better than anyone I knew—including Grayson. I'd pinned my hopes on that being enough to convince him to keep me on as a PI intern.

Otherwise, I was totally screwed.

Last night, after leaving my cousin in charge of running my family's auto repair business, I'd jumped out of my old life and into Grayson's RV.

But I hadn't started my life over with a clean slate. Not even close. I'd climbed aboard toting enough baggage to significantly lower the guy's overall gas mileage.

As I lay curled up on the RV's sofa, I thought about my friend Beth-Ann. The last words she'd said to me blasted through my mind like a hurricane siren.

Are you outta your ever-loving gourd?

Maybe I was.

But it didn't matter. It was *way* too late to turn back now.

From the gentle rocking of the RV, I could tell it was rolling down the highway, full steam ahead. I closed my eyes again.

Screw it, I thought. *Life is for living.*

I was a carpetbagger in search of *carpe diem.*

Woohoo. Let the good times roll ....

Chapter Two

It had been way past midnight when Grayson pulled his vintage RV into the parking lot of a Walmart in Inverness, Florida. I'd woken when he stopped, and watched him pass by me silently on his way to his bedroom in the back of the RV.

Exhausted, I'd immediately fallen asleep again on the couch. When I woke up again, it was still dark.

Coffee was on the stove. Amy Winehouse was on the radio.

I fumbled for my cellphone. It was 7:03 a.m. and we were already rolling again.

Ugh.

I dragged myself to sitting and touched the scab in the middle of my forehead. It was almost healed. Not bad for being the target of a ricochet bullet a little over a week ago. I scratched the itchy stubble growing in where my long auburn locks used to be.

My new hairdo was a memento from the overzealous staff at the hospital in Gainesville. They'd shaved my head all the way to my ears, leaving me with a bald spot not even the most ambitious comb-over could hope to cover.

I scanned the RV's tiny kitchen/living room area for Lucky Red. It was the Redman chewing tobacco ball-cap my cousin Earl had lent me to cover my billiard-ball noggin. I spotted it at the end of the couch, perched atop the head of ET, the extraterrestrial. Or in this case, ET, the world's ugliest lamp.

Good one, Grayson.

I leaned over and snatched the cap off ET's gray plaster skull. Lucky Red was my fallback until I could procure another wig. My last one had met its fate at the hands of a frisky Mothman. But that's another story ....

I yawned and pulled the cap over my stubble. My body reminded me I was in dire need of a shower and at least a half a gallon of coffee.

Sitting on the couch, I could almost reach the coffee pot on the kitchen.

Almost.

I groaned and made a Herculean attempt, but the pot of life-inducing go-juice remained irritatingly out of reach.

I scowled at the stove.

Why couldn't I have gotten some useful skill out of getting shot between the eyes? Like The Incredibles' *stretchy arms, maybe. But no. All I got was the knowledge that I had my twin brother's gonad knocking around in my brain.*

And, like all men, he was not being particularly helpful.

I grunted, hauled myself off the couch, and poured myself a jittery mugful of coffee. After gulping half of it down, I refilled my mug and wormed my way up to the RV's cab.

A slim man dressed all in black tipped his vintage fedora at me, giving me a glimpse of his own shaved dome.

He shot me a sideways glance. "Morning, sunshine. Sleep well?"

Grayson's cheery, morning-person tone might as well have been fingernails on a chalkboard.

"Yeah," I said. "Like a balloon animal in a cactus garden."

I flopped into the passenger seat beside Grayson and rubbed my sore neck.

Grayson laughed. "I told you to take the bed."

"Chivalrous of you, but no thanks."

The bedroom in Grayson's RV moonlighted as an electromagnetic monster trap. Call me paranoid, but I wasn't keen on the idea of losing consciousness inside a strange man's small, padded, soundproofed bedroom that had enough locks on the door to restrain Godzilla. I already had enough trust issues, thank you very much.

I blew out a sigh. "What happened to Walmart? I was gonna buy a wig."

Grayson fiddled with the knobs on some electronic contraption mounted to the underside of the dash.

"I wanted to get an early start," Grayson said. "Last night I got an update on that incident in Plant City. And, as you country folks are fond of saying, 'Time's a-wastin.'"

I shot him some serious side-eye. "I've never heard *anybody* say that."

I blew out a breath and took another sip of coffee. "Use that awful country accent one more time and I can't be held responsible for where the contents of my coffee mug fling themselves."

Grayson smirked. "I see you're not a morning person. Duly noted."

I looked out the window and almost smiled. Despite the crick in my neck and the grayish weather, it felt good to see the distance widening between me and my dead-end life back in Point Paradise. I took another slurp of coffee. It was damned good. I'd give Grayson that much.

"What's so interesting in Plant City?" I asked.

Grayson shook his head. "Not so fast, intern. First order of business is to get the boss a refill." He handed me his empty coffee mug.

"Is this part of my P.I. training?"

Grayson shrugged. "Only if you want to *continue* your P.I. training."

I grinned. Grayson was only a few years older than me, but he was already a seasoned private investigator. I was just a P.I. wannabe with a brand-new intern license. I needed two years of on-the-job training to qualify for a full-fledged Class C license. Thanks to Grayson and his traveling investigator show, I only had 103 weeks to go.

I grabbed his coffee mug. "Pinch of salt, right?"

Grayson's eyebrow ticked up. "Gold star, cadet."

I tumbled back to the kitchen, threw a couple of Pop-Tarts in the toaster, and poured us both more coffee. After delivering the mugs to the cup holders on the dashboard, I grabbed the pastries and parked my rear back in the passenger seat.

"Here you go." I handed Grayson a blueberry Pop-Tart.

He raised a suspicious eyebrow. "Already brownnosing, eh?"

I shrugged. "Figured it couldn't hurt. So *now* will you tell me what's going on in Plant City?"

"I got a call from one of my sources."

"Your *sources?*"

Grayson nodded down at the weird-looking equipment installed under the dash. "That's a ham radio. I use it to operate an informal hotline on an obscure channel. People call in with information. If it sounds interesting, I follow up."

I took a bite of Pop-Tart. "What kind of information?"

"You know. Unidentifiable tracks. Weird lights in the sky. Mutilated corpses. That kind of thing."

I sucked the sticky frosting from my front teeth. "Sorry I asked. So what's in it for the informants?"

"*Operatives,*" Grayson corrected. He shot me a grin and batted his eyes. "Why, my undying gratitude, of course." He turned back to face the road. "That, and cold, hard cash."

"So, exactly what kind of strange phenomenon are we looking into?"

"A fellow in Plant City overheard an unusual radio transmission two days ago. A guy named Lester Jenkins got on a frequency and starting screaming, 'They're here! They're here!'"

I took a sip of coffee. "Huh. Maybe his in-laws came into town."

Grayson shot me a sideways glance. "A cop found him dead a few hours later."

I smirked. "Like I said, maybe his in-laws—"

"His head covered in some kind of slime," Grayson said.

"Huh. You've obviously never dealt with in-laws, Grayson."

He snorted. "Shut up and eat your Pop-Tart."

My gut gurgled. "Hey, can we stop at the next rest stop?"

"I guess. Why?"

"Let's just say I've got something I want to get rid of."

"If you mean what I think you mean, the toilet works just fine while we're underway."

I frowned. "Thanks. But that's something I'm going to need a bit more time getting used to."

Grayson eyed me. "Claustrophobic?"

I shrugged and stared at the road ahead. "Sure. Let's go with that."

Get Dr. Prepper now!

https://www.amazon.com/dp/B07RCG6SHX

More Freaky Florida Mysteries

by Margaret Lashley
Moth Busters
Dr. Prepper
Oral Robbers
Ape Shift
More to Come!

*"The things a girl's gotta do to get a lousy
PI license. Geez!"*

Bobbie Drex

About the Author

WHY DO I LOVE UNDERDOGS? Well, it takes one to know one. Like the main characters in my novels, I haven't lead a life of wealth or luxury. In fact, as it stands now, I'm set to inherit a half-eaten jar of Cheez Whiz...if my siblings don't beat me to it.

During my illustrious career, I've been a roller-skating waitress, an actuarial assistant, an advertising copywriter, a real estate agent, a house flipper, an organic farmer, and a traveling vagabond/truth seeker. But no matter where I've gone or what I've done, I've always felt like a weirdo.

I've learned a heck of a lot in my life. But getting to know myself has been my greatest journey. Today, I know I'm smart. I'm direct. I'm jaded. I'm hopeful. I'm funny. I'm fierce. I'm a pushover. And I have a laugh that lures strangers over, wanting to join in the fun.

In other words, I'm a jumble of opposing talents and flaws and emotions. And it's all good.

I enjoy underdogs because we've got spunk. And hope. And secrets that drive us to be different from the rest.

So dare to be different. It's the only way to be!

Happy reading!

Made in the USA
Columbia, SC
14 October 2021

47209628R00181